Destiny's

Destiny's Daughters

Donna Hill

Parry "EbonySatin" Brown

Gwynne Forster

Dafina
BOOKS

KENSINGTON PUBLISHING CORP.
http://www.kensingtonbooks.com

DAFINA BOOKS are published by

Kensington Publishing Corp.
850 Third Avenue
New York, NY 10022

All Kensington titles, imprints and distributed lines are available at special
quantity discounts for bulk purchases for sales promotion, premiums, fund-
raising, educational or institutional use.

Special book excerpts or customized printings can also be created to fit spe-
cific needs. For details, write or phone the office of the Kensington Special
Sales Manager: Kensington Publishing Corp., 850 Third Avenue, New York,
NY 10022. Attn. Special Sales Department. Phone: 1-800-221-2647.

Dafina Books and the Dafina logo Reg. U.S. Pat. & TM Off.

ISBN 0-7582-1238-0

First Kensington Trade Paperback Printing: February 2006
10 9 8 7 6 5 4 3 2 1

Printed in the United States of America

CONTENTS

PROLOGUE

Essie Mae Holmes wiped dime-sized sweat beads from her forehead as she pulled the third and final baby from Minnie Lou. Her sixteen-year-old great niece stopped pushing when the second baby girl failed to yield to her efforts and had appeared only halfway out of the birth canal. Thirty-three hours of labor had left Minnie Lou Holmes limp and incoherent. "Lord, child, I tried to tell you, but your head was so hard, you wouldn't listen to a soul."

Essie Mae finally freed the precious little pink thing from the birth canal and severed her connection to her mother. Midwifery with one baby was hard enough. Tending to the mother and baby always left her exhausted; she needed at least one other set of hands to help her with these three screaming little ones. After cleaning their air passages, she placed them side by side on the clean white sheet that she had spread on the floor next to the makeshift delivery bed. She rubbed her hands up and down her sides as the three of them screamed, each in a slightly different pitch, while the child/woman who gave them life lay still.

She moved as fast as her feeble body would carry her to the other side of the small kitchen where she had boiled a large pot of water and laid out clean towels. She had known Minnie Lou's belly was too round for her to be with only one baby.

That first baby didn't need any help cranking up her lungs. Her little voice started off slow and mellow like a clarinet and was soon going full blast like a tuba in a marching band. Essie Mae took another look at her oldest sister's baby girl and saw that she still hadn't moved. "I think your mama should name you Clarissa Mae, she said to the one with lungs like a tuba. I bet you gonna be a singer." She bathed Clarissa carefully and wrapped her tight in the towel that felt too stiff and hard for the new baby's tender skin.

She moved to the next baby and bathed her with the same care. "Now, weren't *you* the stubborn one. It was like you were jammed up in there. I think your mama should name you Jamilla." She kissed the baby as she fell asleep sucking her tiny fist. "I bet that's not going to be the last time you're in a tight spot before it's all over for you." She wrapped Jamilla in the towel and laid her next to her sister on the table.

The tired old woman picked up the last of the beautiful baby girls. Her skin was thin and seemed as fragile as a lettuce leaf. She washed her with more care than the others. She worried about wrapping her in the rough towel, but circumstances and energy prevented her from doing anything different. "Well, little one, I guess I'm gonna have to name you Leticia." She began to hum "Amazing Grace" as she took Leticia to her bedroom and placed her in the center of the small bed.

She took the twenty steps back to the kitchen, refusing to look in the direction of Minnie Lou as she picked up Jamilla and Clarissa, and then placed them next to their sister. She said a short prayer before she went back to the kitchen to do what she knew she had to do. "Lord, these here babies gonna have a hard row to hoe. You know my condition, and you know I just can't take care of them. Help me find them a good home. In Jesus' name. Amen."

Essie Mae's weakened condition and fatigue weighed her down. She looked around the kitchen. Beneath her feet the daylight found its way through the naked floorboards. The shelves around the wall held meal, flour, sugar, a grease can, and a few jars of canning from her friend and neighbor, Gertrude Jefferson. The two chairs neatly placed at the wood table looked like even a child's weight could make them collapse.

"Lord, I just don't have no means to take care of these babies. She finally moved to where Minnie Lou lay on the soiled old bunk bed, her legs still in the birthing position. Essie Mae gently put them down and covered her. She touched her skin. It felt cool, the sweat long ago dried. She was still, too still. She placed her left index finger beneath her niece's nostrils and confirmed what she already knew. Those three little girls were orphans.

"Lord, what am I going to do with these babies? I can hardly feed myself, and I'm too sick to take care of one, much less three," she said aloud again. Now she spoke to Minnie Lou. "I told you to leave that no-count Hosea alone. I knew you'd end up with a heap of trouble. Now your trouble's my trouble." With much effort she picked up the rags from the floor, went back to the table and retrieved the washcloth she'd used on the babies, and began to bathe Minnie Lou. She didn't have the strength to move her body so she could change the bloody bottom sheet, so she simply covered her with a clean one.

She heard a faint whimper from the other room and thought she'd have to find something for nourishment. She went to her change purse and counted out forty-three cents. Even if she had money for baby's milk, she had neither a way to get to a store nor the strength to carry three babies. Gertrude had gone to town and wouldn't be back until after dark. She boiled some water in a clean pot and added a teaspoon of Karo syrup. She didn't have a baby bottle, so she found a dropper from a bottle of iodine, washed it, then boiled it in another pot and prepared to feed her charges.

God being merciful to an old woman with a big heart, the babies only woke up once, and all at the same time. At daylight she fed them again before she walked the quarter-mile to Gertrude Jefferson's. Moving around the mud puddles put there by the previous night's rainstorm added steps that Essie Mae just couldn't afford to take.

"Minnie Lou's dead," she told Gertrude as she opened the screen door, "and she left three little girls."

"For the Lord's sake!" Gertrude grabbed her chest as though to protect her heart.

With almost no emotion, Essie Mae asked, "Can you ask your husband to take her to the funeral home in his wagon?"

"Three?" Gertrude needed to catch up. "Uh . . . he sure will. No need to even ask such a thing."

"Much obliged." Essie Mae swayed a little.

"Come on in and sit a spell." Gertrude moved to the side so Essie Mae could enter the kitchen. "Let me make you some tea."

Essie Mae stepped inside. The neat house had splashes of color thrown in with the modest furnishings. Gertrude took in laundry, and her husband, Willie, was a blacksmith in town. Far from rich, or even well off, Essie Mae would guess that Gertrude had more than forty-three cents to her name.

Gertrude set a cup in front of her friend, and then sat in the chair across from hers. "If you knew who the father is, he might give you a little help."

"Ain't no fathers in this family—yours, neither."

Ignoring Essie Mae's sarcasm, she said, "Too bad. I wish there was something we could do, but you know how it is with us. We're just making it."

Essie Mae blew on the hot liquid as she looked around the room and grunted, "Humph."

"You want me to let Miss Jennifer, the town clerk over in Dale, know so she can make up the birth certificates?"

"Yeah, I reckon. Can't do it myself, 'cause I don't want to leave 'em alone long enough to go into town, and I sure can't carry three babies."

"I understand." She touched her friend's hand. "You don't worry none now, ya hear? You gonna be blessed."

Essie Mae only sighed.

"Let me get a pencil and paper so I can write down the names," Gertrude said as she got up from the table.

"Leticia, Jamilla, and Clarissa Holmes," Essie Mae said as soon as Gertrude sat down. "Please put it on their birth certificates that they's triplets."

Gertrude handed her a box of Farina and a five-dollar bill. "What are you going to do with them?"

"Thanks, Gertrude. Nobody wants three babies." Essie Mae pushed herself up with both hands. "People ain't got that kind of money, and especially nobody around here. If you hear of anybody who'll take a baby girl, let me know."

"I will." Gertrude looked closely at her. "You look as if you need to see a doctor."

"Ain't no doctor coming out here in these Georgia sticks, and I can't leave these children by themselves."

As the days dragged on slowly, Essie Mae became despondent over her rapidly deteriorating health; she asked Gertrude if she could watch the babies overnight so she could get a full night's sleep. "I don't have the strength to even feed them tonight," she said weakly. The kindness of her neighbors had brought bottles and a few baby clothes, which she had packed for the girls' night with Gertrude. As she left, Essie Mae hugged and thanked Gertrude. That night she died peacefully in her sleep.

Alarmed at the fact that she now had Essie Mae's burden, Gertrude set out to rid herself of the children as quickly as possible. Through a neighbor she found out there was a woman in California who wanted a baby in the worst way and would pay. Gertrude gave the woman one week to come get the baby. If she played her cards right, she'd be able to collect more than two thousand dollars. When the woman came with her husband and less than the bounty she required, she sold her only Jamilla because she was the fussiest. Within a week she'd found a woman at her church who worked in a group home in New Orleans who had space for only one of the sisters, and she took Leticia.

After more than a month, she hadn't found a home for Clarissa, so she took her to Atlanta and left her in the bathroom of the courthouse. The Department of Children and Family Services was notified, and Clarissa became an entity in the Georgia Foster Care system.

MORE THAN THIS

Donna Hill

Chapter 1

Leticia turned gently onto her side. Slowly her eyes fluttered open against the early summer sun that pushed its way through the slits of the bronze-toned blinds. She emitted a slow, deep sigh. The call from her friend in the police department warned her that her days were numbered. They were close to shutting her down, and she needed to make herself scarce—and fast.

Car horns and the sound of sirens floated up from the street ten stories below, overlooking fashionable Central Park West. Even at six A.M., the city was wide awake, pulsing with energy. Her city, the one she'd made her own fifteen years earlier. Today she would put it all behind her. She had no choice.

The left side of her bed bounced slightly with the movement of weight from the body next to hers. She glanced over her shoulder. Too bad she would have to leave Norman. He was one of the nice ones. Generally she didn't allow her clients to stay overnight. Once she'd been paid and they'd had their evening together, she sent them smiling on their merry way with promises of more. It had been that way since she took up residence in New York, having moved her "business" from Atlanta. She'd foolishly believed that she could finally make a home in the Big Apple, but that was not to be. Last night she'd made an exception, and Norman couldn't have been happier. It was the least she could do, since she knew they would never set eyes on each other again.

She turned onto her back and stared up at the mirror set in her ceiling. At thirty-three, she still looked good, she absently mused. Her thighs were toned, her breasts still sat up firmly on her chest, her stomach was flat and devoid of any stretch marks. Her face was ordinary by most people's standards, but she knew all the tricks of makeup and the magic that they could wield. As a result, she was more than attractive.

However, it wasn't her looks that got her through life—it was her street smarts and natural charisma. Leticia knew the potency of a smile, a look, the right word, a touch in the perfect spot—all as powerful as manna from heaven. She used them to her advantage.

Everything many dreamed of, she possessed: important friends, a sizeable bank account, the ability to travel at will, live well, drive a new car every year, and more clothes and shoes than she could wear in a lifetime. Yes, she had everything—and nothing at all.

The life she lived was filled with excitement, surely, but the secrets and the loneliness outweighed the benefits. The women whom she worked with couldn't be considered friends, merely business associates, and the men—they were simply ships passing in the night. Most days she didn't think about it much, but as she'd grown older, the desire to have something tangible grew with each passing year.

She stared at her reflection and wondered if her estranged sisters had fared as well as she over the years. A heaviness settled in the center of her stomach. Did they have families? Were they happy? Did they ever think about her? Did it even matter after all this time? Never once did her sisters try to find her. They'd probably forgotten all about her years ago. Most of the time she forgot about them as well. Truth be told, she really knew no more about them than their last name Holmes and that their mother died in childbirth. At times she wasn't really certain if the story the case worker at the group home told her about her family was the truth or some hurtful fiction. It had to be a lie, she often told herself. She couldn't allow herself to believe that she had two sisters somewhere out in the world and each of the three had been sold off like cattle. If that was true, then Leticia certainly lived up to her heritage: she was sold for money and she was still selling herself for money decades later. Damn shame.

She eased up and reached for her silk robe at the foot of the bed, careful not to disturb Norman. Standing, she slipped into it and went into the master bath, one of her favorite rooms in the spacious loft. It was a tropical paradise—a riot of brilliant colored flora and white orchids graced the sills and corners of the white walls. It was equipped with a Jacuzzi, sunken bathtub, double sink, and shower stall. It was her haven, where she went to think as her body was massaged by the jets of the Jacuzzi and she listened to the soft music piped in from hidden speakers. She turned on the water and poured in a cupful of jasmine-scented oil. Jazz saxophonist Kurt Whalum played discreetly in the background.

As she slipped into the water and relaxed her head against the pillow, she closed her eyes. Quickly all the steps she'd put into place ran through her mind like a grocery list. She'd all but emptied her bank accounts. Her car was in storage. Her passport and identity papers were in order. She would leave most of her clothes and buy what she needed when she reached her destination. She had enough money to tide her over until she found something adequate to do with her time. Yes, everything was in place. The water pulsed around her.

Quietly reentering her bedroom, she pulled her two packed suitcases from the closet and sat them by the door. Her carryall contained her paperwork, and her money was sewn into the panels of her suitcases. She dressed soundlessly, put the right touches of makeup on her face, took her dark glasses from the dresser, looked once over her shoulder. Norman wouldn't wake up for a few more hours from the sedative she'd slipped into his drink in the wee hours of the morning; by then she would be long gone. She hated good-byes. She'd said too many of them over the years.

With suitcases in hand, her bag over her shoulder, she walked out and would never look back. Yet another new life lay ahead of her. What she would make of it only time would tell. But she was ready for the ride.

Several hours later, the plane touched down in Florida. After retrieving her bags, she went directly to the car rental console and picked up the car that awaited her. The two-door Ford sedan was not what she was accustomed to, but it would have to do for the time being. Settling behind the wheel, she pulled out her map and studied her course. She would be in the heart of South Beach in less than an hour, barring any heavy traffic. South Beach, the East Coast getaway for the wealthy and wanna-bes, was the perfect place to get lost. Anytime of day or night the streets teemed with people, the hotels were constantly filled with stars of every ilk, and the concert halls and theaters couldn't keep up with the number of shows and events that vied for space. Yes, she would fit right in. Smiling, she eased out into the traffic and wondered for a moment what Norman would think when he woke up and found her gone.

As she drove along the streets of Miami, the array of hard, young, beautiful bodies filled the avenues. Color bursts before the eyes. Palm trees swayed ever so gently in the balmy breeze. High-end boutiques lined the streets, music blared from lounges, cafes, and clubs. The city vibrated with a barely controlled energy. Hot, hot, hot was the only thought that ran through her mind. She bobbed her head to the music of it all.

Forty minutes later she pulled up in front of the Loews Miami Beach Hotel, the restored St. Moritz. She'd barely come to a complete stop before a valet was at her window. She depressed the button and the window slid down.

"Guest of the hotel, ma'am?"

"Yes, I am." She smiled.

"I'll take your car for you. Do you need help with your bags?"

"That would be lovely. Thank you." She stepped out into the humid air and looked around as the bellman came to remove her bags from the trunk. The valet handed her a ticket.

"Enjoy your stay," he said, before getting in behind the wheel.

"I'm sure I will."

Following the bellman inside, the welcome chill from the central air greeted her. Several guests of the hotel sat on antique sofas that graced the patterned walls. The ceiling was endless, gold and glass were everywhere. A giant palm tree, the likes of which she'd never seen before, sat in an enormous white marble pool. Uniformed staff hurried about, pushing luggage and giving directions. The glass façade opened to a view of startling blue ocean.

Leticia's predatory instincts shifted into high gear watching the parade of beautiful men who strolled through the lobby, alone or at the side of a woman. The pickings were plentiful, she mused, as she walked to the reception desk, catching the eye of several handsome possibilities. She ran her tongue seductively across her lips when one gave her an extra long look.

"Welcome to the St. Moritz, Loews. How may I help you?" a young woman in a navy blue uniform asked.

Leticia turned her attention to the woman behind the desk. She smiled.

"I have a reservation. Pamela Armstrong," she said, slipping easily into her pseudonym.

The young woman focused on the computer in front of her, quickly stroking the keys. She looked up at Leticia. "I see you'll be with us for a while, Ms. Armstrong?"

"I'm on vacation. I believe I'm reserved for a month."

"Yes. I see that." She hit a few more strokes. "How many keys will you need?"

"One."

The receptionist processed the key, but before handing it over, she said, "We have your credit card on file, but I'll need to see some identification, please, and get an imprint of your card."

"Of course." Leticia dug in her purse, took out her wallet, and handed over her passport and credit card, all in the name of Pamela Armstrong.

The young woman reviewed the identification, made an imprint of the credit card, and handed both back to Leticia. "Thank you, Ms. Armstrong." She gave Leticia her card key. "You'll be in room 1875." She looked over Leticia's shoulder and signaled for a bellman. "Felix will take you to your room. If you need anything at all, we're here to serve you."

"Thank you." She put her information back in her purse and followed Felix to the bank of elevators.

Felix was the epitome of Latin masculinity, of medium height with ink-black hair swept away from his broad forehead and skin the color of lightly toasted bread. He was an almost dead ringer for a young Antonio Banderas. Hmm. *Edible*.

When Felix opened the door to her suite, Leticia instantly knew she was going to love it here. She kicked off her kitten-heeled sandals, dropped her purse on the entry table, and crossed the plush white carpeted floor to the balcony. The pile was so deep and thick, it caressed her ankles. Opening the glass balcony doors, she took in the breathtaking view across Miami and out onto the sandy white beach below. No more snow, winter coats, or turning up the thermostat. She spread her arms, tossed her head back, and sucked in the ocean-washed air. This would be home, she decided then and there.

She spun around, a broad smile highlighting her hazel eyes, courtesy of expensive contacts. "Thank you, Felix." She came toward him, her hips swaying beneath the short swing skirt of white and pale blue gauze. She picked up her discarded purse, dug inside her wallet, and handed him a twenty-dollar bill. "For your trouble." She pressed the bill into his palm and held it there.

"Thank you. If there is *anything* I can do for you . . ."

Leticia reached out and stroked his arm with her free hand. Her voice dropped an octave. "I'll be sure to let you know." She stepped back.

Felix's right brow arched ever so slightly in understanding. He gave a short bow of his head, turned, and walked away.

Leticia stood for a moment, facing the now-closed door, her lips pursed in thought. If all the men in Miami were going to be as potentially accommodating as Felix, she would have plenty to keep her occupied.

Room by room, Leticia inspected her space. Totally pleased with her new digs, she opted for a shower, change of clothes, and a visit to the hotel bar. Anyone who is anyone eventually finds their way to the bar, and she wanted to be there to sample the menu.

*   *   *

White was one of Leticia's favorite colors for the summer and she wore it well. For her foray to the hotel bar and lounge she chose a Grecian white dress, short, waist-hugging with a neckline that plunged dangerously close to her navel, the crisscrossing shirred bodice barely contained her size D's. A tap of her favorite oil, African Musk, behind her ears, on her wrists, and deep in the valley of her cleavage had her smelling edible. Diamond studs dotted her ears, and barely there makeup had her pecan-toned skin looking silky and flawless. She pressed closer toward the makeup mirror, popped in her contacts, and added a stroke of clear lip gloss that gave her mouth a dewy look. Turning her head from side to side, she patted her neatly tapered short 'do and, pleased with all she saw, she stepped out of the dressing room, picked up her white Kate Spade purse with the gold handle, and headed out.

Leticia Holmes was difficult to miss, even in a crowded room. For as long as she could remember, she was able to draw attention to herself. Perhaps it was from the years of trying not to be ignored in the countless group homes she was subjected to. She'd never wanted to be considered just another unfortunate black kid that nobody wanted. So she worked hard on her speech and her looks. She watched the white folks who ran the homes, along with the big shots who came around once a month to check on things, and learned how to shake hands, sit properly, which fork was which at the table, and basically to appear more important, more poised, educated, and worldly than she really was. It was all perception, she discovered by the time she was ten. You could make folks believe whatever the hell you wanted them to with the right words, attitude, and attire. Lessons she never forgot.

Her striking appearance was not lost on the men or the women whom she passed en route to a vacant table by the window. She smiled politely and took a seat shown to her by a too-young-looking-to-be-working waitress.

"That dress is banging," the young woman said.

Leticia grinned. "Thank you. And what is your name?"

"Cynthia," she responded, surprised that anyone would take an interest.

"Well, Cynthia, you are a lovely young woman. I'd love to see what you look like all dressed up."

Cynthia beamed, her light-skinned complexion turning rosy. "I can put it on when I have to," she said.

"I'm sure you can."

"What kin I get you?"

Leticia turned halfway in her seat, crossed her legs, and then her arms over her knees. She focused totally on Cynthia. "I'm sure you know the menu inside and out, what's good and what's not. Why don't you suggest something?"

Cynthia's light brown eyes widened. Most of the customers that came to the hotel lounge barely acknowledged her, but this lady was different.

She cleared her throat, stuck out her small breasts, and poised her order pad in her hand. "The grilled salmon is to die for, ma'am."

"Then I'll have the grilled salmon, and a tossed salad with vinaigrette. And a glass of your best wine. I'll leave that up to you."

"Yes, ma'am." She quickly jotted down the order and started to turn away.

"And Cynthia?"

She stopped and looked expectantly at Leticia. "Yes, ma'am?"

"Please call me Pamela or Pam. 'Ma'am' sounds so . . . old." She grinned and patted Cynthia's hand.

Cynthia bobbed her head. "Yes, ma . . . I mean, Pamela." She scooted away.

Leticia subtly watched the guests and knew before a certain man did that he would be coming her way in no time.

Chapter 2

Nathan Spencer was a man who knew what he wanted and how to get it. The moment he saw Leticia, he knew he wanted her. He waited for the waitress to leave Leticia's table before he got up from the bar and approached her.

Leticia pretended to be engrossed in the dessert menu.

"May I buy you a drink while you wait for your meal?"

With slow deliberance, Leticia put down the menu and turned her head to look up at him. She waited a beat, letting her gaze drift up, then down, his long body. Finally she settled on his face.

"No. You can't," she said, enjoying the look of surprise on his face. "But you can sit down and join me for dinner if you don't have other plans."

Nathan tossed his head back and chuckled deep in his throat. "You drive a hard bargain."

"Only a matter of opinion." She extended her hand toward the vacant seat. "Please—sit."

"Nathan Spencer," he said, pulling out the chair and sitting down.

"Pamela Armstrong."

"So Pamela, let me get the one-liner clichés out of the way. What is a beautiful woman like you doing eating alone?"

"Now, Nathan, if I wasn't alone, you and I would never have the opportunity to meet."

"Touché." He looked her over. "Business or pleasure?"

"A little of both. What about you?" She raised her water goblet to her lips and took a dainty sip, letting her long lashes drift over her eyes.

"Business. I'm closing several building deals in the area."

"Really. So you're in real estate."

"A broker. Mostly commercial properties."

"Do you live in Miami?"

"Yes, I have a house near the beach."

She frowned slightly. "Do you always hang out in bars?"

He grinned, and she noticed how his eyes crinkled in the corners like one who enjoys laughing and laughter. Nathan Spencer was certainly good looking; solid build, a delectable chocolate brown complexion, clean-shaven with a sleek, bald head that had her immediately imagining all manner of erotic images.

"I was having drinks with a client," he said in answer to her question.

Leticia looked around. "Male or female?"

"Male."

"Hmm. Hope it went well." She reached for her water again.

"It did. What kind of business are you in?"

"Entertainment."

"What kind?"

"Management. But let's not talk about business. This is my first time to South Beach. Suggest some highlights."

Nathan leaned forward. "I have a better suggestion."

"And what might that be?"

"If you're not busy tomorrow, I'd be happy to show you around."

She faked surprise with a hand to her chest. "Why, Nathan, I barely know you."

"Then it's the perfect opportunity for us to fix that."

The waitress returned with Leticia's wine and placed it on the table, looking at Leticia expectantly.

Leticia smiled up at her, lifted the glass to her lips, and sipped. A slow smile moved across her wide mouth. "Very good choice."

Cynthia beamed.

Leticia introduced Nathan. "This is Nathan Spencer. He'll be joining me for dinner."

"Would you like a drink to start?"

"Courvoisier on the rocks."

"Right away."

Nathan turned his attention back to Leticia. "What time would you like me to pick you up?"

"I'm an early riser. Why don't we meet for breakfast and take it from there?"

"I like how you think."

"Ahh, a man who is intrigued by the female mind. How appealing." She gave him a seductive smile.

"It's going to be very interesting getting to know you."

"That's the plan, Nathan."

After a very pleasant dinner with Nathan, Leticia excused herself with promises of tomorrow and returned to her room. Unpacking her belongings, she turned on the tub and sprinkled in drops of jasmine-scented oil. But before she had a chance to step into the water, there was a knock on her door.

Frowning at being disturbed during her ritual, she tightened the belt on her red silk robe, turned off the faucets, and went to answer the door.

"Felix. What a pleasant surprise."

Felix had a rolling table, topped with a sterling silver bucket and a bottle of Cristal bedded in chipped ice.

She leaned against the doorframe, folded her arms, and smiled slowly. "Felix, you shouldn't have," she teased.

Felix blushed beneath his golden complexion. "I wish I could say it was me, Ms. Armstrong."

Her right brow arched in question. That's when she noticed the card

perched on the white-linen-covered tray. She picked it up. *"Dining with
you was my pleasure. I look forward to tomorrow. N."*

Hmm, a man with class.

She offered a pretty pout. "How thoughtful." She rolled her eyes
over Felix's chiseled frame and exotic features.

"Care to join me? I see there are two flutes and I hate to drink
alone."

Felix looked over his shoulder, then at both ends of the hallway.
"I'm still on duty . . ."

"How long can a drink take?" She played with the opening of her
robe, running her finger absently up and down the valley of her breasts.

He hesitated, transfixed by the journey of her finger. Swallowing
hard, he said, "I suppose no one will miss me for a few minutes . . ."

Leticia stepped aside and let him wheel in the table, which gave her
a great view of his rear. She smiled, then shut and locked the door behind him. A *man like you—I'm sure you can last for more than a few
minutes*.

An hour later, Felix struggled with his bow tie while hunting frantically around for his shoes.

Leticia watched him from her reclining position on the bed, her
head held up in her palm. "They're in the corner," she said, her voice
thick and dreamy.

He looked over his shoulder at her, and she could see the desire re-
light in his eyes while her long fingers stroked the wetness that clung
to her sex. Her smile invited his return.

She moved onto her back, her legs spread wide and bent at the
knees while her fingers continued their exploration—in and out. Her
eyes closed and she moaned. She ran her tongue over her lips as her
pelvis moved in a sensual rhythm.

Leticia heard movement, but she was too engrossed in what she was
doing until she felt Felix's body atop hers. He pulled her hand away
and buried himself deep inside her, making her groan with pleasure.
She draped her legs across his back, pulling him firmly against her as
she met him stroke for stroke. The bed banged viciously against the

wall as Felix called out in Spanish and pushed them blissfully over the edge of reason.

Alone now in her tub, Leticia leaned back and let the hot, scented water ripple over her. She thought back to her little tryst with Felix. Not bad, and certainly a pleasant way to get acquainted with the natives. It's only sex. The one thing men are good for. She sighed, contented, closed her eyes, and remained in the cleansing waters until they cooled.

Chapter 3

Nathan had expected Leticia to call him when she received her token of his thanks. He'd gone so far as to check with the front desk to make sure it was delivered. That was more than two hours ago. He hadn't heard a word. It shouldn't bother him one way or the other, but it did.

He got up from the couch, turned off the television with the remote, and walked out onto the deck. The sun was setting in a blaze of orange glory across the endless blue horizon as the waves danced gently against the sandy shore. In the distance seagulls dove and rose above the water in a ritualistic dance, daring the fish below to peek above the foam to become entrée or dessert.

It was a calming scene, picture perfect, a movie director's dream.

Nathan leaned down and opened the cooler, removed an icy bottle of Coors, and effortlessly twisted off the top. He took two long, refreshing swallows, then leaned against the cedar railing staring out at forever, thoughts of his impromptu dinner with Pamela Armstrong creasing his brow.

He'd had his share of women. He changed them as often as his tailor-made shirts, wearing them as long as they fit and continued to make him feel good about having them around. When the fit and the feel were no longer appealing, he moved on and traded in for another make and model.

Pamela Armstrong was different. No doubt about that. He was certain that she wasn't playing hard to get. She was simply a woman who didn't give a damn. That intrigued him. She couldn't have cared less if he'd spoken to her or not. She would have been content to eat alone and not feel lonely or out of place. She came across as the type of woman who could make herself at home virtually anywhere she set her feet. He liked that, too—a woman who was sure of herself. She wore her sexuality like a good perfume—teasing, all over but not overpowering.

The corner of his mouth curved into a grin. Pamela Armstrong.

The ringing phone pulled him away from the images he'd begun to conjure in his head—and just in time.

He put down the bottle, pushed open the glass sliding doors, and stepped inside, shutting the door behind him.

"Hello?" Anticipation laced his voice.

"Hey, man, it's Cal."

"Hey."

"Don't sound so excited to hear my voice. I can't take it."

"My bad, brotha—long day, that's all."

"I hear that. Wheeling and dealing or humping and bumping?"

Nathan laughed. He took the cordless phone, crossed the room, and sprawled out on the couch, tossing his right leg over the back. "Quiet as it's kept, I do work for a living."

"That's the rumor."

"So what's up?" He wished he'd brought his beer with him.

"Marcia is having some friends and business associates over for a dinner party, and for some reason she insists that I invite your sorry ass."

Nathan grinned. "Marcia knows I'm charming. A fact that has apparently escaped you."

"With good reason," he joked back.

"Tell my sister-in-law that I'll be there. What time?"

"Around eight, last Friday of the month. And bring one of your lovely ladies, or you know Marcia is gonna try and hook you up with one of her friends."

"Gotta give her credit for trying. She doesn't give up."

"She wants you to be just as miserable as I am."

Calvin and Marcia married right out of college and there were no two people who were happier. Marcia was perfect for his frat brother. She settled Calvin down in a way that no other woman before her could, and there had been plenty. When they got married, Nathan felt a certain kind of loss. His running buddy was off the market. Their days of hanging out and swapping stories of their romantic trysts came to an abrupt end—at least it did for Calvin. He now lived vicariously through Nathan's escapades. In a way, Nathan envied Calvin. He had yet to feel about any woman the way Calvin felt about his wife, and often wondered if he ever would. In the meantime, he'd keep having fun and looking.

"If you're miserable, then I believe in Santa Claus," Nathan said.

Calvin chuckled. "I got to play the role."

"Only for those who don't know any better." He leaned his head against the cushions. "So what's been happening? I haven't seen you in a minute."

"Oh, you know, the usual—working. We have a new pilot set to launch in the spring, and everyone in production is going crazy."

"But you love it. Television is in your blood, and putting on a new program and all the madness that goes with it keeps you young."

"True dat. Speaking of television, did you see the fight on Friday night?"

"Aw, man . . . did I . . ."

They talked about sports, segued to music, friends they'd run into, and wrapped it up nearly an hour later with promises to make plans to have a boys' night out with some of the fellas.

"So, I can count you in for dinner?"

"For sure. Wouldn't miss it. Besides, I don't want Marcia to come looking for me. Blow my whole program!"

Calvin laughed. "You got that right. Who do you plan to bring?"

"Hmmm, not sure yet. Maybe I'll surprise you."

"You always do. Coming!" he shouted out. "Well, that's my cue. Duty calls. See you soon."

"Will do. Tell Marcia hello for me."

"Sure. Later."

Nathan slowly hung up the phone, the shadow of a smile still playing around his mouth. It would be good to see Calvin and Marcia, and if things worked out with Pamela, maybe he'd ask her to be his date.

He checked his watch. Eleven-thirty. Not a word from her.

He was more intrigued than before.

Chapter 4

A habitual early riser, Leticia was up with the sun and in the hotel gym. She'd put in a good two-hour workout by the time any other guests arrived.

Returning to her room, she took a hot, then cold, shower, then lathered on her favorite lotion, Papaya Mango, created by this small, one-woman company called *Pamper Me, Pamper You* that she'd stumbled upon in Brooklyn. She smiled as she watched herself in the full-length wall mirror. She turned from side to side, checking herself from every angle. What man wouldn't want this body? It's what women were made for, wasn't it? To bring and receive pleasure.

Yet, even with her internal mantra constantly playing in her mind, the hollowness in the center of her being was never filled, not with men, money, clothes . . . She turned away from the damning reflection.

A drink and a compliment from a handsome man were sure to lift her mood. It always did. She was confident that Nathan Spencer was a man who could easily make her forget the things she didn't want to remember.

She selected a soft-peach wrap dress in a clingy jersey that did lovely things for her figure. Gold hoops for her ears, a hint of makeup, and peach-and-yellow back-out sandals, and she was ready to go.

* * *

Leticia arrived in the hotel dining room, and quickly scanned the space to see if Nathan had arrived. When she didn't see him, she experienced a moment of disenchantment. She was certain that her nonresponse to his thank-you gift would have piqued his interest.

She lifted her chin, shook off the momentary flutter of disappointment, and walked up to the waiter to be seated. She perused the menu.

"I didn't think you would show up this morning." Nathan pulled out a seat opposite her and sat down.

Slowly she put down her menu. "I generally do what I say, especially when an intelligent, handsome man is involved."

"Is that right? So can I conclude that you consider me a handsome and intelligent man?"

"You could . . . if you like."

Nathan chuckled. "What are you having for breakfast?" he asked, changing the direction of the conversation. He had yet to have his coffee for the morning and instinctively knew that he wasn't ready to go toe-to-toe with Pamela.

"I was going to start with a fruit salad. What about you?"

"Sounds good. We can make that two." He signaled for the waiter, who quickly took their orders. "So . . . how did you spend the rest of your evening?"

A flash of Felix's hot flesh and whispers in Spanish skipped through her head. She shrugged. "Nothing special. Watched a little television and went to bed."

He looked at her for a moment. "Hmm."

"And thank you for the champagne, by the way. I should have called."

"Glad you liked it."

"Do you always send champagne to women you've just met?" She picked up her glass of orange juice and brought it to her lips.

"Depends on the woman and how much of an impression she made on me."

"I take it I made an impression . . . of some sort?"

"You definitely did that."

She took a sip of her juice, then put the glass down. "Did you decide what you're going to show me today?"

He had plenty he wanted to show this woman, but it would have to wait. "Thought I'd take you on a tour of South Beach, then lunch, then take you back to your hotel so that you can change for dinner and some music."

"I love the sound of that. A full day."

The waiter arrived with their food.

"I hope you're up to it."

She glanced at him from beneath slightly lowered lids. "Oh, Nathan, I work out. I'm always ready."

"I'm sure you are." He raised his glass in a toast. "To beginnings."

Chapter 5

"You never did tell me what kind of entertainment business you're in," Nathan said as he wound his way around the Miami traffic. They'd been spending all their free time together during the past weeks, but he'd never gotten a clear answer to his question. He took a quick glance at her before veering around a tan Lexus sedan.

"I book clients for . . . special performances."

"That must be interesting. Music, art, what?"

"Music," she lied smoothly. "Is that the Versace mansion?" She pointed to the grand edifice guarded by a ten-foot white fence.

"Yep. Sometimes they offer tours."

"I've heard so much about it." She smiled.

"It's definitely impressive. His sister is there quite a bit, Donnatella."

"Hmm." If she met the right people during her stay, she was sure she could get a peek inside.

They drove slowly down the crowded streets, teeming with people. Every restaurant had an outdoor café setting and practically every seat was filled with young, tanned bodies.

Palm trees swayed gently against the offshore breezes, and from certain points you could see right down onto the white sandy beaches dotted with sunbathers.

"That building on your right. It's one of the projects that I'm working on."

"What is it going to be?"

"The top ten floors are residential co-ops. The bottom five are offices."

"How soon will it be available?"

"Construction is completed, actually. The closing with the owner should wrap up next week. All of the office floors have been leased and ready for occupancy."

"Are all of the co-ops purchased?" She stared up at the building, imagining herself ensconced on the top floor, looking out on the city below. It wasn't New York, but . . .

"I believe there are about three vacancies. The prices are pretty steep."

She turned to him. "What do you consider steep?"

"Five hundred thousand for one bedroom on the top floor."

"Hmm. Not bad."

His brow arched. "I guess not, if you have it like that. I personally prefer some land for my money."

"I don't want the headache of having to mow lawns, water grass, and chase kids off my front yard."

"You have a point. But there's nothing like walking out onto your own property. I never really understood the purpose of spending that kind of money to live in a high-priced apartment building."

"Do you share your sentiments with all your potential buyers?"

He chuckled. "First and foremost, I'm a businessman. If clients want to spend a million bucks on three rooms with a view, I'm more than happy to take their money."

"Can you take me inside?"

He stopped at the red light. "Sure."

"Then let's go. I want to see up close what you do."

He made a quick right turn and headed toward the building.

Just as she'd thought, the view from the fifteenth floor was spectacular. The rooms were spacious with high ceilings and glass everywhere. Wood floors, plenty of closet space, and a sunken living room. Perfect.

She spun toward him, hands on her hips. "I'll take it. Who do I need to speak with to make that happen?"

Nathan's eyes widened. "Just like that?"

"I don't dawdle on making decisions, especially when things feel right to me."

"I can get you an appointment with the owner and have the papers written up. You're sure about this? I didn't realize you wanted to stay in Miami. I got the impression it was temporary."

"Even if it is," she turned and began walking through the space again, "I'd like somewhere to call home." She ran her hand across the black marble countertop in the kitchen. "I can see myself here. Can't you?" She gave him a slow smile.

He walked toward her. "I can see you being at home in any place you chose."

She rested her elbows on the counter and leaned forward. "I can see you visiting here . . . often."

"Can you, now?" He was right in front of her. The tantalizing view of her cleavage called out to him. *Touch me, go ahead.* Reluctantly he pulled his gaze away and focused on the teasing smile that played around her moist lips. That wasn't much better. If he kept looking at her looking at him that way, he was going to have to keep his hands in his pockets for the rest of the afternoon. He turned away.

"If you're sure about it, I'll make an appointment for you to meet with the owners. What day is good for you?"

"My time is my own, Nathan. Get the date and I'll be there." She came from around the table and stood in front of him. She looked up into his eyes, saw the desire there. "Is something wrong?" Her voice was a caress, not a question.

He cleared his throat. "Nothing that spending the rest of the day with you won't cure."

"I like the sound of that." She glanced around. "I know exactly where I'll put everything." She turned back to him. "The bedroom is always my favorite room to design. Do you have a favorite color?"

"Nude."

She chuckled. Her brow arched. "Touché." She touched his arm. "Let's go before we get ourselves into trouble." She headed for the door.

Nathan followed her out. The view from behind was just as tempting. This was going to be a long day.

Chapter 6

Nathan and Leticia spent the rest of the afternoon roaming the streets of South Beach, darting in and out of boutiques and art galleries, stopping off periodically for a cool drink.

"I'm famished," Nathan said after coming out of the florist where Leticia had put in an order for some exotic plants to be delivered to her hotel.

"Do you have someplace in mind?"

"Why don't I fix us something on my grill?"

"A man who can cook! How can I say no?"

"Do you like steak?"

"I love meat." She grinned.

Nathan shook his head and chuckled. "I aim to please."

By the time they arrived at Nathan's beach house, the temperature had cooled considerably. The warm breeze off the ocean gently rustled the trees that braced his home.

"Let me give you the grand tour, then you can relax while I get things together for dinner." He opened the front door and stepped aside to let her pass.

* * *

In a sweeping glance, Leticia took in the rustic and contemporary mix. Wood and smoked glass dominated the rooms. Heavy beamed rafters gave the space an outdoor yet secured feeling. The stone fireplace was perfect for stormy nights or after a cool evening swim.

She turned to him with a smile of approval. "Very nice."

"Glad you like it. Come, I'll show you the rest of the house."

He took her to the kitchen, which looked like it was straight out of a cooking show. Sparkling pots hung from ceiling hooks. The center island was black and stainless steel, matching the industrial refrigerator and freezer. The kitchen opened onto the wraparound deck with a laundry room on the side. Speakers tucked neatly into the high ceilings played soft jazz. Upstairs was a guest bedroom down the hall from the master bath, complete with a Jacuzzi tub, that led to the master bedroom.

It was much as she imagined, strong and masculine, like Nathan. Rich browns and soft tans complemented the space. There was no television or a telephone in the room, she noted. Nothing distracting. The large windows looked right out on the water.

"This is definitely you. It looks comfortable."

"I spend a lot of time here. I want to be able to relax and shut out the world."

"Without interruptions," she added.

"Exactly."

"That's pretty much it, except for the deck. That's where I'll do the cooking tonight."

"Can I help with anything?"

"What are you good at?"

"Whatever I set my mind to."

"I bet you are." He took her by the hand and led her back downstairs.

"Ever been married?" he asked while cutting peppers and onions on the cutting board.

"No. Never found anyone that could put up with me or vice versa." She emptied several ice trays into the ice bucket and put it on the side counter.

"There're several different wines in the cabinet in the living room. Pick what you want."

"How 'bout I make us some margaritas—if you have the ingredients."

"Sounds like a plan. Everything you need is inside."

She went into the living room and found the bottle of tequila and margarita mix and noticed a photograph on the mantel. For an instant her heart thumped in her chest. It was a picture of Nathan and Norman Conyers. She stepped closer and picked up the framed photograph. Yes, it was him. And the background looked like Nathan's house. "Damn."

"Find everything?" he called out from the kitchen.

Leticia put the picture back. "Yes. Coming."

Most times it didn't matter to her if some of her clients knew each other. A good referral was what kept her business thriving. But in this case it was different. She didn't want Nathan to know about her other life, what she'd done before fleeing New York. She wanted him to know her as Pamela, a wealthy entertainment manager, and that was all.

Nathan looked up from his chopping when she reentered the room. "You okay?"

"Yeah, yeah, I'm fine." She forced a smile. "Where's your blender? I think I'll make frozen margaritas."

"In the cabinet over the sink."

"Thanks."

She kept her back to him as she worked and wondered how long it would be before he found out who she really was. Inhaling deeply, she decided to just go with the flow and ride the wave as long as she could. She'd cross those troubled waters should the need arise. But a part of her hoped that it wouldn't.

With the steaks seasoned and sizzling on the grill, Nathan and Leticia relaxed on the deck chairs, taking in the atmosphere and each other.

"Did you always live in New York?" He took a long swallow of his margarita. "These are excellent, by the way."

"Thanks. They'll sneak up on you if you're not careful. To answer your question, no, not always, but I feel like a New Yorker. I lived there for more than ten years."

"Where before that?"

"Atlanta. What about you?"

"Homegrown southern boy. I grew up in Mississippi during the height of the civil rights movement."

"You were in the thick of it."

"Tell me about it." He polished off his drink and went for a refill from the crystal carafe. "I grew up seeing so much ugliness, I believed it was the way of life."

"What changed your mind?"

He leaned forward, resting his forearms on his thighs, and stared out toward the ocean. "I met Martin Luther King one day at a rally. My folks took me. I guess I was about five or six. He was . . ." He paused, searching for the words. "The most powerful presence I'd ever encountered and not in a threatening way, but in a way that reached inside and touched you, made you believe that all things were possible if you had faith." He turned and looked at Leticia with a sheepish expression. "I know that sounds corny, but it was truly a spiritual experience, even for a little kid."

"I'm sure it's something you'll never forget."

"I haven't." He drew in a breath. "After that I decided to take a walk on faith and leave Mississippi when I graduated, build a business. Much of the profits I make from real estate I send back home. I have a foundation there that I personally fund for poor families."

Her eyes widened in surprise. "Now I really am impressed."

He leaned back. "I make more money than I will ever be able to spend. So why not share some of my rewards." He shrugged. "Besides, I get it back in other ways."

"Such as?"

"Meeting someone like you."

Leticia felt her face heat. Sure, she'd been told all manner of bullshit from men over the years, mainly as a way to get between her legs or to stay there once they were in. But this she knew was sincere, and she didn't know what to do about that.

"Are you blushing?" He reached for her but she slipped out of his way and stood.

"Don't be silly." She walked to the railing and pressed her palms against it. She felt him come up behind her and her heart began to race.

Nathan reached out and gently caressed her back, feeling the muscles tighten beneath his fingertips. She closed her eyes and inhaled, slow and deep, enjoying the innocent moment.

"You're beautiful," he whispered. "And I want you. But I'm willing to wait until you say it's all right."

She turned into his arms and faced him. "Do you really mean that?"

He nodded. "Yeah, I do. It's killing me." He grinned. "But I mean it."

She reached up and stroked his chin, then gently touched her lips to his. "Thank you."

"I gotta be going straight to heaven for this one."

Leticia laughed, releasing the hot thread of tension that bound them. "I hear it's a fun place."

"So you say!" He tapped his finger on the tip of her nose. "Let's eat."

"Yeah, I'm starved."

"Have you ever been married?" Leticia cut into her steak.

"Once."

She stopped short of putting a piece in her mouth. "Oh. What happened? If you don't mind me asking."

"No, I don't mind. She left me for another man."

"Oh, I'm sorry."

"Naw, don't be. It would have never worked out anyway. We wanted different things in life and, obviously, different people."

"Hmm."

"How's your steak?"

"Perfect!"

"Great. Uh, a good friend of mine and his wife are having a little party next Friday night. If you don't have plans, I'd love to take you."

"Next Friday?'

"Um-hmm."

She smiled. "I'd like that. Thanks."

"I'll pick you up at the hotel around eight."

"Great." She glanced at him over the rim of her glass. His head was bowed. She'd never been asked to accompany a man for the evening as a real date or without being paid up front. This was all new to her, and she suddenly felt out of her element. Well, she'd just have to play it by ear.

The wind slowly began to pick up, blowing the napkins off the table. Nathan looked toward the horizon.

"Uh-oh, looks like a storm is coming. We'd better get this stuff inside."

She helped him gather everything up and they got settled in the living room, just as the first bolt of lightning zinged across the sky. The sound of thunder seemed to rock the house.

Within moments, a deluge of water pounded against the room, slashing across the windows as the sky grew black and ominous. They stood at the deck window and watched nature whip up a frenzy on the beach.

"Looks like you'll have to stay the night. This could last for a while, and there's no way I'd risk driving back into town in this weather." He looked at her.

"Are you sure you didn't arrange all this?" she teased.

"I only wish I had that kind of power. But I promise to be a perfect gentleman. You're safe with me." He crossed his heart.

Standing next him with the storm holding them captive, she felt as if she were on a deserted island, with just the two of them battling against the forces of nature and their own desires. And she wasn't sure if she wanted him to be a gentleman or not.

"Everything you need is in the closet in the bathroom. I could give you a big T-shirt to sleep in if you want." He stood outside the door of the guest room.

"I'll be fine, thanks." She turned to him. "See you in the morning," she said, a note of hesitation in her voice.

He cleared his throat and shoved his hands in his pockets. "Yeah, rest well. Holler if you need anything."

"I will."

"Well . . . good night, Pam."

"Good night."

He turned and walked down the hall to his room. Slowly she closed the door, but not all the way. Just in case.

Nathan went to his room and walked out onto the deck adjacent to his bedroom and sat down under the overhang as the storm raged on. He heard the shower running in her bathroom, and his mind went into overdrive. He could see her nude body as clearly as if she stood in front of him. He knew she would slip under the covers just the way God had made her. He adjusted himself in the seat as the image resulted in an immediate and intense hard-on. He blew out a long breath. This was going to be one long night.

Chapter 7

Leticia awoke the following morning to a blaze of brilliant sunshine and crystal-clear skies. Slowly she stretched, looked around, and was momentarily confused. This wasn't her hotel room. *Nathan.*

She sat up and looked toward the door. It was still slightly ajar, just the way she'd left it. Tossing the sheet aside, she got out of bed and closed the door fully. A mixture of disappointment and surprise filled her. Disappointment in that she and Nathan had not shared the night that she'd envisioned once it was clear that she was spending the night. Maybe he wasn't as attracted to her as she'd thought. Yet she was surprised that, whether he was attracted to her or not, he did remain a gentleman. How many men would have missed the opportunity to at least attempt to make a play for a woman who was spending the night in the very next room? Hmm, there was more to Nathan Spencer than she gave him credit for.

She found a spare toothbrush in the medicine cabinet, brushed her teeth, washed, and got dressed. When she came downstairs, Nathan was already in the kitchen. He smiled when she entered.

"Good morning. Hope I didn't wake you, banging around down here."

"No, not at all." She sat down on the stool beneath the island counter.

"How did you sleep?"

"Very well, thanks. And you?"

He grinned. "I've had better nights."

"Did the storm keep you up?" she asked innocently.

"You could say that." He put a bowl of fresh fruit on the table. "I'm not a heavy eater in the morning. But I can fix whatever you like."

"Fruit is fine with me."

He passed her a bowl and spoon. She scooped out slices of watermelon, pineapple, and cantaloupe.

"Coffee, tea, juice, water?"

"Coffee."

He poured her a cup and sat down. "What are your plans for today?"

"Go back to the hotel and change out of yesterday's getup, for starters." She laughed.

"Whenever you're ready, I can take you back." He paused. "I really enjoyed your company."

"Likewise."

Nathan tugged in a deep breath. 'I'd like to keep seeing you.'

She arched a brow. "Really?"

"Yes, beyond our 'official date' next Friday. If that's all right with you."

She had no business even thinking about getting involved with anyone. That was in her M.O. She was freewheeling, doing her own thing. Besides, when you made attachments it was harder to say good-bye, and she knew she would at some point. She was a businesswoman, and her business didn't have room for relationships. Judging from the kind of man Nathan Spencer showed himself to be, he wouldn't take too kindly to finding out how she really made her money. And she never wanted to see the look on his face when he did.

"Why don't we take it slow? One day at a time."

"Fair enough." He took a bite of pineapple and chewed slowly before speaking again. "I made the call to the building owner this morning. If you haven't changed your mind, you can meet with him later this afternoon."

"You don't waste time, do you?"

"I'm a businessman. This is business. I think I'd like it to be more, but I'll settle for this for the time being."

"You don't seem like the kind of man who would simply settle for anything."

"There are exceptions to every rule. You happen to be one exceptional exception." He stood. "Now, before I go and say something totally inappropriate, let me get you back to your hotel."

He turned and walked out of the room, leaving Leticia to struggle with her conscience.

Nathan pulled his black Lincoln Navigator to a stop in front of Leticia's hotel. He turned to her.

"I'll be back to pick you up at two-thirty."

"Fine. I'll be out front waiting." She opened her door, stepped out, then turned back to him. "Thank you."

He nodded and watched her walk inside.

Leticia entered the lobby, and the first face she saw was that of Felix. She put a bit more swing in her hips and slowly approached him.

"Felix, how are you?"

"Hmm, *muy bien*, and you?"

"Actually, I have a little problem in my room." She rolled her eyes down to his crotch then back to his face. "I'm hoping you can fix it . . . if you have some time."

"I see. The gentleman that dropped you off could not feex your *problemo*?"

She absently glanced toward the door, waved her hand in dismissal. "Oh, that." She shrugged her right shoulder. "Do you have time or don't you?" She checked her watch. "I'm going up to take a shower. I'll leave the door unlocked." She walked away and knew he was watching her every move. Felix was just what she needed to take her mind off of what she knew she could not have.

Promptly at two-thirty, Nathan pulled up in front of the hotel. She'd barely had enough time to shower and change after her romp with Felix. Already, he was getting possessive. Not good. She didn't need him and didn't want him for anything more than diversionary sex. She'd have to deal with it. She put on her smile and walked toward the car. This time he was driving his BMW.

Nathan got out at her approach, dressed totally for business in a navy pinstriped suit, stark white shirt, and power tie in a rich burgundy.

"Well, don't you look impressive," she said, taking his hand as he helped her into the car.

"So do you."

She'd decided on a fitted off-white pantsuit with a waist-length jacket with gold buttons, simple black Jimmy Choo sling backs, and matching purse. Small gold hoops hung from her ears and a gold cuff bracelet graced her wrist. She got in the car and gently sat down. Felix had been a little more than rough on their third go-round, and she was feeling its effects. She adjusted the short black silk scarf around her neck, a last-minute accessory when she'd noticed the angry red marks popping up on the left and right sides. Ice and relaxation would diminish them, and she hoped they'd be gone by morning.

Nathan eased out into traffic and headed to the center of town. "The office is on Palm Court, about ten minutes from here."

Leticia nodded. "How was your morning after you dropped me off?"

"Actually, kind of busy. The paperwork kind. Needed to get some information together for a client."

"Another commercial building?"

"Yes, an upscale beauty salon."

"My kind of spot."

He turned to her and grinned. "When it opens in about two months, I'll take you by there, see if it meets your high standards."

"I'm actually pretty easy to please."

"Are you? That's good to know. Now I won't have to bring in my stable of character witnesses."

She tossed her head back and laughed. "Do they get a salary or are they on retainer?"

"Retainer. I never know when I have someone I need to impress. You'll meet some of them soon."

"And I can't wait to hear what they have to say about you."

*   *   *

They pulled up to the complex and got out.

"Ready?"

"Yes."

"All right, let's go."

They got off the elevator on the tenth floor and walked down the hushed corridor to the offices of Graham and Associates. Nathan opened the door for her and stepped up to the desk of the receptionist.

"Good afternoon, Ginny."

"Hello, Mr. Spencer. Mr. Graham is waiting for you—go right in."

"Thanks." He placed his hand at the small of Leticia's back and ushered her inside.

Miles Graham stood, a dead ringer for a young Mickey Rourke during his 9½ *Weeks* fame.

"Miles." Nathan approached with his hand outstretched. They shook hands, but Miles's eyes stayed focused on Leticia. "This is Pamela Armstrong."

"Ms. Armstrong." He extended his hand to Leticia and held it a little longer than needed.

"Thank you for seeing me on such short notice."

"Not a problem at all. Please, have a seat."

Nathan held the chair for Leticia. "I'll leave you two to discuss business. I'll be out front when you're done." He walked out, closing the door behind him.

"So, you're interested in the penthouse apartment."

"Yes, it's perfect."

Miles opened a folder and turned it to face Leticia. "These are the specs for the apartment, along with the asking price, which is expensive. I have to be honest—I wasn't interested in having a single woman take over the property." He folded his hands atop the desk. "If it weren't for Nathan's recommendation, I doubt if I would have seen you."

Leticia looked into his eyes. "Why is that?" She arched a brow.

"The asking price is quite high and I need to be sure that the payments can be made."

"What makes you think that a single woman wouldn't be able to make the payments?"

"Not that she wouldn't, just that I believe from experience that it may prove to be more difficult."

"I've never had any difficulty holding up my end of anything, Miles. Can I call you Miles?" Her gaze locked onto Miles, her eyes darkened, and a gradual flush rose from his neck to his cheeks. He cleared his throat, obviously flustered, and Leticia crossed her legs in a scene right out of *Basic Instinct*. She gave him a slow smile, leaned slightly forward, and slid the file toward her.

She nodded her head slowly as she read the contents, flipping the pages unhurriedly. Several minutes later, she closed the folder and pushed it back across the desk. "Looks fine."

He tugged a bit at his tie.

"What do you want from me to make this happen?" she asked, the question simple, the innuendo loaded. "Would you like to see my papers?" She uncrossed her legs, waited a beat, and crossed them back.

"I'll have to run a credit check," he said, almost apologetically.

"Of course." She folded her hands over her crossed knees, drawing his eyes to just where she wanted them to be. "I'll definitely have to invite you up for drinks once I get settled. I have some great ideas on how I'm going to decorate. I think even you would be impressed, Miles."

"I'm sure I would." He flipped through the papers on his desk until he found the form he was looking for. "If you would fill this out . . ."

She leaned across the desk, offering him a hint of a glimpse. "I really love that place. I'd hate for it to go to someone else. I feel as if it were made for me. You ever feel like that, Miles, that something was simply made for you?"

"I—"

"Are you married, Miles?"

"No, I'm not."

"Oh, then I guess you'll be coming alone for drinks."

A thin line of perspiration popped up on his forehead as he ran his tongue across his lips. "Do you want me to come alone?"

She tilted her head to the side. "Sounds perfect." She reached for a pen on his desk and completed the application, then passed it back to Miles.

He barely looked it over. "I'm sure everything is fine. I'll be sure to expedite the application. I should have an answer back for you tomorrow."

Languidly, she stood, looking down on him. "That long?" She pouted. "Can't you do it faster? Isn't the final decision yours?"

"Yes, it is."

"You don't strike me as the kind of man who doesn't trust his instincts. What are your instincts about me?"

He rose and came around the desk to her side. "My instincts about you are that you would be a lovely addition to the building."

"Of course I would. You'll love having me."

His nostrils flared. His voice dropped a note. "Would I?"

"I guarantee it." She smiled up at him. *Fool. Just like a man when it comes to the scent of pussy.* "Now, about these papers." She held them up between them.

He took them from her hand. "I'm sure they're fine. You can make your check out to Graham Management Corporation. You'll sign your lease as soon as the check clears, and then you can move in."

"What a pleasure it is doing business with you, Miles," she purred.

"Pleasure is something I thoroughly enjoy giving."

She laughed deep in her throat. *Asshole.* She wrote out the check for the down payment.

"The apartment will be leased to you for six months. After that time, if you decide to stay, you can apply for purchase."

"Works for me." She handed him the check for the first six months for thirty thousand dollars.

He looked it over, then slid it into the breast pocket of his jacket and gave it a pat. "I'll put this through today."

Leticia reached for her purse on the desk. "I really look forward to hearing from you." She turned ever so slowly until she faced him, chest to breasts. Her gaze ran over his face, settled on his mouth.

"You definitely will."

"I'm sure," she said, before walking to the door. She stopped and turned halfway. "It's been a pleasure." She opened the door and walked out.

Nathan was sitting in the reception area. He stood as she approached. "How'd it go?"

She tucked her purse under her arm. "Oh, quite well. Looks like I'll be staying for a while."

He put his arm around her waist and they walked out.

Chapter 8

Back at her hotel room, Leticia quietly relished her successful endeavor. It had taken her years to create her "other self." Pamela Armstrong was everything that she was not: a hardworking, tax-paying citizen. She'd used her connections in the state government in Atlanta and New York to secure a social security number, birth certificate, and an impressive list of job experiences and checkable references. Pamela Armstrong had a family, a good American education, and a sizeable bank account. All very legitimate for those who didn't know any better. Her credit rating was impeccable, as Miles would soon discover.

She stretched out across her bed and folded her hands across her stomach. Maybe being Pamela Armstrong for a while would be a good thing, after all. Perhaps she could become in real life all the things that she'd created for Pamela and leave her old life behind. But old habits died hard. Felix and the stunts she pulled with Miles were perfect examples. Oh well, she thought. She'd ride this one out as long as she desired or until circumstances dictated otherwise.

Hmm. A little room service would be the perfect ending to the perfect day. She reached for the phone.

* * *

Nathan returned to his office after dropping Leticia off at her hotel. They'd made tentative plans for dinner. She promised to call. He hoped that she would.

He was reviewing some documents on the computer when his secretary buzzed him.

"Mr. Spencer, you have a call on 307. A Mr. Conyers."

"Thanks." He pressed the flashing red light on the desk phone. "Norm, how's it going, man?"

"Everything is fine. I was planning on coming into town this weekend. I thought we could get together."

"Of course. When are you coming in?"

"My flight arrives on Friday morning. How are you for dinner?"

"Aw, man—actually I have plans for Friday night."

"Hmm, then maybe Saturday."

"Absolutely. Hey, why don't you join us?"

"Maybe another time. I don't want to intrude."

"You wouldn't be. Anyway, think about it and give me a call. Where are you staying?"

"At the Hilton, downtown."

"You're welcome to stay with me if you want."

"Thanks, but I live for room service." He chuckled.

"I hear ya. Well, it will be good to see you. We have catching up to do."

"I'll give you a call."

"Safe travels." Nathan hung up.

He and Norman had met at a brokers' conference several years earlier and became fast friends. Norman was a good guy, hardworking and honest. He'd lost his wife ten years earlier to cancer and had never remarried. He'd said he'd never find anyone to replace Virginia, so he took his pleasure where he could find it, drifting in and out of relationships and one-night stands. Not the ideal life, but it seemed to work for Norman.

Nathan returned to his computer files. He couldn't wait to introduce him to Pam. He'd love to hear what Norman thought of her.

*   *   *

Disappointed that they'd sent a woman instead of Felix to deliver room service, Leticia slowly chewed on her fresh fruit as she sat on the balcony overlooking the city of Miami. In a few weeks she'd be able to relocate to her new home. She'd deal with Miles then, certain that he would be looking for some kind of payment. She only hoped that he wouldn't become troublesome. She so detested troublesome men, which brought her thoughts to Norman Conyers.

It wasn't that Norman was particularly troublesome, but his connection to Nathan was. Her gut instincts told her it was only a matter of time before the Norman Conyers shoe fell, but until then she was going to make the most of it and try to pretend to have a semblance of a real life.

She pushed her fruit plate aside and stood. One thing was certain: until that shoe fell, she wanted as much of Nathan Spencer as he could handle. She longed to be "the girlfriend," not the escort, to be treated like a lady and not the paid whore, and she wanted to be made love to, not fucked. Was that too much to ask?

Entering the living area, she went to the phone and dialed Nathan's number. She was never one for wasting time, as tomorrow was not promised.

Nathan made reservations for dinner aboard a cruise ship, complete with a live band.

"This is wonderful," Leticia said as they walked on the top deck as the ship pulled off for its three-hour cruise.

"I thought you'd like it. Do you want a drink before dinner?"

"Yes, I'd love an apple martini."

"Don't move, I'll be right back." He went off toward the bar on the lower level.

Leticia leaned against the railing and watched the city of Miami slip away as the ship moved gently across the still waters. She tugged in a lungful of sea air and for a moment closed her eyes, imagining a life with Nathan Spencer. He was handsome, intelligent, comfortably well-off, sexy as hell, and he treated her like a lady. When she was in his presence she could almost forget the life she'd lived, the things she'd done.

Almost.

"Here you go."

She turned and his smile and her drink greeted her. "Thanks." She took the glass and a sip. "Mmm. Very good. Just the way I like it."

Nathan braced his back against the railing to better look at her. "I'm really glad you agreed to dinner."

"Really? And why is that? I'm sure a man like you has an assortment of women to have dinner with."

"Maybe I do. But I wanted to have dinner with you. Does that make a difference?"

She grinned. "I feel special."

They both laughed.

"Tell me about you, Pam. I want to know everything."

"Everything! Ha. Trust me, my life is not that interesting."

"Let me be the judge. How'd you get started in the entertainment field?"

She took a sip of her drink and then another. She'd rehearsed this hundreds of times. "I majored in Marketing and Communications in college and was lucky enough to get an internship in my senior year with a public relations firm that specialized in the music industry. I loved it. Loved the excitement, the scandals we had to cover up." She smiled as the story took on a life of its own. "Even then, I was a savvy businesswoman," she said with a hint of laughter in her voice. "I decided to leave school before graduation." Just in case he decided to look up her graduating class.

He frowned. "Why?"

Her expression sobered. Momentarily she lowered her head. "My grandmother passed. She left me a large amount of money and the opportunity to start my own business presented itself. I had a client list and inside experience. So I took a chance, tapped into some of my contacts, and I've never looked back."

"Sounds like a fairy tale."

She snatched a glance at him to see if he was serious or testing her. She smiled. "Sometimes life is charmed. I guess things just fell into place for me."

"And you've made the most of it."

"I've tried. I like what I do." She finished off her drink and handed it to a passing waiter. "What about you, Nathan?" She played with his tie. "What made you the man you are today?"

"I can't say my life was as charmed as yours. I'm one of five kids. The oldest, the one who had to set the example. Did pretty good in school and was able to get a partial academic scholarship. I majored in Economics and Finance. Unlike you," he said without rancor, "I didn't land my dream job right out of school."

"What did you end up doing?"

"Worked in construction for about four years. In a way it was a good thing. It really gave me a close-up look at the building industry. That knowledge is crucial to me now. A building owner can't razzle-dazzle me when I can run my hand across a wall and know what kind of beams are behind it." He took a long swallow of his drink as if suddenly caught up in thought. He pushed out a breath and looked at Leticia. "I was in a bar one night after a tough day and wound up sitting next to a guy who worked on Wall Street. We got to talking and he told me about a friend of his who was opening a real estate office that dealt strictly in commercial property." He shrugged slightly. "The rest is history." The corner of his mouth lifted in a grin.

"Where's your family now?"

"My two sisters live in Chicago. One is a nurse, the other a social worker. My youngest brother is a doctor in Houston, and my brother under me is a teacher in Brooklyn."

"Were you and your siblings close?"

He chuckled as he nodded. "Yeah, when we weren't trying to kill each other. We had a pretty good life. My mom and dad worked hard to make sure we had the best they could provide for us. Holidays were always great, and we still all get together every year for Christmas. Both of my sisters have kids and my youngest brother's wife is expecting any day now."

Family. She had no idea what that was, what it was like to have a Christmas dinner in a house that she could call home, have siblings that she could tease and tell her troubles to, share secrets with. She looked away. Family. Hump. It was overrated.

"Sounds wonderful."

"Maybe you'll get to meet them one day."

"Hmm, maybe." She took a breath and looked around. "Shouldn't we be going in for dinner?" She started to walk off and missed the curious look that Nathan flashed at her.

"I had a wonderful evening," Leticia said as they disembarked. "This was a great idea. Thank you."

"I enjoyed every minute. He paused. I don't want it to end." He gently clasped her by the arm. "What do you say we continue our evening out on the beach . . . my place?"

She stepped up to him. "I like how you think, Mr. Spencer."

"How 'bout a swim?" Nathan asked once they'd arrived at his beach house.

"I don't have a swimsuit."

His eyes spoke volumes. "This is a private beach. It's dark, and I won't wear a suit since you don't have one."

Her laughter danced in the night air. "Last one in," she sang out as she ran toward the ocean, discarding her clothing as she went.

Nathan followed suit, and they swam the way God made them. The water seemed to heat as they played, swam, brushed against each other, the waves exciting their bare flesh. Finally they emerged, two bronze gods under the moonlight.

Nathan wrapped her in an oversized towel before tucking one around his waist.

"I turned on the fire before we got in." He looked into her eyes, then put his arm around her waist and guided her inside.

The warm fire blazed, the only other illumination in the room save for the moonlight and stars. Soft music played in the background.

"Can I fix you a drink?"

"Some wine would be great," she said, her voice thick and sensual as she took in the expanse of his chest, the long, lean muscles of his calves.

Nathan poured two glasses of wine and brought them back to the couch, where Leticia was curled up.

"Thanks." She brought the glass to her lips, but Nathan stopped her.

"I want to make a toast. To new beginnings and happy endings." He touched his glass to hers.

"I like the beginning part," she whispered.

"So do I." He took her glass from her hand and put it on the table. He looked at her for a long moment. "I want to kiss you, Pam."

"I want you to."

Gently he put his hand behind her head and drew her to him until his lips were only a breath away from hers. When they met, Leticia felt as if she were being kissed for the first time. It was gentle, sweet, and caring. Nothing like anything she'd previously experienced. When the tip of his tongue stroked her lips, shock waves of bliss coursed through her. A low moan rose up from her chest as he pressed a bit harder, compelling her lips to yield to his.

Nathan's arms embraced her, pulling her into an erotic dance of lips and tongues that found its own unique beat.

Leticia's fingers played with his chest as his trailed up and down her back, loosening her towel until her breasts were freed and pulsing against his chest.

"You're so beautiful," he murmured against her mouth. "I want to see all of you."

Slowly he stood, pulling her gently to her feet, letting the towel pool at her ankles. His eyes ran over her and heated her body like hot coals. She shivered under the intensity of his gaze and nearly crumpled to the cool wood floor when his mouth captured a hardened nipple.

"God, I want you," he groaned as he eased down her body, his mouth and tongue taunting every inch of skin. He pressed his mouth against the dark hairs at her center and had her crying out when his mouth tenderly suckled her throbbing clit.

Her knees weakened and she clung to him to keep from falling, tossing her head back in joy as wave after wave of unspeakable sensations jettisoned through her. Just as she was at the threshold of her climax, Nathan drew back and stood. Her entire body vibrated.

"Not here," he whispered. He took her hand and led her to his bedroom.

Once inside, he continued the titillating assault on her body until he had her on his bed. For what seemed like forever, he braced himself above her.

"I've thought about this moment from the instant I set eyes on you." He reached across her to his dresser drawer and took out a condom.

"Let me." She ripped open the packet and skillfully slid it on his erect penis, using her fingers and her mouth to make the simple act become a symphony of the senses.

Nathan shuddered and groaned as she teased and played with him, licking, sucking, taunting, drawing out the moment until neither of them could hold out any longer.

He moved her away, his eyes dark and dangerous as he pushed inside of her all the way.

Leticia drew in a long, tight breath as he filled her, moving inside her with the artistry of a Caribbean dancer. She came after little more than a dozen expert strokes, but he didn't stop. He lifted her legs higher, pushed deeper, rotating his hips to elicit even more pleasure. She exploded again and again until she was weak, limp with tears of incredible joy slipping from behind her closed lids.

Nathan slowly, methodically, increased the tempo until it seemed as if the world moved beneath them.

"This is for you," he groaned, pulling her raised hips hard against him as he thrust into her one final time before slumping into the welcoming valley of her breasts.

Chapter 9

Leticia had slept with many men in her life, too many to count. For the most part it was just a job. Periodically, she allowed herself to feel pleasure, to screw simply for the fun and thrill of it. This with Nathan was something different. She didn't understand it. She didn't like it. She didn't like the sudden feeling of being connected, as if what they'd just done to and with each other really mattered. It didn't.

She turned onto her side, and was surprised to find that Nathan was awake and looking back at her.

"Hey," he whispered. He pushed damp hair away from her forehead and trailed his finger down her cheek. "You okay?"

She nodded instead of speaking, thinking she might say something really stupid like she was falling for him or something equally ridiculous, like it was the first time in her life that she'd been made love to. Her throat tightened.

He leaned over and kissed her tenderly. "I'll be right back." He got up from the bed and walked into the bathroom.

Leticia listened to the water running, and for just a moment, she allowed herself the joy of simply relishing the moment, letting her imagination explore the improbable possibilities of being a part of Nathan's life, being cared about by him, waking up with him in the morning, sitting across a dinner table from him at night.

Fool. This is not your life. It is only a temporary diversion. You're a

*paid whore. It's who you are, all you will ever be. But be of good cheer—
you're great at it.*

Nathan returned with a basin in his hand and a towel draped over
his arm. He sat next to her on the bed after setting the basin filled with
water on the nightstand. He eased the sheet off of her.

"Let me take care of you." He dipped the washcloth into the water
and wrung it out before running it tenderly across her face. He repeated the process, washing her hands, her neck, her breasts, her stomach, the still-pulsing crown of her sex.

It took all Leticia had not to weep. He was treating her as if she
mattered. Not showering her with gifts or money, but with warm,
cleansing water, the most profound gift she'd ever received.

"It doesn't replace a shower." He chuckled lightly, almost self-
consciously, Leticia thought. "But it'll help you to rest more comfortably."

"Thank you."

"I'm gonna get something to drink. Can I get you anything?"

"Some fruit juice or water would be fine," she said, barely able to
find her voice.

"You got it."

Leticia stared up at the ceiling. She'd simply ease out of his life.
Before long, he'd never know she'd been there.

After trying unsuccessfully to get Leticia to spend the day with him,
Nathan opted to catch up on some work in his home office. Settled in
the small but well-equipped space, he turned on his computer and was
just about to begin some research on a less-than-upstanding contrac-
tor when his cell phone rang. He checked the number and saw that it
was Miles. Must be good news.

"Hey, Miles. How are you?"

"Good. And thank you for bringing Ms. Armstrong."

Nathan leaned back in his seat and smiled. "Did everything go
through okay?"

"Smooth as silk. Almost too smooth."

"Too smooth? Is there such a thing?"

"Well, in her case, yes. Not a spot, not a stain on her credit. Her references are impeccable. She's never been late with a bill and she has a nice chunk of cash in the bank."

"And that's a bad thing?"

"No," he drew the word out. "Just surprising. Everyone has a ding or two."

"What's your point, Miles?"

"How well do you know her?"

After last night, pretty damned well. "We're getting to know each other. Why?"

"Personal or business?"

"I don't think that's any of yours." He pushed up in the chair, his patience running thin.

"Hey, relax. That's one hot lady and . . . well, all roads lead to Rome, as they say."

"Do they?" His jaw clenched. He and Miles had shared more than business deals on occasion. Miles had no conscience when it came to women, a standing joke between the fellas; if it has two legs and wears a skirt, Miles was in there. Not this time.

"Look, she acted like she was on the market and ready for whatever I wanted to give her. I just wanted the inside scoop on whether or not you've tapped it or not. Maybe give me some tips."

Nathan shot up from the chair, turning it over on its side. He began pacing the room, trying to clear his head and make sense out of the nonsense Miles was spinning.

"She actually came on to you in your office?" His nostrils flared as he tugged in air.

"Man, she all but came out of her clothes. If she wasn't a friend of yours, I'da been scared it was some kind of sting." He chuckled. "She's hot, man."

"Yeah," he said absently. "Well, you go for it if that's what you want to do. Free country." He stared at the wall.

"Now you know, I know, and they know that ain't shit free in this country." He laughed. "For a piece like that, humph, I'd be willing to pay top dollar."

Nathan sat down on the edge of the desk, feeling the gut punch that knocked the air out of him. "Yeah, I hear you," he mumbled. "Listen, Miles, I have to run. Meeting in a few minutes."

"Sure. Once again, partner, thanks for sending the lady my way."

"Yeah." Nathan hung up the phone, feeling suddenly ill. The combination of disbelief mixed with possibility had his head throbbing. *Pam and Miles?* He stood. *Coming on to him in his office?* He shook his head. *No.* But then he thought back to the night he'd met her. She oozed fire and sex. She knew it. At times she acted as if she'd give it to him right there on the table, and he would have been more than willing to take it. But something happened in the ensuing weeks, something that he couldn't remember happening since college; he actually wanted to get to know her, not just get her in the bed. And he'd been foolish enough to believe that she wanted the same thing, even though she never admitted as much.

He paced the floor. So what was last night about? He couldn't believe it was all show on her part. Those were real tears in her eyes, that was real joy on her face. He knew it.

Or did he?

Leticia sat on the side of the hotel pool, dipping her toes in and out of the mild, waveless water. A young woman swam effortlessly along the length of the Olympic-sized pool. A few hotel guests walked along the sides or lounged in chairs.

Today was one of the few times that she wished she'd had a girlfriend, just someone she could talk to about the turmoil that was going on in her head, the new emotions that she was experiencing. But what more could she expect from the hand that life dealt her?

From birth she'd been alone, abandoned by her mother in death and her siblings through circumstances. Fending for herself was a way of life from the moment she'd been given away and into the hands of strangers. Strangers one after another, their names and faces becoming a blur, her hopes for her life fading until there was nothing left inside, no feeling of worth or value. How could you feel worthy or validated if people only wanted you for "a little while" or until they no longer needed or wanted the government checks they received in payment for putting a roof over her head? Payment for services—she learned that early. She learned it from the age of eight when "Uncle Lou," her foster mother's brother, told her she needed to do something for her keep, and if she wanted to stay there, she needed to make it worth his while.

So at eight years old, she learned, in silent agony, what it was like to be opened and pillaged and given a dollar for her pain, humiliation, and her silence. As she grew older, there were more "Uncle Lou's", but she'd learned to get what she wanted for her time and her body. Five dollars instead of one, twenty instead of ten, fifty instead of thirty. By the time she was sixteen years old, she understood her body was a viable business and she dealt with it as such, disconnecting her emotions and adding up her dollars. Dollars leveled the playing field. She could buy her way into places where before she was unwelcome. She could pay for the clothes she saw in magazines, travel to the places she'd only read about.

By the time she was twenty-two, she owned her own town house in Atlanta. She had more clothes than she could ever wear. Men lined up to be with her, leaving handfuls of money, jewelry, and confidences behind.

She made a life for herself, she made acquaintances and allies, but she'd never made a friend. That's what she needed most, right now, right this minute.

"Where is your smile today?"

Leticia looked up into the dark, smoldering eyes of Felix. She forced a smile and some cheer into her voice.

"Felix, I missed you the other night."

"I'm here now." He looked around. "We could go to your room . . ."

And they'd romp around in her bed, sweat, climax in biblical proportions, and it would mean absolutely nothing. Felix wouldn't care if she was all right afterward, he wouldn't touch her body as if it was a treasure, he wouldn't bathe her afterwards, or tenderly kiss her to make her heart swell. No, it would just be another fuck, and poor Felix certainly didn't have the money to even rate this brief conversation.

"Sounds like a great idea, Felix. But maybe later." She smiled.

Felix stared at her for a moment. "Women like you—"

She jumped up. "I'm not going to continue this conversation." She started to walk away. He grabbed her arm.

"Take your hand off of me," she said from between her teeth.

"Bitch." He tossed her arm aside and stormed off.

She drew in a long breath. Her eyes darted around to see if anyone else had witnessed what transpired. One woman was frowning in her direction, then shook her head and walked away. Leticia snatched up her towel from the deck and returned to her room.

Felix was going to be a problem. She could feel it. She'd had other situations like this, where they became possessive. But before she'd had the luxury of simply not letting them in, or calling upon one of her law enforcement friends to put a little scare in them. Here, she was on her own.

She went to the bar and fixed herself a glass of wine, finishing it off in two swallows. She poured another. If she could steer clear of Felix until she moved into her apartment, everything would be fine. She was a fool to get entangled with someone who worked at the hotel. She'd let desire overshadow reason.

She walked out onto the terrace—that's when she heard her front door open. She spun around and Felix was standing in her living room.

"Get out!"

He came closer. "You think you can use people. Oh, no, *señorita*, not this time." He unzipped his pants and snatched the belt from around his waist.

She was paralyzed. Paralyzed with fear and the memories that froze her mind and body—images of all the "uncle Lou's" who'd come before him. Paralyzed when he pushed her down on the floor, wrapped his belt around her throat, and buried his anger and frustration inside her.

Leticia didn't utter a word, not a sound. She remembered what she'd been told: *"Scream and I'll have to hurt you. Don't say a word, this is our secret. Tell and I'll come back and finish you off."* The mantras ran over and over through her mind as Felix had her every which way but loose.

When he finally got up, staggering to his feet, he looked down on her with such repulsion her own stomach roiled.

Without a word, he fixed his clothing, smoothed his hair, and walked out as quietly as he'd entered.

* * *

She didn't know how long she lay there on the floor. When a semblance of time and place found its way to her, it had grown dark outside. Inch by painful inch, she pulled herself up from the floor and stumbled into the bathroom.

The reflection that stared back at her was a face she did not recognize. Her eyes were swollen, her lip busted, the skin around her neck was raw from the belt that kept cutting off her air, taking her in and out of consciousness. Her dressing gown was torn and dotted with semen and blood.

Trance-like, she turned on the tub and in a ritual that she'd performed countless times, she got in with the vain hope that the waters would somehow wash away her memories and her pain.

Chapter 10

Nathan hung up the phone. He'd tried Leticia at her hotel room all afternoon with no answer. He'd left several messages on her cell phone with no return call.

Was she with another man right now? Was she with Miles?

He flipped on the television as the sun settled down beyond the horizon. What did he really know about her? Only what she told him, which had been minimal at best. He'd been so enamored of her and her apparent attraction to him that he'd cast all caution to the wind.

"Get it together, man," he said aloud. You barely know the woman, and there are plenty more where she came from.

Unable to sit still, not wanting to rest, he went and found his PDA and looked up the number of Simone, a hot model that he'd dated off and on. She was home, not busy, and would be happy to see him. Was he planning to stay the night, she wanted to know? *Of course.*

As he dressed in preparation for his night out, he was sure that Simone would be more than happy to take his mind off anyone else but her.

Leticia sat in one of the local bars, nursing her second apple martini. She'd been periodically listening to a conversation between a young woman and man who were discussing their jobs on a cruise ship that was ready to set sail in two days. To be young and carefree, Leticia thought as she paid her tab and gingerly rose from the barstool.

It was near eleven, and the streets of South Beach were bustling with activity. Neon lights from shops, restaurants, and mammoth billboards competed for the eye's attention. Couples strolled and laughed, car horns blared, music of every genre blended into its own unique sound.

Leticia strolled the avenues, her still-red-rimmed, puffy eyes shielded behind wide, dark shades—nothing odd about that in chic Miami. A brilliant, multicolored scarf covered the welts on her neck. Her legs still weak and her inner thighs still trembling, she forced herself to stay on her feet, breathe the air, and become simply one of the pulsing throng of nighthawks.

Never before had she felt so desperately alone, even in the midst of all this humanity. For all that she had, she had nothing at all. Thinking that she could begin a new life was a foolish, childish dream. Who she was, what she had become, would follow her to her grave.

"Leticia!"

Her heart leapt in her chest and she nearly stumbled but kept looking ahead. She knew the voice.

"Leticia."

The voice was closer, coming from behind her. She dared not respond. She approached the corner just as a cab pulled up. She jumped in and took a chance on glancing back. And there he was—Norman Conyers.

Leticia gave the driver the name of her hotel. She sat back and closed her eyes, letting speed and distance do their job, but her past was never far behind her.

Norman stood in the middle of the bustling street, momentarily confused. He was certain that it was Leticia he'd seen. He'd know that walk and that body anywhere in the world. But could he have been wrong? Did he want to see her so much that he actually imagined that he did? Miami was filled with beautiful women. But one who looked exactly like Leticia? He shook his head and absently paid the driver, who was waiting patiently by the side of the cab that Norman had gotten out of.

"I can drive you right up to the front door, sir."

He'd commanded the driver to stop in the middle of the street when he saw a woman he thought was Leticia. "Uh, I'm fine. Thanks," he muttered, still looking off toward where he'd seen the apparition. He picked up his bags from the curb and proceeded toward the entrance of his hotel.

Once he was settled in his room, he called Nathan and left him a message that he was in town a couple of days early and maybe he would take him up on his offer for dinner with his friends on Friday night after all. He left his room number and hung up.

Norman walked over to the terrace that looked down on the city and wondered what Leticia was doing in Miami. More important, why had she left without a word?

That morning when he'd awakened and found her gone he'd been devastated. At first he didn't want to believe it. He kept telling himself that any moment she was going to call, walk in the door, put her arms around him and tell him that "she'd just needed some space." Then everything would be right with his world again.

But as the days turned to weeks and the weeks into months, his worst nightmare became reality—Leticia was gone. Simply gone.

He knew who Leticia was, what she was, and it didn't matter to him. He'd sat in his car outside her brownstone in Manhattan on numerous occasions and watched as the men came and went. He'd seen her prepare for elaborate dates, then be picked up by chauffeur-driven limos. But none of it mattered. When he was with her, none of the other men, and what she may have done with them, mattered.

He laughed derisively at himself. He lived a good, upstanding life, was married to a good woman until the day she died. He had a business, friends, a close-knit family, and traveled at will. He could have just about any woman he wanted, but he was in love with a whore. How sad was that?

Maybe he should have told her long ago how he felt about her. Told her that he didn't care about her past, that they could make a new future together anywhere in the world. But he hadn't said a word. He'd been afraid, afraid that she would laugh at his naivete. No one fell in love with a whore, not really, she would say. Some men simply had grand illusions of somehow turning them into honest women. Yes, Leticia would have said that.

He'd never told anyone about his relationship with Leticia. It was his dirty little secret. And the only person he would trust to understand was Nathan.

Chapter 11

Nathan returned to his beach house the following afternoon. Simone had been a tigress from the moment he'd walked in the door. The night was filled with wine, cocaine, and hot, steamy, sticky sex until both of them were past the point of exhaustion.

He tossed his small overnight bag onto the bed and saw the flashing light on his answering machine. Bone weary, he sat down on the side of the bed and listened to his messages. Two were from his office, one from Cal reminding him about the dinner party, and the last one was from Norman.

Nathan listened to the message again, jotted down the phone number of the hotel and Norman's room number, then dialed.

Norman picked up just as the answering service kicked in.

"Nate, glad you called, man."

"Thought you weren't getting in until the weekend."

"Yeah, I know. Changed my mind at the last minute and hopped a plane. What are you up to today? Can we get together?"

Nathan ran a hand across his face. The stubble on his cheeks and chin bristled against his palm.

"To be honest, man, I had a pretty rough night."

Norman chuckled, reading in between the lines. "Some things never change. You're still an old hound."

"Hmm. Yeah. But, uh, maybe later on. Why don't you come out here?"

"Thought you'd never ask."

"You remember where I am, right?"

"Sure. How's eight, nine o'clock?"

"Works for me. See you then."

Nathan hung up and stared at the phone. Still no word from Pam. He pushed up from the bed and headed for the shower, determined to get the scent of sex out of his skin.

The steamy water sloshed over him. He lathered and scrubbed. He turned his face up to the water. Why was she avoiding him? What had gone wrong?

Finished with his shower, Nathan decided to kill a few hours at the office. But once there, he couldn't concentrate. Every few minutes he was checking the dial tone on the phone and on his cell to assure himself that they were working. Still no word from Pam, and he was determined not to call her again.

His intercom buzzed.

"Yes?"

"You have a call. A Ms. Fleming."

Simone. "Could you tell her I'm busy and that I'll call her later?"

"Yes, Mr. Spencer."

The last thing he needed right now was to have an inane conversation with Simone Fleming. He pushed away from his desk and stood.

He walked to the coffeemaker on the side table and poured himself a cup of black coffee. He felt a headache coming on and hoped the jolt of caffeine would offset it.

His intercom buzzed again. He returned to his desk and pressed the flashing button. "Yes?"

"It's Mr. Graham."

"Thanks. Miles, what can I do for you?"

"For starters, you can tell me where Ms. Armstrong is."

"Excuse me?"

"I've been trying to reach her since yesterday so she can come in and sign her lease, but she hasn't called back. I figured maybe you knew how to reach her."

Nathan clenched his jaw before speaking. "I couldn't tell you, Miles.

I know about as much as you do regarding Ms. Armstrong. I already told you, it's not that kind of party between us."

"Hmm. Well, if I don't hear from her by Monday, I'll have to cancel the contract and return the money, something I'm loath to do, but this is business."

"Do what you have to do—that's all I can tell you."

"This was your recommendation. If this deal falls through . . ."

"If this deal falls through, then *what?*" he snapped, spoiling for a fight, someone to take his frustration out on.

"Then I'm going to have to think twice about doing business with you if your sources are unreliable. And you know how much money I bring to you."

"Is that right? Is this about business or pussy?"

"Both."

"Well, seems to me that you lost out on both counts." He slammed down the phone and stormed out of his office, briefly stopping at his secretary's desk to inform her that he would be out of the office until Monday. If there was an emergency he could be reached on his cell; if not, she could handle it. With that, he walked out.

By the time he'd reached his beach house, he'd calmed down considerably. He went straight to the fridge and took out an icy-cold Coors and gulped it down while leaning against the kitchen counter.

Miles was willing to use not getting with Pamela as leverage against him in doing business? He still couldn't believe that he'd actually come out and admitted it. What in the world could Pam have possibly said or done to get Miles so twisted?

At this point, he had no answers and trying to figure them out was only making him crazy. He'd deal with Miles if and when he had to, but whatever semblance of a friendship they had was dead.

He tossed his empty beer bottle into the recycle bin, then went to his bedroom to change clothes before pulling out some steaks from the fridge to throw on the grill. As he seasoned the meat and put some beers on ice, he realized he was beginning to look forward to hanging out with Norman for a few hours. It would take his mind off of Pam, something he sorely needed to do.

*   *   *

Nathan turned the steaks on the grill. "So how's it been, man? I haven't seen you in ages."

"The usual. Business is great, busy as all hell, but a good busy." Norman chuckled, then took a swallow of beer. He looked around. "I really like it out here. Been thinking of getting a place here."

Nathan turned to look at him. As long as he'd known Norman, he'd been a die-hard New Yorker. He'd never thought an atom bomb could blast Norman out of his Central Park West digs.

"You're thinking of moving to Florida? I don't believe it."

Norman nodded. "Yeah, I've been tossing the idea around for a while. There's really nothing for me in New York anymore."

Nathan closed the cover of the grill and took a seat on the lounge chair opposite Norman. "Look, this is me, man. I know how much you love the city. I mean, even after your wife . . ." He paused. "So you want to tell me the real reason? You're not sick or anything?" His voice rose a note in alarm.

Norman waved off his concern. "Naw, nothing like that." He put his beer down and rested his arms on his thighs, leaning forward. He blew out a breath and looked at Nathan. "I, uh, need to talk to you about something. Just between us. I mean, you're the only one who wouldn't think I needed my head examined." He laughed nervously.

"Well, I might, but I'd never tell you," he joked, trying to lighten the suddenly tense moment between them. "So . . . what is it?"

What Norman told him was the last thing he'd even think he'd hear.

Chapter 12

After Norman left, Nathan was barely able to sleep. The things Norman told him danced in his head, taunting him throughout the night. He didn't want to believe it, but the more he thought about it, the more it seemed true. The photo that Norman shared was the final bit of evidence.

"This is her picture. She didn't know I took it months ago." Norman had opened his wallet, taken out the picture, and handed it to Nathan.

It took all he had to hide his astonishment. It was a picture of Pam, the woman Norman referred to as Leticia Holmes.

"Good-looking woman," Nathan said, nearly choking. "I can see why you can't get her out of your head."

Norman took the picture back, stared at it for a long time before returning it to his wallet. "I never thought I'd feel this way about any woman ever again." He sucked in a breath. "But I haven't told you everything."

What more could he possibly say? Nathan swallowed. "I'm listening."

"She's a, uh, hooker."

Nathan nearly spit out his beer. He started to cough.

"You okay?"

Nathan nodded, unable to speak. He pounded a couple of times on his chest, coughed some more to buy himself some time before asking the question he didn't really want the answer to. "Are you sure?"

Norman nodded. "That's how we met. I was introduced to her through a mutual friend."

He wanted to jump up and bust Norman in the face for making up such a vile story, but in his gut he knew it was the truth.

"Damn, man," he finally managed to say. "How long have you . . . known her?"

"Almost two years. We saw each other about three times a week. I knew what she was doing . . . the other men, but . . ." He heaved a heavy, disheartened sigh. "I fell in love with her."

"Shit."

"Yeah, exactly."

"I wanted to tell her how I felt, that we could put all that stuff behind us and start fresh. I wanted to marry her. The last time I saw her was the time I was going to ask her to marry me. When I woke up, she was gone—lock, stock, and barrel. Not a note or anything." He reached into his jacket pocket and pulled out a small jewelry box. "I was going to give her this." He opened the box to reveal a brilliant diamond solitaire set in platinum. "Hump, never got the chance."

Nathan didn't know which way to look, what to say. A part of him still refused to believe it. There were hundreds, thousands of folks who looked alike. They said all black folks looked alike anyway. Maybe that was it. The picture of the woman was just somebody who looked like Pam. That had to be it. It had to be. After all, didn't Miles say he'd done a thorough check on her—Pamela Armstrong, not this Leticia Holmes? Pam had a history, credit, job references. It had to be a mistake. Some macabre, twisted mistake.

"So I came out here," Norman was saying, jarring Nathan away from his spinning thoughts. "After so much time of not hearing from her, I tried to go over everything she'd ever said to me. Then I remembered that she'd once said, if she had the chance she'd come to Miami, the one place she'd heard so much about but had never been to."

Nathan's stomach turned. It was the same thing she'd told him when they'd first met.

"I was hoping that if I could find her, tell her how I felt, that maybe she would change her mind." He laughed sadly. "Stupid, huh?"

"Naw, man, it's what you felt you needed to do. But Miami is a big place and . . ."

"I know, I know," he said, suddenly excited. "But last night when I was pulling up to the hotel, I saw her."

"What?"

"Yeah, I saw her right on the boulevard. I jumped out of the cab and called her."

"What did she do?" His heart pounded.

Norman eased back down. "Nothing. She didn't even turn around."

Nathan didn't realize he was holding his breath until he felt it swoosh out of his chest. "See, what'd I tell ya? Miami is big and filled with beautiful women. You probably just thought it was her."

Norman shrugged. "At first I figured the same thing. But the more I ran it through my head, the more I knew that it was Leticia. She's here. I know she is."

And the more Nathan ran it through *his* head, the more the improbable became probable. The prior night and all of Norman's revelations dogged him all the way to the front desk of the Loew's Hotel. He wanted to hear her tell him to his face.

"Yes, sir. How may I help you?"

"Can you ring Ms. Armstrong's room, please?"

"One moment." The desk clerk hit some keys on the computer, frowned, and hit some more. She looked up at Nathan. "How are you spelling Armstrong?"

Nathan nearly spat out the letters.

"Oh, yes, I'm sorry. Ms. Armstrong actually checked out last night. Can I help you with anything else?"

"Uh, no. Thank you."

Confused and angry, he turned away and went back to his car. For several moments he sat there in the parking lot, trying to figure out what to do. Where had she gone?

Miles.

He pulled out his cell phone and dialed Miles's office.

"Graham and Associates. How may I direct your call?"

"Miles Graham, please. This is Nathan Spencer."

"One moment."

Nathan held on for what seemed like forever, before the cultured voice returned to the line.

"I'm sorry, Mr. Spencer, Mr. Graham is busy. He said he would call you."

"Yeah, thanks." He disconnected the call, wishing he could slam it down instead. He banged his fist against the steering wheel.

So . . . she was gone, she was a whore, and he was the other fool who fell for her.

Chapter 13

Leticia stood on the deck of cruise ship *Excursion* as it pulled away from the Miami dock. Happy travelers waved and blew kisses to the friends and family on the boardwalk that they were temporarily leaving behind.

The ship was en route to Aruba. She'd paid a pretty penny to purchase the last-minute ticket, but it had been worth it. She may have been able to deal with what happened to her with Felix, but she knew she could never face Nathan when he found out who she really was. And with Norman in town, it was only a matter of time.

As the city of Miami grew distant, Leticia roamed the decks, checking out the amenities, familiarizing herself with her surroundings.

When she reached the lower-deck level by the pool, she stopped short. Near the bar, waiting for a drink, was one of her former clients. She turned away and hurried toward her room. Obviously she couldn't spend the duration of the trip holed up in her room. But she didn't have the stamina to deal with Winston Barnes. He was a loud, obnoxious clod. She'd been glad to be rid of him. And now, halfway across the country and in open waters, here he was. What the hell was she going to do now?

Leticia closed her room door and looked around. Could she actually spend the next three days trapped in this tiny space? She'd go out of her mind. But she'd been in worse situations before. The hellhole of foster care was far worse than anything she'd have to deal with for the time being. Her room on board was immaculate. She could watch movies, get room service, and have someone clean up whatever mess she made. She wouldn't complain, just ride it out and at the first opportunity, she would be gone.

When the boat docked in Nassau the following morning, Leticia had her bags ready. As she went along the gangplank, a crew member stopped her.

"Miss, we will only be on the island overnight." He looked at all the luggage she was pulling behind her on a cart.

Leticia looked at him over the top of her sunglasses and beneath the shade of her wide-brimmed hat. "Yes, I know." She grinned. "A lady never knows what might pop up, and I always want to be prepared."

"Do you need some help?"

She looked him over: young, good-looking, virile, and she was sure by the looks he was giving her, ready, willing, and able. Hmm, a quick fling on a sandy beach—every woman's fantasy.

"No, thank you, handsome. Maybe some other time." She continued on until she reached solid ground.

She'd been to the Bahamas dozens of times and knew which hotels were the best. She'd stay at least overnight, while she figured out what her next move would be. She had plenty of cash and easy access to it, but at some point she was going to have to start bringing in some income. She looked around at all the handsome, buff men that strolled along the island paradise, each and every one who passed giving her an appraising look.

Hmm, maybe she would stay a little longer than she planned.

Leticia checked into the Oasis, taking a suite on the tenth floor. After getting settled, she took a short tour of the hotel, her last stop being the outside bar and café. She didn't realize how hungry she was until she inhaled the tempting aromas of island cuisine.

She took a table near the railing so she could look out on the beach.

"What can I get the pretty lady today?"

He couldn't be more than twenty-two, with the body of Adonis, skin as smooth and rich as maple, and brilliant white teeth. Hmm, edible.

"What do you recommend?" She looked him up and down and smiled.

"All of our guests love our piña coladas." He grinned.

"Then I'll start with that."

He turned and walked away, and that's when she noticed that Mr. Handsome and Delectable had a little sugar in his tank. Oh, well.

When he returned with her drink, she was pleasant but for the most part ignored him as she gave him her dinner order.

While she waited, she watched the small cruise ships that went back and forth from Florida to the islands of the Bahamas. A small part of her wished that somehow, by some miracle, Nathan would put all the crazy pieces of her puzzled life together and come walking off one of the boats and they'd sail off into forever.

She sipped her drink. *Stupid, silly girl. No one is coming to rescue you. No one ever has. The only person you have ever been able to rely on is yourself. This is your life, the only life you know—so live it and stop whining.*

She finished off her drink and signaled the "sweet" waiter for another. *The only one who can save you is you.*

Leticia spent the next few weeks in Nassau, wandering through the shops during the day and the nightclubs by night. But the longer she stayed, the more she realized how utterly alone she was. She watched couples, old and young, mothers with their children, sisters with the brothers, dads playing with their sons. Even strangers seemed to find a way to connect. But she . . . she had no idea what it meant to have something or someone to call your own. In her dreams she always imagined being part of a family. Sometimes she could almost see the faces of the sisters she was told she'd had. And they were happy.

Why had they been separated? Didn't they have anyone in the world who cared enough about three innocent baby girls to keep them together? Where were her sisters? Were they even alive? Did they have lives better than hers?

The questions, which she struggled daily to force to the back of her head, had begun of late to rise constantly, pushing her, prodding her to answer them. But she had nowhere to begin. She didn't even know her sisters' names, where they lived, or even if they lived at all.

"Are you all right, Miss?"

She glanced up into the concerned face of an older woman with the crisscrossed lines of age and wisdom making a roadmap of her face. Her smile was gentle.

Leticia didn't even realize that she'd been sobbing alone at the table until the woman came up to her. She grabbed a napkin from the table and wiped her eyes and nose. She sniffed loudly and gave an embarrassed smile.

"I'm sorry. I . . ."

"No need to apologize. Tears are good for the soul. Do you mind if an old lady sits down for a moment?"

"No, please." She was actually glad for the company. The woman would be the first person she'd had a conversation with since her arrival.

The woman eased down into the rattan seat. "My name is Olivia. Most of the folks around here call me Livie."

"Nice to meet you. Leticia. Leticia Holmes."

The woman looked at her closely, studying her face. "I knew a woman named Holmes once. Stayed on the island for about six months. Looked a lot like you. That was one of the reasons I stopped. The resemblance."

Leticia's heart began to race and she felt heat flow in waves through her body. She cleared her throat. "You met someone who looked like me?" She tried to keep her voice calm.

Livie nodded. "You could have passed for twins, except for the chin. She was a little taller, I think, and thinner, and always had that same sad look in her eyes that you do."

Leticia could barely breathe. She laughed lightly so as not to scream. "Wow, how long ago was that?" She clenched her hands into fists beneath the table.

"Hmm." She frowned in thought. "Must be going on five, maybe six years now. I always thought she would come back, and I thought she did when I saw you."

Leticia's head was spinning. "Where was she from?"

"I sure wish I could remember. Somewhere in the states in the South."

"Do you remember her first name? Maybe she's a cousin or something." She chuckled, her nerves ready to snap.

"Everyone around here always called her C. That's all I remember, but she had a voice that could shake your soul." She smiled and nodded with the memory.

Leticia's mind was running wild. A woman who looked enough like her to be mistaken for her. Lived somewhere in the South. Her last name was Holmes. Could it be possible, or had she become so despondent over her life that she was simply hoping for some kind of miracle?

"Did this woman say where she was going when she left, by any chance?"

"No. One night I came out to hear her sing in the little club about a mile away and she was gone. Owner said she simply left."

"The club, is it still there?"

"Burned to the ground about two years ago. Owner took his wife and kids and moved away."

Leticia's stomach was reeling.

"Well, I didn't mean to disturb you," Livie said, pushing herself to her feet. "It's just that I thought you were her. You take care of yourself."

Leticia nodded. "Did she ever mention anywhere she might go?" she called out, almost in desperation.

Slowly, Livie turned around, frowning, straining, trying to remember. "I think she might have mentioned New York or Chicago a few times. Can't be sure."

Leticia released a breath of defeat. "Thanks."

Could it be possible that her sister had been there? That she was alive somewhere? Even more disturbing, they could very well have lived in the same city for years and never run across each other.

She paid for her drink and dinner and returned to her room. The following morning she was on a plane to New York. She was taking a big chance going back, but it was one she was willing to take. Hopefully, the police had found someone more interesting than her to investigate. She had to start somewhere, and maybe the time to put the pieces of her life together was now.

Chapter 14

"What do you have for me, Wil?" Nathan paced the floors of his office as he listened to the P.I.'s answers. Leticia had been gone for almost four months. There hadn't been a day that went by that he didn't think about her, think about what Norman told him. But he needed his own answers, and he believed deep in his gut that there was so much more to Pam . . . Leticia . . . than either of them was aware of.

"Are you sitting down?" Wil asked.

"No. Should I be?"

"You may want to. I don't know how much you know about this Pamela Armstrong, aka Leticia Holmes, but it's not a pretty picture."

"Just give it to me."

As he listened, Nathan did sit down. The information was not only enlightening but painful to hear. He couldn't begin to imagine what Leticia had gone through all those years, what she was still going through. But at least now he understood how she became the woman she was.

"I tracked her as far as the Bahamas. By the time I got there, she'd already left."

"Does anyone have any idea where she went?"

"No. But from my experience in the biz, folks always return to what is familiar. My bet is New York."

"Thanks, Wil, for everything. I'll put a little something extra in your check."

"All donations are appreciated." He chuckled. "Good luck."

"Thanks." He hung up, then buzzed his secretary. "Lisa, book me on the next available flight to New York."

Leticia sat in her new apartment with a stack of newspapers on the table. She searched every single entertainment section in the hope of finding something about a singer named C Holmes. It was a task she carried out every day since she'd been back. She'd even gone so far as to search the archives of the library for any clues.

Frustrated that her search was pointless and insurmountable, she picked up a copy of the *Village Voice*. Page by page, she looked. Just when she was about to give up, a small photo and a column-length story caught her attention.

Clarissa Holmes to debut at Radio City Music Hall. Her hands began to shake as she read on.

Jazz stylist Clarissa Holmes will make her first New York appearance at the famed Radio City Music Hall.

The words began to blur as she read on. But her eyes kept coming back to the smiling face of a woman who looked enough like her to be her. This must be her sister. It had to be.

The concert will begin at eight P.M. on Friday night. Tickets are available . . .

She jumped up from her seat, paced the floor, looked back at the photo, and paced some more. What should she do?

Nathan walked the streets of midtown Manhattan, studying each and every face, hoping to find Leticia in one of them. He needed to tell her, make her understand, that nothing she had done in the past mattered to him. And that if she gave him the chance, they could make a life together, work together to find her family and build one of her own.

Before he'd left Miami, he'd called Norman and told him everything, including the story of his relationship with Leticia. He told

Norman that he was in love with her and that he was going to find her and tell her. For a long moment, Norman was totally silent.

"We've been friends for a long time, Nate. I've never known you to be a man to stab another in the back."

"Norm, I—"

"No, listen. I realized after all this time that it wasn't real love that I had for Leticia. I did care about her deeply, but I was putting all the emotions I didn't know what to do with into her." He chuckled sadly. "I hate to admit this, but she never gave me an inkling that she felt the same way." He paused a beat. "Go for it, man. If she is the one for you, go for it. Life is too short, so make the most of it."

"Thanks, Norm."

"Yeah. And don't forget to send me an invitation to the wedding."

Nathan released a relieved laugh. "Will do."

That had been several weeks earlier. He was glad he'd come clean with Norman; he deserved as much, and he was equally as glad that there were no hard feelings between them.

He continued his stroll down Sixth Avenue toward Forty-ninth Street when the marquee at Radio City Music Hall caught and held his attention.

CLARISSA HOLMES, FRIDAY, 8 P.M.

Nathan stopped dead in his tracks, then ran up to the ticket window. A big color picture of Clarissa, announcing her appearance, was posted on the glass doors. The resemblance to Leticia was stunning. They could easily be mistaken for twins. This had to be her missing sister. If Leticia was anywhere in the city, maybe, just maybe, she would find her way here.

He went up to the window and purchased a ticket for Friday night.

Chapter 15

The crowd outside Radio City Music Hall swelled as the curtain time drew closer.

Leticia had hired a car to take her to the event. It sat parked across the street as she watched the crowd file in. She gripped her ticket in her hand, tormented about the right or wrong of what she was doing.

If she went inside, how would she even get to meet her? And if she did, there was no telling how Clarissa would respond. What if it wasn't her sister, but just some freaky twist of nature that had two women looking so much alike?

She felt ill with anxiety.

The last of the concertgoers filed inside. She looked at her watch: 7:55. She drew in a long, deep breath, hoping to slow the erratic racing of her heart—to no avail.

The white-gloved doorman stepped outside the theater, looked right and left, then stepped inside and pulled the glass doors closed behind him.

"Um, driver, you can park somewhere—I'll call you when I'm ready to be picked up."

"Yes, ma'am."

Drawing on the strength that had pulled her through many an adversity, she stepped out of the car and slowly crossed the street.

She stood in front of the closed doors, suddenly unable to move, unable to think.

The doorman came to the door and opened it.

"Do you have a ticket, Miss? The show has begun."

Leticia blinked several times, bringing him into focus. No. She couldn't do it. She couldn't risk being turned away. She simply could not.

"Thank you. I—" She suddenly spun away, only to come face-to-face with Nathan.

He reached out for her, bracing her shoulders. He looked steadily into her eyes as hers asked a million questions that her voice could not express.

"I know everything, Leticia."

The sound of her name coming from his lips made her feel weak.

"And I don't give a damn." His eyes ran over her face. "You can't keep running. I love you, and I'm not going to let you run away from that. Your future, and your past, are on the other side of that door. If you choose to walk away now, you will always regret it." He took a breath, then pulled the concert ticket out of his pocket and held it up. The only choice I'm giving you right now is to walk in there alone or with me. But in either case, I'll be waiting for you."

At that, the tears that she'd been battling back spilled over her lids and down her cheeks.

"Just like a man to make a woman ruin her makeup," she choked out.

He pulled a handkerchief from his pocket and dabbed at her eyes.

She took his hand and pulled him to her side, then looked up at him, fear, hope, acceptance, and love in her eyes. "We're going to miss everything if we don't hurry."

The doorman stepped aside and let them in.

LIFE'S LITTLE MYSTERIES

Parry "EbonySatin" Brown

Chapter 1

"MaDear, this was such a fun birthday!" Jamilla clapped her hands together as she matched her mother step for step in the small but immaculate kitchen.

Augusta Dixon turned her petite, round body to face her daughter and smiled broadly. "Baby girl, that's exactly what I wanted to hear. Your daddy and I want so much for you to be happy."

"Oh," Jamilla hugged her mother, "I am!"

Johnny Dixon strolled into the kitchen carrying a large trash bag filled with the remnants of his daughter's twelfth birthday celebration. "What's an old man gotta do to get some of that?"

Jamilla ran to her dad, reaching up to throw her arms around his neck. As he lifted her off the floor, he planted a kiss on her shelled-pecan-colored cheek. "I love you, PopPop."

"I love you, too, sweetie." Johnny set the bag close to the back door. "I'm really glad to hear that you had a good time today. Your friends seemed to have had a good time, too."

"Oh, they did!" Jamilla squealed. "They all told me so."

Augusta stole a glance at her husband of almost twenty-five years as her eyes shared her thoughts. When she and Johnny had decided today would be the day almost twelve years ago, it seemed an eternity away. A day so far in the future, there was never any need for her to be concerned with any of its details. Where had all the time gone? She had planned to tell Jamilla when she woke up on her special day, but then she seemed so happy and full of delight, she was afraid the news would steal her joy. Now, as Jamilla danced around the modest kitchen with appliances in need of updating, the time still didn't seem right.

As her daughter's birthday drew near, an increased trepidation filled her heart with every beat. *What will she think? Will she understand that we loved her in a way so special that we didn't believe we could breathe without her?*

"MaDear," Jamilla broke into her guarded thoughts, "what do you want me to do with the rest of the birthday cake? Cover it with aluminum foil?"

Struggling to force the words over the lump in her throat, Augusta managed a smile. "No, baby girl, let's put it in a plastic container so that good frosting doesn't get all messed up."

Johnny cleared his throat to get his wife's attention. "It's time," was all he could manage in his low, deep baritone voice.

"Time for what?" Jamilla stopped with her hand in midair as she reached into the cupboard neatly filled with Tupperware containers that were older than she was. "Do I have more presents?"

Augusta dried her hands on her yellow floral apron as she slowly said, "We truly hope you'll think it's a gift."

With her chore forgotten, Jamilla clapped her hands together and began jumping up and down. "What is it? Is it a new bike?"

Augusta almost laughed as she thought of her tomboy daughter riding through the streets of Los Angeles to the baseball park where she'd play with boys two or three years her senior, beating them at their own game. "No, baby, it's not a new bike."

Johnny rubbed his snow-white, perfectly manicured beard and sighed deeply. "Come sit in the living room with us."

Jamilla's smile vanished. They *never* sat in the living room. The last time she had been told to *come sit in the living room* they had told her that her beloved grandma Rose had died. She wanted to ask who had died, but her words were held hostage by fear. The solemn look on her parents' faces did little to comfort her. She grabbed her mother's hand as they walked slowly in silence to the room filled with all things French Provincial.

As Jamilla entered the room, she wondered why the off-white furniture was covered in plastic, since they never were allowed to sit in her mother's showplace. On the few occasions she had sat on the sofa, the plastic had stuck to her skin, making her sweat. She looked at the two side chairs, realizing she had never sat in either one of them. Her mind had taken her on a journey through a child's trivia rather than focus on the reason for the visit into the neatly cluttered sanctum.

Johnny sat in the high-backed side chair and crossed his long legs. Augusta sat in the middle of the sofa and motioned for Jamilla to sit on the end between her mother and father. Jamilla obeyed silently, though she knew they could hear her heart pounding.

Jamilla looked from one to the other as she impatiently waited for them to speak. Augusta toyed with the green zigzag border on her apron as she stared at the Oriental rug. Johnny picked up a small crystal object that didn't serve any purpose but to gather dust. The silence choked the life out of Jamilla as she began rubbing her hands up and down her thighs until her hands burned.

Johnny drew a deep breath and began to speak, each word more labored than the last. "Baby girl, you know we love you with all our hearts."

Augusta suddenly looked up as though she'd had an epiphany. "There's nothing we wouldn't do for you."

"I know, MaDear." Jamilla's heart pounded a little harder. "You're scaring me."

Her mother placed her hand on Jamilla's and turned to face her. "Johnny and I," Augusta's words rushed forth with the force of a ruptured dam after a torrential rain, "aren't your real mother and father."

Looking rapidly from one to the other, Jamilla finally managed, "What do you mean?"

"What your mother is trying to say is that we didn't give you life." Johnny leaned forward, resting his forearm on his knees. "You didn't live in Augusta's stomach for nine months."

Seconds ticked by like hours before Jamilla finally found her voice. "Whose stomach did I live in?"

Augusta laughed nervously. "You've always gotten right to the point, haven't you?"

Jamilla only stared.

"Minnie Lou Holmes."

"Holmes?"

"Yes, baby girl," Johnny answered. "We kept that part of your name when we adopted you."

"Who is she?"

"I really can't answer that." Augusta spoke quietly, as though whispering would make this twelve-year-old secret easier to digest. "We don't know anything about her."

"Where did I come from?"

"You were born in a small town in Georgia," Augusta answered laboriously.

"How did you get me, then?"

Augusta shot Johnny a glance and he nodded. She continued. "There was a lady down in Georgia who knew your people. She knew that I couldn't have a baby naturally, and she told me about you. You were living with her cousin, but she couldn't take care of you and my friend wanted you to have a good home.

"Your daddy and I drove down there to see you and we fell in love with you instantly." The tension around Augusta's temple felt like a too-tight baseball cap. "You were so tiny."

"How old was I?" Jamilla whispered.

"Seven weeks old." Johnny's eyes locked with his wife's, though he spoke to Jamilla. "We need to tell her the rest."

Jamilla looked from her mother to her father and back again. "What rest?"

Augusta drew a long breath. "There were two other baby girls there that day."

Confusion clouded Jamilla's big brown eyes. "Your friend's cousin had other babies, too?"

"Yes." Anxiety robbed Johnny of a more eloquent response.

"How many babies? How old were they?" Jamilla addressed her questions to whoever could give her the quickest answers.

Augusta's tongue lay paralyzed on the floor of her mouth. She had suddenly lost the confidence from twelve years ago when she was assured she and Johnny were making the right decision.

She didn't know how long she had been silent when Jamilla asked, "MaDear? Did you hear me?"

Blinking as though she had been in a trance, Augusta hesitated before answering. "Yes, baby. I heard you."

Johnny rescued her. "Yes, she had other baby girls." It wasn't so easy for Johnny to continue, either.

"How many?"

"Two." Augusta's response was barely audible.

"How old were they?" Jamilla's curiosity fueled her enthusiasm. Neither parent wanted to answer.

"MaDear, why won't you answer me?"

Johnny cleared his throat and sighed deeply. "They were seven weeks old."

"Wow! The same age as me?"

Exchanging glances again with Johnny, Augusta answered this time. "Yes, baby. They were the same age as you because . . ."

Time and space stood still. Augusta was suddenly standing in the tiny shack in the Georgia backwoods with outdoor plumbing. The old woman rocked back and forth, spitting into a Maxwell House coffee can occasionally.

"This one has a humble spirit." The lump in her left cheek shifted slightly. "She ain't gon' be much trouble." *Spit.* "That one over there, she gon' be a singer. She croons all day and night. Right fussy, though." *Chew.* "That one," the old woman pointed to the dresser-drawer-turned-baby-cradle in the furthest corner, "gon' be real trouble."

Augusta and Johnny searched the three identical faces. "How can we ever decide?"

"Then take all three. Buy two and I'll throw the third one in for free." The old woman smiled, showing her rotting, uneven teeth.

Augusta's heart ached because she wanted to rescue all of the babies from this wretched place. She clutched her purse to her side. She feared the old woman could see into her soul, or at least into her wallet, seeing that she didn't even have the seven-hundred-and-fifty-dollar bounty for one child. She and Johnny had scraped and borrowed every penny they could to come up with the four hundred and thirty-eight dollars that lay neatly tied in the bottom of her purse.

She had packed food for the round trip and filled their bottles with water at each stop along the route from Los Angeles to Atlanta. After they had ridden for more than three days, they'd hired someone to drive them for another three hours into a place that still bore the marks of slavery with its dilapidated shacks and outhouses.

When Augusta and Johnny had approached the rickety old house, there was nothing that could have prepared them for such poverty. If these had been the living conditions that the mother of the babies had endured, it was no surprise that she hadn't survived.

"MaDear?"

Augusta shook her head slightly and tried to bring Jamilla into focus. "Yes, dear?"

"You stopped in the middle of a sentence." Jamilla pulled herself to the edge of the sofa cushion. "You were going to tell me why the other babies were the same age as me."

Augusta nervously continued to toy with the edge of her apron. She took one final glance at Johnny before she continued. "They were the same age as you because they were your sisters." There—she'd said it. It could never be taken back.

"I have sisters?" Jamilla was on her feet.

Johnny took over. "You had two other sisters born at the same time. Your mother had triplets."

"What happened to my *real* mother?"

Augusta cringed at the thought that her precious baby girl thought of anyone else as her mother. "Your birth mother was very young, and the trauma of giving birth to three babies was more than her body could handle."

Jamilla looked puzzled at the explanation.

"What your mother is trying to say is that she passed away the day you were born."

The words weighed so heavily on Jamilla, she was forced to take a seat. "She died?"

"Yes," Augusta answered weakly.

Jamilla's parents sat silently as they waited for the reality to catch up with the shock. Augusta wanted to hug her, but she thought she should leave her alone, at least for the time being.

Johnny rubbed his ample belly, needing a beer. He wanted to run from this room and out the door to his favorite watering hole. In that haven there would be no eyes pleading for answers to unasked questions.

"Baby girl?"

Jamilla turned to her father with sad, accusing eyes. Her lips remained sealed.

"Are you going to say anything?" Johnny asked pensively.

Jamilla's thoughts of her short life scurried through her head. She'd always wanted a baby sister or brother. She wanted to be the big sister who could help them learn to color between the lines. She wanted to have tea parties with a real person instead of the sister she'd make up in her imagination. Confusion balled up in her chest as she wondered what it would've been like to have grown up with a sibling or even two.

"Where are my sisters?"

Chapter 2

Sweat drenched the Egyptian cotton sheets as Jamilla bolted upright from a deep sleep. The dream was the same as always. But then, why would tonight be any different? Throwing the covers back, she slipped the baby-doll pajama top over her head, tossing it onto the animal-print bench at the foot of the four-poster maple bed. As she padded off to the bathroom, she wondered for the zillionth time how and when this nightmare would stop.

Refusing to flip the switch, the night-light distorted her image slightly as she stared at her reflection, searching for answers. The thought of the two crying babies with her face reaching up from the swamp, calling her name, had haunted her for twenty years while she slumbered, but now she was beginning to see them during her waking hours.

"How ridiculous is this?" Jamilla faked a smile just as she turned on the water faucet to splash her face with cold water. The tiny clock on the shelf to the left of the beveled medicine cabinet showed 3:12. She knew trying to return to sleep was futile, and she decided, as she dried her face with the sunshine-yellow, extra-thick towel, she'd best try her hand at the outline that was due for her next mystery project.

Jamilla Holmes Dixon began writing mysteries when she was thirteen as a way to deal with the overwhelming sense of foreboding that always loomed around her. The *present* she'd received from her parents on her twelfth birthday was more of a burden than a gift. Reading the confusion on their only child's face, they explained as best they could. Though they had tried to help her understand that they'd chosen her special, she couldn't help but wonder why her beloved MaDear and PopPop hadn't thought at least one of her other sisters special too.

The knowledge that she had been born with two other baby girls haunted her almost constantly until she turned her energies to writing. Her parents gave her a typewriter for her fourteenth birthday when they realized she was serious about developing her craft.

Johnny had served the University of Southern California as a mechanical engineer, while Augusta was a clerk at the post office, not far from their Crenshaw District home. He wanted nothing more than for his babygirl to become a judge; her mother, on the other hand, only wanted her to be happy. Both parents had insisted she take full advantage of the free education that her father's many years of service had earned.

Despite her heartfelt desire to major in Literature, Jamilla graduated with honors as she received a Criminal Justice degree. She happily headed off to law school. From the very start she knew she would never make it in the profession. Though she wanted her beloved father to realize his dream, the problem with being a judge is one had to be a lawyer first. From everything she'd learned in her Criminal Justice classes, she knew that the practice of molding the truth for one's own purpose was not for her.

Not wanting to break her daddy's heart, she went through the motions, but her first love was writing. The same classes that had caused others hair-graying, ulcer-manifesting stress, she had breezed through. When she received her Jurist Doctorate, she knew without a doubt that she would never practice law. By the end of her third and final year of law school, she had managed to crank out a five-hundred-and-twenty-five-page manuscript. And the dashingly handsome doctor-by-day, super-sleuth-by-night Wilton Portofino was born.

Each summer she'd interned proved what she'd believed since her first year in law school—practicing law had nothing to do with justice. Armed with the prestigious degrees but no certification for the California Bar Association, she'd sought employment within the criminal justice system. Jamilla was always amazed at the lengths parolees would go to, thinking they were deceiving her. Though she was one of the youngest in her unit, her supervisor often said she had the potential to be one of the best officers he'd seen come through the doors in a number of years.

Before the end of her first year as a parole officer, where her idealism made her believe she could effect change, she had been lied to, cursed at, hit on, spit on, stalked, mocked, and threatened. But it was the being shot at that made her turn in her resignation. There were still days, however, when she missed the challenge.

Jamilla rode the elevator to the fifth floor of the trendy office building in Los Angeles' high-rent district's Century City. As she stepped up to the reception desk in the suite of offices, the woman looked up and offered a warm and seemingly genuine smile. "Good afternoon— how may I help you?"

Jamilla returned the smile. "Jamilla Holmes Dixon to see Mr. Brewington."

"You may have a seat right over there, and I'll let him know that you're here," the pleasant redhead with expressive green eyes and the slightest hint of freckles said.

Jamilla obediently sat in the comfortable black leather side chair with a yellow lumbar pillow. She nervously crossed and uncrossed her legs. Her dreams had brought her to this office. She had searched for answers to the mysteries of her life since her parents had shared the news that she wasn't born alone. Frederick Brewington had come highly recommended by a friend of a friend, and Jamilla hoped he could help her fill the empty space in her soul.

"Ms. Dixon?" The stocky man in the Sears off-the-rack suit in need of pressing reminded Jamilla of an Afrocentric Columbo.

Jamilla stood, extending her hand. "Mr. Brewington?"

"Right this way."

Jamilla followed the man, who walked with a slight limp. Her James Bond façade had been shattered as she wondered how this man was an effective private investigator. They walked down a long, ultramodern hallway past several wood doors with art deco windows. Mr. Brewington stopped in front of the door with the numbers 554 affixed to plastic with press-on numbers. "Please come in."

"Thank you." Jamilla stepped inside the very neat office with state-of-the-art computer equipment, still and video cameras, as well as other equipment she didn't quite recognize.

Mr. Brewington pointed to one of the two chairs in front of the moderate-sized desk. "Please have a seat." He took a seat with his back to the window with a view of the mall. He moved a file from the center of the desk and folded his hands before saying, "Ms. Dixon, how can I help you?"

Suddenly Jamilla started to second-guess her decision. What information did she have to give him? Why couldn't she just leave well enough alone? She didn't know how long she'd sat staring at nothing when Mr. Brewington cleared his throat. She blinked quickly, as though trying to focus. "I'm sorry, Mr. Brewington, I guess I'm a little nervous."

He smiled reassuringly. "It's quite all right. Take your time."

"I need you to help me find my sisters," Jamilla blurted before she lost her nerve.

"You've come to the right place, Ms. Dixon." He sat back, placing his elbows on the arms of the chair, and pressed his fingertips together. "If I must say so myself, I have a very impressive track record."

Jamilla began to relax. Her parents had literally no information about her sisters, not even their names. She only knew when and where they were born. She prayed that these challenges wouldn't lessen his confidence. "Please call me Jamilla, Mr. Brewington."

"Only if you call me Fred."

"Well, Fred, my sisters and I were separated at birth, and there's a part of me that's so empty despite the wonderful life I've had."

Fred pulled a yellow pad from his top left desk drawer and a Mont Blanc from his jacket pocket. "So tell me, Jamilla, how many sisters are we talking about?"

"Two."

"Where's the last place you know that your sisters lived?"

"A little town outside of Dale, Georgia."

He wrote. "And when was that?"

She squirmed. "Nineteen seventy-three."

He looked up momentarily. "And how old were your sisters when you were separated?"

"A few weeks old."

Again hesitation. "Both of them?"

"Yes."

"So they are twins?"

"Actually, no."

Fred looked up from his pad questioningly. "How's that?"

"*We're* triplets."

Fred sat back, tossing his glasses onto the desk. "I see." He gathered his thoughts for a moment before he continued. "Under what circumstances were you separated?"

"According to my parents, my birth mother died while giving birth and her aunt couldn't take care of us. Because my parents couldn't have children, a friend told them about us and they went to Georgia to pick me up. My sisters were still there when my parents left, so we don't really know if they were adopted or what."

"Have you tried to make contact with your great aunt?"

"According to the woman who gave me to my parents, Essie Mae Holmes died shortly after we were born."

"What about other relatives?"

If I were able to find other relatives to give me answers, would I be sitting here in front of you today? Jamilla thought but said, "There's none to speak of."

"What are your sisters' names?"

Jamilla toyed with her fingers, wondering if she sounded as pathetic to Fred as she did to herself. "I don't know." She answered so softly, Fred wasn't sure what she said.

"Excuse me?"

"I don't know." This time Jamilla almost yelled, then repeated in a defeated tone, "I don't even know my sisters' names."

Fred Brewington had been at this game for a long time, and it never ceased to amaze him how people thought he was a miracle worker, yet his heart always went out to those like Jamilla. Those who only wanted to find a long lost, or never even known, loved one. "Do you know if your births were recorded by the county clerk?"

Jamilla thought for a moment before she responded. "I believe so." She went to her purse, removed an envelope, and passed it to Fred.

Fred quickly opened the envelope and looked up at Jamilla and smiled. "This is a good start."

"My birth certificate, of course, has my adoptive parents' names on it, but it does have the county where I was born, which I think means the county clerk must have entered our births into the record."

Fred smiled broadly. "Indeed it does."

"My parents told me that they kept my birth surname."

"So Holmes is the name you believe appeared on your original birth certificate?" Fred's confidence was building.

"Yes."

Fred relaxed and smiled. "Now we're getting somewhere. There couldn't have been too many sets of triplets born on October 17."

Relief washed over Jamilla as a tiny flicker of hope was ignited. Would it be possible to find her sisters with such limited information? Would Fred have to travel to Dale, Georgia? How much would all of this cost? And did it really matter? She'd set aside half of her advance for the delivery and acceptance of her next book to be used solely to find her sisters. "So you think you can find them?"

"I'd be foolish to guarantee you that I would, but I've been in this business for almost twenty years and you don't have that kind of staying power from a poor success rate."

"How long do you think it will take?"

"I could get lucky and find them in a matter of days or it could take years."

"Years?"

"Years. There are those that don't want to be found, you know. I'm sure that's not the case with your sisters. But, God forbid, they could even be dead."

Jamilla blinked rapidly and grabbed the arms of the chair to keep from flying out of her seat and slapping Fred for even suggesting such a thing. "Please don't say that, Mr. Brewington!"

Fred hadn't meant for it to come out the way that it had, but he also wanted her to know and understand the challenges before them. "I just want you to be prepared for whatever news I bring you."

Jamilla stared at him long and hard before she continued. "How much do you think this will cost me?"

"Again, there is no way for me to know—let's say you give me a retainer of twenty and I'll keep you informed each week of how much you have remaining to see if you want me to continue."

"Twenty what?" Jamilla surely didn't think he meant dollars.

"Thousand."

This time Jamilla shot out of her seat before she could stop herself. "Dollars?" she exclaimed.

"I thought you were aware of what something like this would cost." This will require me traveling to Georgia, talking to a lot of people. All of that takes time." Fred stood also. "And as an intelligent woman like yourself knows, time is money."

Jamilla sat heavily back into the chair. "I just had no idea it would be that much money." She sighed and picked up her purse. "I'm sorry I wasted your time."

As she began to leave, Fred spoke up. "Let's not be too hasty."

"What's the point in continuing?"

"What can you afford?"

Jamilla eyed him suspiciously. "Not twenty thousand dollars."

"We've established that." Fred motioned for her to take a seat again. "I want to work with you. I'm intrigued by the challenge."

Taking a seat warily, Jamilla remembered what her daddy had told her about buying a car. If the salesperson comes after you when you walk away you've got him with his pants down. "I need to see your fee schedule."

Fred opened a drawer behind him, removed a piece of paper, and slid it across the desk. Jamilla picked it up and studied it, glancing up at the investigator occasionally. Fred began to squirm.

"Understand, these are our published rates. I'm in a position to discount them."

Jamilla placed the piece of paper in front of her on the desk, crossed her legs, then said, "I'm listening."

"I'm thinking perhaps I can go as high as twenty-five percent and reduce the retainer to ten."

Jamilla waited a beat before saying, "I like the way you think." She looked him in his eyes for the first time. "You're hired."

Chapter 3

The drive from Century City to Rancho Cucamonga was laborious, yet hope and fantasy seemed to lighten the very air in the blue Honda Accord. As Jamilla inched along I-10, her mind wandered back to her college years. Her haunting dreams had become more pronounced and filled with images of babies that pulled at her, begging to be rescued.

In an attempt to block out the images of the babies, Jamilla let her mind roam to the days gone by. She'd wondered why she didn't have any girlfriends. Over the years she made attempts at relationships, but soon after, the excuses would start. Something would come up and they'd cancel lunch, then movies or dinner, until they'd stop returning her calls.

Now she wondered if all along she was only trying to replace her sisters with girlfriends. She had come to the realization that she was forcing what didn't fit.

She'd dated off and on during and since college, but nothing ever seemed to click—until Maxwell.

Maxwell had been the police officer who'd taken the report after one of her parolees had taken a shot at her that came so close to killing her, she heard the bullet whiz past her ear. He'd worked hard to try to smooth out her frayed nerves and to convince her not to quit a department so short on quality officers, especially those with heart. He'd made it his mission to find the woman who'd caused her so many sleepless nights.

One evening more than six weeks after the incident and a month after she left the employ of the County of Los Angeles, Maxwell had shown up on her doorstep unannounced, bearing tropical flowers and a brown envelope.

"Are you going to leave me out here all night?" Maxwell stood back from the door, wearing a confident smile.

"What are you doing here?" Jamilla asked, stunned. "How did you get my address?"

Maxwell looked disappointed. "Do I have to answer all your questions before you ask me in?"

Jamilla stepped to one side to allow him entry. Maxwell looked around and nodded with approval. "Very nice."

"Thank you. I was lucky enough to buy before Rancho became the place to be. I couldn't even afford to buy this place now." Jamilla was confused yet intrigued by her unexpected guest. "Please have a seat." She pointed to the green faux suede sofa. She took a seat in the matching side chair.

Maxwell suddenly handed the flowers to Jamilla, startling her. "These are for you," he said awkwardly.

"Thanks." Jamilla laid the flowers across her lap after she took a whiff. The scent of the flowers made her think of piña coladas. She turned her attention back to the average looking man with the extraordinary eyes and asked pointedly, "Maxwell, why are you here?"

"I thought you'd never ask." He handed her the brown envelope that had her name neatly printed on it with a felt marker.

Jamilla slowly turned the envelope over and opened it. She couldn't control the tremble in her hands as she removed the single sheet of neatly folded white paper. It vibrated slightly as she unfolded it. She looked once again at Maxwell before she began reading. He smiled.

Jamilla read quickly, and when she'd finished she leapt up moved to the sofa and hugged Maxwell. "You didn't have to bring this all the way out here. You could have called me."

"But then I wouldn't have gotten that hug, now would I?" Maxwell winked.

Despite herself, Jamilla smiled. She looked down again at the arrest report of Shaniqua Aleze' Johnson, the woman who'd shot at her. "Yeah, I guess that's true."

Jamilla had offered Maxwell a glass of wine, but he'd refused and had asked for a rain check. They stood in the doorway for a long moment while Maxwell searched her eyes before he asked, "Now will you come back?"

A little stunned, Jamilla asked, "Come back where?"

"To work. We need you."

"We?"

"Okay, I need to see you more often."

"You know where I live."

"Is that a no?"

"My mother introduced me to a literary agent friend of hers who liked my manuscript. She sold it. I signed the contract earlier this week. I'm going to write full time. So the answer *is* no. I won't be coming back to the department, but I'd like it . . ." Jamilla hesitated.

"You'd like what?" Maxwell toyed with her.

"I'd like it a lot if you'd come back here again."

Maxwell beamed. "I think I can do that."

That night had been the beginning of a friendship that had blossomed into true love. Maxwell was patient with her emotional ups and downs, all while he encouraged her to find her sisters. Jamilla was amazed at his insistence when she was discouraged about the possibility of ever finding them. It was Maxwell who made her believe that a private investigator could help her cause. Fear of failure, or perhaps it was success, seemed to always get in the way, and she'd put off moving forward until last week when she'd seen the babies during her waking hours. She was anxious to share the good news about the investigator.

She ran her hand across the soft leather seat as she thought of the last time Maxwell had sat there. Her heart and soul longed to see him, hear his voice. She touched the button on the hands-free device for her cell phone and spoke the command, "Max at work."

He picked up on the first ring. "Maxwell."

Jamilla liked the sound of his baritone voice—smooth as warm butterscotch. She smiled whenever she thought of how much he hated his first name. She thought "Habakkuk" had unique style. He definitely was one of a very few. "Well, hey, Detective Maxwell," Jamilla cooed.

She could feel him smiling. "Hey yourself." Maxwell lost the official tone in his voice. "I've been thinking about you a lot this afternoon. How'd it go?"

"He was a nice enough man," Jamilla began. "He made no promises, but he did give me a glimmer of hope."

"That's wonderful." Maxwell leaned back in the rickety chair, placing his leg on the desk. "But I don't want you to get your hopes up too high. This is little more than a crapshoot. I had him checked out. He's strictly legit, like I told you. But it's still not going to be easy."

"Since I gave him a ten-thousand-dollar check," Jamilla faked a laugh, "I surely hope it's better than that." Her voice wavered slightly as she continued, "It just has to be."

"I know how important it is to you to find your sisters, so you know whatever you need, it's yours. And I do mean anything."

"I know." Jamilla needed to change her focus. Finding her sisters had occupied so much of her thoughts, it had gotten in the way of her writing. "What time are you getting off? I thought maybe we could meet for dinner."

"Looks like it'll be around eight or so." There was an apology in Maxwell's voice. "How about I pick up some Chinese and come by around nine?"

As much as Jamilla wanted to see him, she hated the late-night drop-bys when he was so tired he often fell asleep before she'd cleared the table. "How about we do it another night—I need to get some writing done anyway, and you know the nighttime is the right time."

Maxwell sighed his disappointment but also knew she was right. He wouldn't be the best company. "How about we shoot for Sunday afternoon?"

"It's a date." Jamilla almost said *I love you*, but caught the words in her throat. "I'll talk to you tomorrow."

"You can count on that." Maxwell hung up and Jamilla's cell phone disconnected. He'd come to care so much for this woman who seemed so elusive. As he'd watched her at work, he knew there was something fresh and different about her from the other parole officers. It was more than her idealism—it was her passion. She wanted to show those put in her charge that things could be different if they'd only put feet to their faith and wings to their dreams. No matter what others around her said, she refused to give up. Which made Maxwell know she wouldn't give up until she was face-to-face with her past.

Traffic still crept along, and Jamilla took a deep breath, shifted her hips in the well-padded seat, and did some breathing exercises she'd learned in yoga to help her relax. The technique must have worked, because before she knew it she was making the exit onto Vineyard, and home was only a few short minutes away.

With newfound determination to meet her daily writing quota, Jamilla pulled into the garage and quickly closed the door. She removed her white blouse and blue slacks, tossing them into the hamper next to the washer. As she stepped into the kitchen she opened the refrigerator, grabbed a bottle of water, removed the cap, and guzzled half of it before she took a breath.

Opening the freezer and peering inside, she decided a TV dinner wouldn't do tonight. Jamilla removed a seasoned chicken breast and placed it in a bowl of cold water before she ran up the stairs to her bedroom. Once inside, she grabbed her sweatpants and baggy t-shirt off the chaise. She was now uniformed for work.

As Jamilla descended the stairs, she let her mind wander again to the backwoods of Georgia. This time she wondered what it must have been like for her birth mother. With little or no medical attention, no husband, and way too young to deal with any of it. How old was her mother when she conceived not just one, but three babies? And who was her father? Was he still alive, and why hadn't he stepped up and taken on his responsibility like a man? Despite her determination and good intentions, the questions moved her creative thoughts out of the way, and she felt hopelessly at a loss for the words she needed to fill five hundred pages. She touched the power button on the stereo and Luther Vandross's voice filled the air around her.

Luther's music always soothed her soul. She'd cried real tears when he died. The thought of never hearing a new song from him put a hole in the pit of her soul. There wasn't one romantic scene in her books that hadn't been inspired by the late crooner's unmistakable style. But today the words to "Dance with My Father Again" made her yearn even more for her sisters.

What would it feel like to laugh and cry with women who shared so much of who she is? Were the three of them identical or fraternal? Were they as anxious to know her as she them? Did they even know she existed? If her MaDear and PopPop had been selfish and kept this all a secret, she might have never known. That thought made her wonder if perhaps not knowing would have been even better.

Chapter 4

Jamilla pulled her long, thick hair up, wiping her neck with a napkin. She picked up the coffee cup and put it down before she blurted, "I'm going to cut my hair for the summer."

Maxwell turned his head and stared into the blue waters of the Pacific instead of commenting. Jamilla's thick tresses were one of the many things that attracted him to her. In a time when those who couldn't achieve, weaved, her long, dark hair made her even more beautiful.

"You're not going to say anything?"

"What is there for me to say?" Maxwell turned to stare at her. "It's your hair—do as you please with it."

Maxwell had refused to bite. Jamilla didn't understand why she always tried to pick a fight with him. She cared for him—a lot. She wasn't sure if she was in love, but she was in serious like. "You just don't understand how hot this hair is on my neck."

The waiter interrupted them with a spinach salad for her and chicken wild rice soup for him. Although Pedals was the casual-dining restaurant at the Shutters on the Beach Hotel, the service was only surpassed by the food. The warm May sun kissed Jamilla's skin, making it tingle slightly. She hated the heat, and the direct sun was what had started this whole conversation.

"Can I get you anything else?" Joel, the young waiter who, like most of his contemporaries, was doing this only until his big break in Hollywood came, asked.

Maxwell looked at Jamilla's coffee cup before he replied, "No, I think we're good for now."

Joel disappeared inside the restaurant and Jamilla began again to plead her case. "I know how much you love my hair—it's the only reason I even bring it up."

"You know, Milla," Maxwell blew on his soup between words, "you're a big girl. Do as you wish."

Uh-oh. He called me Milla. This discussion is over. "Thank you for understanding."

Maxwell stared at her with a *yeah, whatever* look before he smiled and said, "I know it's a little soon, but has there been any word from the P.I.?"

Disappointed that Maxwell had changed the subject, Jamilla reluctantly shared her news. She loathed always seeming to vent her frustrations on the one person who believed she could do anything she set her mind to do. Fear of angering him outweighed her need for conflict. "He's actually started working on the case." She picked at the salad. "He said he thinks he was able to locate my mother's obituary in the newspaper. So that's a good start. We're going to have a phone meeting tomorrow afternoon."

"That *is* great news." Maxwell dipped Italian bread into the olive oil and pesto mixture in front of them. "If your sisters weren't legally adopted, then they'll be easier to find with that information."

"Do you really think so?"

"I'm really hoping so, for your sake."

Jamilla smiled and leaned back from her salad as she gave Maxwell a piercing look.

He returned her stare, and then said, "What?"

"I don't know," Jamilla hesitated, "but at this moment I think I . . ."

With all interest lost in the delectable concoction, Maxwell dropped his spoon and said, "Go on."

Panic constricted Jamilla's throat. She couldn't force herself to finish the sentence. She'd looked into the swimming pool after stepping off the diving board, only to find it was the shallow end. She'd purposely avoided uttering those three little words. It was always safer to keep him guessing. "I like you . . . a lot."

Maxwell scooted to the edge of his seat as he leaned forward onto the table. "That's not what you were going to say, and you know it!"

Blinking to fight back panic, Jamilla stammered, "I guess, I, well . . ."

Maxwell touched her hand this time as he whispered, "I just want to hear you say it."

There was something in his eyes that told her it was safe. That perhaps there was more water in the pool than she had first perceived. "Say what?" She pretended not to know what he meant.

"Come on Jamilla, you can say it," Maxwell almost pleaded. "Say the words I've longed to hear."

Jamilla dropped her head just as the waiter appeared with salmon and chicken plates. "The chicken for the lady," a server other than Joel said, presenting the platter-sized dishes. "And for you, sir. Will there be anything else?"

Maxwell impatiently dismissed the pleasant-enough young woman. "No, no. We're fine," he said as he stared at Jamilla.

Jamilla looked briefly at the brunette with olive skin and green eyes and smiled. "May I have some hot water with lemon?"

"Certainly."

Jamilla turned sharply as the server disappeared. "Please don't speak for me."

"Don't even try it," Maxwell mused. "I'm not going to let you start an argument trying to weasel your way out of this."

"What do you mean?"

This time he laughed out loud. "You look for any distraction available whenever I start to talk to you about us."

Jamilla started blinking rapidly again as she said, "I don't know what you're talking about." She breathed a sigh of relief when her hot water arrived. "Thank you."

This time the server looked directly at Jamilla as she asked, "May I get you anything else?"

Before she answered, she looked at Maxwell deliberately before asking, "Would you like something else?"

Maxwell just smiled.

"That'll be all for now, thank you." Jamilla took "polite" to new heights.

Unfazed, Maxwell continued, "As I was trying to say, you need to stop running from this."

Jamilla picked up her fork and began eating. "From what?"

With feelings of exasperation, Maxwell sighed, "You know what?" Jamilla looked up from her plate.

"I'm done." Maxwell stabbed his fork into the salmon. "You going to let this good man get away." *Chew.* "Then you go right ahead." *Chew. Chew.* "I'm tired of chasing you."

Jamilla moved the garlic-mashed potatoes around with her fork, refusing to look at Maxwell. She wanted so much to love him with abandonment, but what if he left her, too?

Too? Who else had left her? Surely she wasn't talking about her birth mother. She had died! She wouldn't have left her otherwise. Jamilla's mind took her back to what it must have been like for her. She was hot and felt sweat beginning to form on the bridge of her nose. Then suddenly she saw them in her plate, two babies with her adult face. She leapt from her seat, tossing the plate as she moved. Chicken and potatoes rained down on the Hollywood-looking couple seated across from them. All eyes, including Maxwell's, were on her. She wanted to break and run, but her feet felt bolted to the ground. She was fighting for air but she couldn't seem to get any. Panic began to consume her. The more she struggled for air, the less she seem to have.

Maxwell was on his feet, standing next to Jamilla, when he asked in a low voice, "What the hell is wrong with you?" As he placed his arm around her, he could feel her trembling. The slight tremors gave way to the shakes.

Jamilla felt totally out of control as she stood, stunned, looking at the mess she'd caused. She looked at the blond woman and her companion, who seemed almost hysterical as she cleaned chicken and potatoes from her hair and lap. "I don't . . ."

Before she could answer, the manager had joined them. "Is there a problem here?" he asked in a stern yet concerned tone.

"I'm so sorry." Jamilla had moved to where the woman sat, visibly angry. "I . . ." Words abandoned her. She wanted to tell Maxwell, the woman, the manager, and the world that she'd seen two babies smiling with her face in her plate, but who'd believe her?

"My girlfriend has been under a tremendous strain lately." Maxwell reached into his breast pocket and removed his badge. "Please let me pay for this couple's meal and any damages."

The manager examined the badge closely before looking at Maxwell, then at Jamilla. "Are you sure you're all right, Miss?"

Jamilla managed to nod her head.

The manager moved to the table where the other couple sat, the woman still brushing food from her hair with the assistance of the waitstaff. The manager spoke too softly for Maxwell and Jamilla to hear, but the couple looked in their direction several times before the man nodded his head yes.

The manager returned half-smiling and said, "Your apology has been accepted and they have agreed that you can pay for their meal. But I must warn you, if there is any further disturbance, LAPD or not, I *will* ask you to leave."

Maxwell breathed a sigh of relief. "Understood." He helped Jamilla back to her seat before he went to the table where the other couple sat. "I just want to apologize personally. My girlfriend has just been going through some things lately, and I don't know what happened here today. But please, have whatever you wish and I'm picking up the tab."

The woman was openly hostile, but the man seemed more forgiving. "Thank you for your generous offer. My wife and I accept."

Maxwell reached into his back pocket and pulled out his wallet, opened it, and removed two crisp twenty-dollar bills. "This should also cover your dry cleaning."

"That won't be necessary," the man said as the woman snatched the money.

Maxwell looked between the two of them and smiled. "I insist."

Without further words, Maxwell returned to Jamilla, who sat quietly crying. Joel and crew had cleaned the area and reset the place setting. "Are you okay?"

"Can we just leave?" Jamilla didn't make eye contact with him.

Maxwell knew she was embarrassed, but he was hungry. "Everything will be fine." He reached across and patted her hand. "I've taken care of everything."

Jamilla withdrew her hand angrily. "You've taken care of what?" She leaned across the table, her voice growing louder with each word. "You've found my sisters?"

Chapter 5

The car ride wasn't as quiet as the wait for the valet to bring Maxwell's pearlescent white Hyundai Sonata. Jamilla was mortified to the point that she didn't even want to look at Maxwell. She was equally as angry.

His insistence that they stay and finish the meal had made her utterly miserable. The couple that had been innocent victims of her tirade kept stealing glances at her, whispering. Why hadn't she driven her own car? She would have taken a cab home if it hadn't been more than sixty miles away. How dare he hold her hostage! She had a good mind to file a police report.

Jamilla almost laughed at herself and how irrationally she was thinking. How absolutely stupid she'd look to the police if she reported one of their own for refusing her request to leave an upscale restaurant without finishing their meal. Maxwell interrupted her revelry in lunacy.

"I think you need to get some professional help, Milla." Maxwell never took his eyes off the road as he spoke. "I've been worried about you for a while now."

Jamilla stared out of the passenger window.

"You haven't been sleeping. You've lost a ton of weight. And now this . . ."

Jamilla turned quickly to face Maxwell. "And what?" she shouted.

"We should have left. I was humiliated, and all you could think about was finishing your dinner."

"You need to face your demons." Maxwell turned to her as he came to the light just before the freeway entrance. "You can't continue like this. You're having some sort of breakdown."

"Go to hell!"

"If I thought it would help you, I'd gladly do exactly that." Maxwell made the right turn to the freeway ramp. "What can I do to help you?"

Tears welled in the corners of her eyes. The sad part about all of this was that Jamilla knew Maxwell was right. She was out of control. The visions and dreams were holding her creativity hostage and there was an APB out on her sanity.

Maxwell stole a glance at her. Her tears broke his heart. He was a man who carried a gun and had vowed to protect and serve perfect strangers, yet he couldn't do anything for the woman he loved. "Let me help you." He took her hand and turned quickly to look at her. "Please."

Jamilla turned again to stare out into the night at nothing. "What is it you think you can help me do?"

Maxwell hadn't expected that particular question because he sure didn't have a well-thought-out answer. "Whatever you need."

In a pain-filled voice Jamilla said, "My needs are simple. I simply need to find my sisters."

"I can do whatever I can, but you've done the right thing by hiring Brewington. I can help you with that financially."

Just like a man, thinking money or sex can fix anything. "I don't need your money."

"I wasn't insinuating that you did." Maxwell had to rein in his anger. "To be honest with you, I don't know what the hell to do. What you need to do is get yourself into some therapy. And several times a week is a good place to start!" The reins broke. "You're going to have to deal with whatever feelings are causing those dreams. And no one can do that except you."

"I haven't asked you for any help, so don't be acting like the great black hope."

"What the hell are you talking about?"

"You're just trying to make yourself feel better. If you swoop in and save a damsel in distress, you get to be the hero." Jamilla spewed pure fire. "I don't need you."

Maxwell made the exit onto National Boulevard. "Well, little lady, rescue your damn self, because you can consider this brother done. I wish you well in whatever it is you think you need to do."

"What are you saying?"

"Have a nice life." The car accelerated slightly. "I'm tired of begging to be your man—your man in the true sense. Taking care of you, protecting you. You like your misery, so I'm leaving you to it."

Jamilla was stunned. Maxwell had never spoken to her in that manner. She didn't know whether to be sad, angry, or flattered. She was ready to plead her case, but he had pulled up next to her car and stared straight ahead. She wasn't sure what to do next. Maxwell helped her out with that decision. He leaned over and opened the passenger door, never looking at her, and said, "Good night."

Jamilla turned and stared first at the opened door and then back at Maxwell. "You're throwing me out of your car?"

Silence.

"I'm talking to you." Though she'd made it up in her mind at the restaurant that she wasn't spending the night, she said, "I thought I was spending the night."

"That's not such a good idea." He never took his eyes off the stop sign straight ahead. "I need to get up early tomorrow to work out before the game."

"So you're just going to let me drive back to Rancho at this hour after what happened at the restaurant?"

"You don't need me, remember?"

Jamilla grabbed her purse and slipped out of the door. She slammed it so hard, Maxwell thought the glass would shatter. He laughed to himself as he thought of the scene when Tina Turner had done just that in *What's Love Got to Do With It*. His laughter stopped abruptly as he realized—everything.

Jamilla was in the car and peeling away from the curb in a matter of seconds. Maxwell *was* worried about her driving home in her condition. What would she do if she saw the babies while she was driving? He shook off the feelings, though his nonchalant attitude was insincere.

Jamilla didn't remember the drive home—only the tears that clouded her vision. Why had she told him she didn't need him when the opposite was so true? He was her only true friend and she'd blown it. What would she do now? As she pulled into the garage, she resisted the temptation to call him.

She refused to turn on the lights but climbed the stairs and fell into bed, still clothed. She was asleep instantly, and for the first time in she couldn't remember how long, she had dreamless sleep.

Chapter 6

Fred picked up on the first ring. "Fred Brewington."

"Mr. Brewington, this is Jamilla Holmes Dixon. I was calling to see if you'd found out anything yet."

"Ms. Holmes, I do love promptness. You're right on time." Fred could be heard moving papers around. "Ah, yes, here we go."

Jamilla held her breath.

"Amazingly enough, I found a Minnie Lou Holmes obituary in a Dale, Georgia, newspaper in July 1973. In that obituary it says that she was survived by her infant daughters, Clarissa, Jamilla, and Leticia."

Jamilla grabbed the end of her desk as the room began to spin out of control. Had she heard him clearly? "What did you just say?"

He laughed a little before he continued. "I believe I found your birth mother's obituary."

"Oh, Mr. Brewington!" Jamilla sang with glee. "That is wonderful."

"Hold on here just a minute, Ms. Dixon. This is a long way from finding your sisters. The trail could be dead cold after this was published. I just don't know at this point."

"Mr. Brewington—I mean, Fred—do you know that I have never even heard my sisters' names before? So please let me have this."

"Okay, I'll admit it's a pretty good start."

"But this is more than I could have hoped for in such a short time," Jamilla rambled on, breathless. "I called because it was easier than sitting here staring at a computer screen willing words to appear magically. I've been watching the clock since I got up at three this morning, waiting for this phone call."

Jamilla's mind went back to the scene at the restaurant and subsequent fight with Maxwell. When she woke she was fully clothed and on top of the covers. Though she hadn't dreamed, she still couldn't fall back to sleep.

"I'm glad to be able to share this news, but I want to warn you that this didn't take any great investigative skills. You could have found this as easily as I did. The real test will come with trying to find where your sisters went from Dale."

"Do you think it's possible that they're still in Georgia? Dale, even?"

"In a town with red dirt and no resources? I don't hardly think so. Although anything's possible, but chances of young people staying in a small town like that in this day and age are pretty slim."

"What'll you do next?" Jamilla dared to hope that soon she'd be looking into eyes so much like her own.

"Now that I have your sisters' names, I'm going to see what public records I can find. If they were adopted and their names changed, that would make it more difficult, but not impossible, to find them."

Jamilla listened intently—all the while, her mind raced. Would Leticia and Clarissa be as happy to find her as she knew she'd be to find them? Did they even know that she existed? Were they together, or had they each grown up with a hole in their soul like she'd had since her twelfth birthday? "When can I call you again?"

"You can call me whenever the spirit moves you, but if I get anything worth telling you, I'll be sure to call you." Fred Brewington paused. "But Ms. Dixon . . . ."

Jamilla interrupted him. "Please, Mr. Brewington. No buts—just find my sisters."

"I was going to say, I needed to warn you that it may be weeks or even months before I uncover another lead. I just don't want you to get your hopes up too high."

Undaunted, Jamilla said, "Mr. Brewington, high hopes is all I have."

For some reason unbeknownst to him, Fred Brewington liked this young woman from the moment she'd stepped into the lobby of the office suite. There was a freshness and innocence about her that he hadn't seen in a lot of years in this business. Most of his cases dealt with cheating spouses and jilted lovers. Occasionally, he'd help a father win custody of his children, but for the most part the rewarding part of his job had long since vanished.

The idealism that had brought him to this business after a motorcycle accident had forced him into early retirement from the Los Angeles County Sheriff's Department had been crushed out like a fully consumed cigarette. He had grown tired of people hiring him to confirm what they knew full well in their hearts in the first place.

The saddest part of all was, even when he'd shown the victim proof in black and white—or even living color—they had refused to believe. So his only motivation for the past several years had been the money until he'd met Jamilla.

"Well, then, Miss Jamilla, I guess I'm just going to have to find your sisters, huh?"

Chapter 7

Jamilla gently tapped the handset on the cordless phone as she pondered whether she should call Maxwell. They hadn't spoken since he'd thrown her out of his car ten days before. He'd left her several messages, but what could she say to him that would sound at all rational?

Sleep had been her enemy since the *episode*. Screaming babies woke her from a sound sleep or caused her to jump suddenly when she tried to concentrate on her manuscript. She took a deep breath and began dialing. Maxwell seemed to answer before it even started to ring.

"I was wondering how much longer you were going to make me suffer," Maxwell said, only half joking.

Sighing, Jamilla regretted making the call. She had nothing to give, yet Maxwell wanted something, anything, from her. "I've had a lot on my mind."

"Don't you understand that I'm your friend?" Maxwell pleaded. "Which means we share everything?"

"What do you mean?"

"It's one of those magical formulas. When we share, you have half the pain and sorrow, but double the joy and happiness."

Jamilla sighed. "I know you're my friend, and that's why I called you." Jamilla's voice began to crack. "Please don't make this hard."

"I'm not trying to, Milla." Exasperated, he went on. "As your friend it's my job to see the first tear, catch the second one, and stop the third."

Jamilla's tears began to stream as he spoke.

"And you know what, girl?"

"What?" she managed.

"You're preventing me from doing my job."

Despite the emptiness and hopelessness she felt inside, she had to laugh. "You know you can always make me laugh."

"Just a part of my charm, my sweet."

"So tell me what's going on with you. I really have been worried, you know."

"The dreams are coming every time I fall asleep. I hear screaming babies when I'm awake. I'm just exhausted."

"Oh baby, I'm so sorry." Maxwell searched for something more profound but there was nothing. "What's the investigator saying?"

"I haven't spoken to him this week, but I'm sure if he had news he'd call me."

"Let me give home skillet a ring—maybe he needs a little inspiration to make something happen." Maxwell searched for relief from his pangs of despondency.

"I don't want to tick him off." Jamilla wiped a single tear from her cheek.

"Just leave this to me." Maxwell smiled to himself. "If he knows you're my girlfriend, then he'll look at all of this differently, I promise you."

Too stunned at the words *my girlfriend* to respond immediately, Jamilla removed the handset from her ear and just stared at it. They'd never talked about being boyfriend-girlfriend. She enjoyed being with him, no doubt, but she wasn't good girlfriend material. She needed to fill the void in her soul before it was worthy of a mate. She didn't have any energy to be his *girlfriend*. "What did you just say?"

A little perplexed, he replied, "If he knows I have a vested interest and I'm the police, he'll be sure that whatever he's doing is fast and ac-curate."

"No, I mean the girlfriend part."

"I don't really understand what you're asking me."

"You said, and I quote, 'If he knows you're my girlfriend, then he'll look at all of this differently'. We've never talked about me being your girlfriend."

"Woman, we've been hanging out for almost two years." Maxwell's voice seemed a little higher than it had been. "What do you call it?"

"Hanging out."

Daunted, Maxwell said, "I see."

Jamilla could feel the disappointment through the phone and it only underscored her point. She didn't have any oomph to give this man and his emotions. She needed desperately to change the subject. "Do you want Mr. Brewington's number?

"Who's Mr. Brewington?" Maxwell was lost in his own selfish thoughts. He didn't know when he'd fallen in love with Jamilla, but he couldn't remember the time before he did. His feeling of impotence only escalated when she was this depressed. There had to be something, anything, he could do to help her find her sisters.

"The investigator, remember? You checked him out."

"Oh yeah, yeah. I'm sorry—I was thinking of other things at the moment. Sure, give me the number."

Jamilla shared the number with him and made a weak excuse to hang up. She was so exhausted. Her lack of sleep alone would make her a hazard if she were operating heavy machinery. She dragged herself up from the comfortable leather chair and into the kitchen. Just as she placed her hand on the refrigerator door, the phone rang.

"Don't tell me you wrote the number down wrong," Jamilla teased.

"Excuse me?" the voice on the other end of the line asked.

"Oh, I'm sorry—I thought you were someone else."

"Ms. Dixon, this is Ayasah Bennett. I work with Fred Brewington. He asked me to give you a call."

Jamilla's pulse began racing instantly. She needed to sit, but the bar stool perched under the granite kitchen counter was too many steps away. Frederick Brewington's words were '. . . if I get anything worth telling you, I'll be sure to call you'. This could only mean that he had *something* to report. Jamilla tried to steady herself so she could speak. "How can I help you?"

"Mr. Brewington wanted me to let you know that he found what he believes to be your sisters' birth records in the county clerk's office in Dale, Georgia. He has found birth records for Clarissa Holmes and

Leticia Holmes, both born on your birth date, and it is listed that they were of multiple birth. But that also means they weren't adopted."

"How do you know that?"

"Because Minnie Lou Holmes is listed as their mother."

Jamilla had turned her back so she could lean against the refrigerator, and as the woman spoke, she began to slowly slide to the floor. She'd just said she believed that her sisters' birth certificates were found. Paper made them real. Minnie Lou Holmes made them hers.

"Are you there, Ms. Dixon?"

Jamilla cleared her throat in an effort to calm her quivering tongue. "Yes."

"Please understand that this is only the beginning—a positive one, but still only the beginning. If they haven't changed their names or hyphenated them like you did, it will make our job so much easier."

"What about my birth certificate?"

"We didn't find your original birth certificate, only the one from your adoption. In most states when someone is adopted, the original birth certificate is sealed."

"My birth certificate doesn't say that I'm of a multiple birth."

"Mr. Brewington was looking at the actual birth records, which contain more information than appears on the actual certificate. But then also remember that once you were adopted, everything about your natural birth was changed in the records."

Jamilla's head began to pound as she tried to comprehend all of the information Ayasah Bennett was imparting. "So what's next?"

"We've started looking for your sisters in hopes they, too, kept the name Holmes."

"Oh my God!" Jamilla had an epiphany. "If their last name is Holmes and he has their birth date, he really *can* find them through their driver's licenses or employment."

"Exactly!" Ayasah's grin could be felt through the phone.

This news was more than Jamilla had ever hoped for—this soon or even ever. The two ladies made idle chitchat for a couple more minutes before Jamilla pressed the END button. A sense of relief mixed with anxiety washed over her. She lifted herself off the floor and ran to her computer. For the first time in days, or had it been weeks, she felt like she could write.

Chapter 8

This time it wasn't screaming babies that jolted Jamilla from her deep sleep. Sleep that had been so sweet in coming had been stolen away by grown women with her face. In her dream she'd been in a country town with streets that weren't paved. Transportation was horse-drawn buggies instead of cars. The women were dressed in modern clothes in this Old West setting. When she approached them and they turned, it was her own face that stared back at her.

"Who are you?" she'd asked frightened.

"I'm Clarissa," the woman in the red dress hissed as she stared back at Jamilla.

"And I'm Leticia," the woman in the black dress whined as she lifted the veil. "Why have you summoned us to this dreadful place?"

"I didn't call you here."

"Indeed you have," Clarissa barked. "We were content in our lives, but you couldn't leave us alone."

"You've been calling us since we were twelve." Leticia moved closer to Jamilla. "But we didn't know how to find you."

"More importantly, we didn't want to be found." Clarissa pulled a gun from her red purse and aimed it at Jamilla. "You're the reason my soul has been empty for so many years. I've had no peace for twenty-one years, and as long as you keep longing for us, we won't."

Jamilla stared at the barrel of the gun that reminded her of Clint

Eastwood in *The Good, the Bad, and the Ugly*. "What are you going to do with that?" Panic engulfed her.

"I'm going to shoot you so you'll leave us alone," Clarissa said calmly as she pulled back the hammer on the Colt .45.

The resounding "No" Jamilla screamed woke her as she sat up suddenly. Her heart pounded so hard she could hear it as she felt her chest to see if she was shot. There was no blood, but pain seemed to surround her. She slowly threw back the covers and swung her body around so her feet would touch the floor.

"What in God's name was that supposed to mean?" Jamilla spoke to her image in the mirror perched above the triple dresser. Even in the darkness she could see that dark circles surrounded sunken eyes with bags big enough to double as a carry-on.

Was her subconscious trying to tell her that she needed to drop the search? She couldn't. She wouldn't! There was no dream that would stop her from searching for her sisters. She only wondered if they wanted to find her as much as she did them. Was it at all possible that they were together, living and loving like sisters, and she was the lone one?

Trying to fall asleep at this point would be futile, so she decided that she might as well try her hand at writing. She glanced at the clock for the first time and saw that she'd been asleep for less than an hour. She couldn't continue this way, she thought, as she fell back onto the bed. She wanted to call Maxwell but thought better of it.

Thoughts of a reunion with her sisters battled in her head as the pros and cons war raged. Until this dream she hadn't thought their reunion would be anything but pleasant. In her mind's eye she had seen them embracing while sharing stories of what their time apart had been like.

Jamilla's eyes fell onto the large white envelope on the nightstand on the opposite side of the bed. She'd read the report from Fred Brewington at least one hundred times, but decided that just once more couldn't possibly hurt. She reached for the envelope and then turned on the light. She sat up in bed and pulled the down comforter up close to her neck as she felt a sudden chill.

She slowly removed the yellow sheets of paper. According to the report, the investigation had taken Fred Brewington to Columbus,

Georgia, where a woman by the name of Clarissa Holmes resided with her teenage son. The woman was a bookkeeper for a dental office where she'd been employed for more than five years. She owned a simple home and drove a late-model Ford. Her skin tone was close to Jamilla's, but she didn't have her face. In all of her visions and dreams her sisters always had her face.

Fred had been confident that he'd completed the job for which she had paid so handsomely. Jamilla ran her finger around the edge of the picture as tears filled her eyes. Though her heart had longed for this moment, her mind had told her it may never come. Fred had offered to make the introduction, but now Jamilla didn't know if she was ready.

She'd played out several scenarios in her mind, but her favorite was to knock on Clarissa Holmes's door early on a Sunday morning. Her sister would take one look at her and know. She would throw her arms around her and they would begin to bridge the thirty-three-year gap.

Then she'd thought of starting with a phone call. She didn't want to give the woman a heart attack and have her die before they even had a chance to meet. She flung the pages to the side as she tossed her tired body back against the maple headboard.

If only she could manage to get a good night's sleep, then maybe making a decision would become an easier task.

Chapter 9

Jamilla didn't know how long she'd been sitting across from 1129 El Domingo Circle, staring at the front door, when the basketball bounced off the hood of the burgundy rental car. She jumped involuntarily as the lad ran up to her, apologizing for overthrowing the ball.

Once she'd gathered her wits, she decided that she hadn't come all the way across the country *not* to meet her sister. She turned the key in the ignition and the engine died. The music continued to play as Luther's voice filled the air around her. She removed the key and slipped it into her purse, then took one last look at the house before she opened the car door.

The blinds opened in the window she presumed to be the living room a short while before—someone was at home. She stood close to the car, trying to fortify her steps. "Put one foot in front of the other," she said aloud.

She'd decided against calling ahead to announce her arrival. She didn't want to be deterred before she got started. It would be a lot harder to reject her in person. Fred had strongly suggested otherwise. She thanked him for his concern and proceeded to make reservations for the trip. She'd arrived the day before. She'd driven past the house several times but never stopped.

Now her mouth tasted like onions. Fear was like her next of kin but she knew she had to press on. She moved her right foot, then her left, and soon she was walking. Her knees wobbled and her ankles shook. *I should have worn flat shoes*, Jamilla thought idly as her body moved toward the house. She didn't remember the final steps that landed her on the porch with the lovers' swing and beautiful potted plants.

She stood before the door with her hands to the side, hoping she could will herself to ring the doorbell when suddenly it opened. The two women startled each other. The woman on the inside blinked several times before she asked, "May I help you?"

"I'm looking for . . ." Jamilla started but suddenly had lost all of her resolve. "I'm a . . ."

The woman eyed her suspiciously. "What can I do for you?" the stranger with the cinnamon complexion and shoulder-length dark hair with blond highlights asked as she placed her hand on the handle of a black wire mesh door that did double duty guarding against winged and two-legged intruders.

Jamilla tried again to state her purpose. "I'm Jamilla Holmes Dixon." She waited for the slightest hint of recognition. There was none.

"Holmes?" The woman relaxed her hand slightly.

"Yes."

"That's my name."

"I know—that's why I'm here." Jamilla let the words spill forward.

"Excuse me?" The woman tensed up again.

Jamilla let her breath escape slowly, then took in more of the warm, moist air into her lungs, trying to slow her pounding heart. "May I come in?"

"What is it that you need?"

"I've searched for you a long time," Jamilla stated nervously.

This time it was the woman on the other side of the door who was getting nervous. "For what?"

Jamilla looked around before she continued. "I'd really rather not discuss this on the front porch."

The woman crossed her arms and leaned back on her left hip.

Sighing, Jamilla knew she'd have to share more information. "I actually found you through a private investigator I hired. I believe we share something very important."

"Don't be coming up in here with none of that *Sittin' in the Front Pew* mess," she snapped.

Confused, Jamilla asked, "What?"

"Don't come up in here telling me my daddy is your daddy. I'm not having it!"

Actually, my mother is your mother. Almost relieved, Jamilla started to laugh. "No, I assure you that isn't the case. But it would be so much easier if I could come in and speak with you."

The woman hesitated, then decided that Jamilla posed no threat. Besides, now her curiosity was getting the better of her. She flipped the latch on the door and opened it. "Come in," she said as she stepped to the side.

Jamilla stepped inside the medium-sized house with the warmth that made it a home. Pictures of Clarissa and a young man Jamilla believed to be her son were generously distributed around the room. There were pictures of Clarissa with a man who had his arm thrown over her shoulder as they both smiled broadly. She took a few steps toward the center of the room before she turned. "You have a lovely home."

"Thank you." The woman moved past her toward the animal-print chaise. "Please have a seat in here."

Jamilla obediently followed her, sitting across from her on the matching sofa. She cleared her throat, trying to find her well-rehearsed words. "I'm sorry to intrude like this. You opened the door like you were about to leave."

Still cautious, the woman said, "I was going to tell Martin that it was time for lunch. That boy would play basketball twenty-four-seven if I'd let him."

The resemblance between this woman and the young man who'd apologized for hitting the car struck her. Martin was her nephew. "I won't keep you, I promise."

Her patience waning, she asked, "What can I do for you, Ms. Dixon?"

Jamilla took a deep breath and began. "I guess I need to first ask if I'm at the right house. Are you the Clarissa Holmes born on October 17, 1973?"

The woman looked shocked. "How do you know my birthday?"

Jamilla worked hard to relax. She needed to calm the battle raging in the pit of her stomach if she was ever going to get through this. "I did a lot of research before I showed up on your doorstep."

"Research?"

Jamilla forced a smile. "As I tried to explain earlier, I hired a private investigator to find you."

"I'm really confused." Clarissa shifted uneasily in her seat. "Why would you hire a private investigator to find me?" She laughed nervously. "I didn't know I was lost. And you said that you weren't trying to say that my father is your father."

"I was born in a little town right outside of Dale, Georgia, thirty-three years ago on October 17." She waited a beat, hoping she'd struck a familiar chord, then continued. "I'm one of three baby girls born that day." Still nothing.

"You're a triplet?"

So are you. "Yes."

"I don't think I've ever met a triplet before." Clarissa relaxed slightly. "Only met twins once."

"My mother died giving birth to us."

"Oh, I'm sorry to hear that. That must have been very difficult on all of you."

This isn't going anything like I thought it would. By now I would have thought she would have thrown herself into my arms and said, 'Oh my God, you're my sister.' "We were all separated." Jamilla struggled to hide her disappointment. "Well, at least I was separated. A wonderful couple in Los Angeles adopted me and I've had a good life, but there's a vital part of me missing. Actually it's more like two vital parts of me."

As though someone had thrown cold water on her, Clarissa leapt from the chaise as she realized why Jamilla was there. "You think I'm one of your sisters?"

Giving the thought a chance to take root to become a realization, Jamilla waited. The look on Clarissa's face made Jamilla believe this had all been a horrible mistake. She should have left well enough alone, gone on with her life, and if it had been meant to be, she would have met her sisters. The syndicated sitcom *Sister-Sister* played out in her mind. The twin girls had been shopping at a mall when they encountered each other. But that was television. In real life if you wanted something to happen, you had to orchestrate it. "I do."

"You're nuts." Clarissa could hear herself screaming but couldn't do anything to control it. "My parents live on the other side of town where I grew up."

"Until my parents told me the whole story on my twelfth birthday, I didn't know, either." Jamilla deliberately spoke softly and slowly. "They just thought it was the time to tell me. But they could have just as easily taken this secret to the grave."

"But I have brothers and sisters. Some younger, some older."

Oh, she's making this so much harder than it has to be. She's fighting the inevitable. Denying it doesn't make it untrue. Jamilla tried to calm her trembling hands, but they refused to cooperate. She had to continue. She'd come much too far to let this woman's disbelief deter her. "Where were you born?"

"Right here in Columbus at St. Francis Hospital. Just like all of us were."

That can't be right. "What's your parents' last name?"

"Holmes."

This time, Jamilla felt like the one who'd been splashed with cold water. "Really?" was all she could manage.

"Really."

"But we were born on the same day." Feelings of desperation caused panic in Jamilla. She was too close to her sisters to have this woman snatch her fulfillment away.

"I think that has already been established." Clarissa began to feel sorry for the stranger. "But on that day I was born to Daisy and Willis Holmes. I have pictures of them bringing me home from the hospital."

"That doesn't prove anything." Finally, this was something Jamilla could rebut. "They could have been bringing you from anywhere."

Clarissa thought for a moment and realized Jamilla was correct—the picture proved nothing. But none of this made any sense. She was and always had been the third child of Mr. and Mrs. Willis Holmes. "You're wrong," she managed, not totally convinced.

"Don't you see, Clarissa, they could have picked you up from Dale."

Clarissa shook her head, refusing to believe her parents would have lied to her for thirty-three years. "Like I said before," she paused for emphasis, "you're nuts. I'm sorry you don't know where your sisters are, but believe me, you haven't found one here."

"Please hear me out."

Clarissa folded her arms across her chest. "I'm done hearing!"

"Please," Jamilla pleaded.

Nothing.

"Give me five minutes. If I haven't convinced you in that time, I'll leave and you'll never hear from me again."

"Five minutes." Clarissa didn't know whether to listen to what she had to say or throw her out. How dare she come into her home spewing such nonsense? "Not another second."

"Let's just suppose Willis Holmes was related to my mother Minnie Lou. When he heard she'd died, he came to rescue you. Maybe I was already gone. Maybe our other sister was gone, too.

"So he and your mother have raised you just like they gave birth to you without making you any the wiser. And I ain't mad. Sometimes I wish my mom and dad hadn't told me."

Clarissa's expression told Jamilla she was pondering what she'd just heard. "But we look nothing alike. How do you explain that?"

"I can't," Jamilla said softly, unable to hide her disappointment. "In all my dreams my sisters always had my face."

"Your dreams?"

Jamilla went on to explain how dreams had plagued her since her twelfth birthday and now they were becoming visions during her waking hours.

"This is all too bizarre."

"I know it seems too much for you to believe. I've been living with it for more than twenty-one years." Jamilla stood and began pacing. "Clarissa . . ."

Clarissa looked up from the pattern she studied in the area rug beneath the coffee table. "Yes?"

"I need you to keep an open mind." Jamilla sat on the chaise next to Clarissa, taking her hand. "Think back. Is there anything that was said or done, given this new information, that makes sense when it didn't before?"

Clarissa sat quietly for a moment in deep thought. She finally raised her eyes and Jamilla could see the tears forming.

Time was no more. The contemporary furnishings seemed to have dropped away and the two of them were suspended in midair. There was no sound as the air around them stood still.

"Not a thing."

Chapter 10

Hot tears poured from Jamilla's eyes as she raced through the city in search of the hotel. She'd passed the freeway entrance and now she was doubling back in hopes of getting as far away from Clarissa Holmes as she could.

When Clarissa had shared the family album with her, Jamilla was convinced that she shared the same parents as her other siblings, who all bore a striking resemblance to *their mother*. How could Fred Brewington have made such a horrific mistake?

Anger blurred her vision as she entered the on-ramp, doing more than seventy miles per hour. She felt relieved that she'd made the dry runs from the hotel to Clarissa's house, because now she didn't have to search for refuge.

The miles that separated her from the nightmare that was Clarissa Holmes was a blur. She pulled into the parking space, turned off the car, and fell onto the steering wheel, beginning to wail. She wallowed in self-pity and despair until she had no tears left to shed. She finally raised her head, wiped her face, and sat up straight. Suddenly, she had a newfound determination. She was sure that this setback was only a test—a test to see if she was really sincere in her quest. The scene replayed in her head like a bad movie that was way too long.

Clarissa's manner had switched from confusion to compassion as she came to realize that this silly woman sitting in front of her had actually thought that they could be sisters—not just sisters but triplets!

"Jamilla, I'm sorry. As much as you want to make me one of your sisters, you know in your heart I am not," she had said.

Jamilla had stared out of the window onto the street where she watched the boys play basketball. "Where does your birth certificate say you were born?" She refused to give up.

Clarissa had sighed. "Columbus."

"Do you know what time you were born?"

"What does that have to do with anything?

"Please, Clarissa."

"Twelve-oh-seven A.M."

Hope flowed from her as she had slowly expelled air. She'd picked up her purse and stood. "I'm sorry I bothered you."

Jamilla had slowly placed the long strap over her shoulder while she stared at the floor. She'd turned and walked toward the door.

"Jamilla, I'm so sorry this didn't turn out the way you'd hoped."

"Me, too." Jamilla's defeated tone had thickened the air with sadness.

Jamilla shook her head to stop the recorder that played in her head. She squared her shoulders and straightened her posture. "Clarissa Holmes, that *is* my sister, I *will* find you!"

She gathered her things, got out of the car, and headed for the hotel lobby. The smell of hot chocolate-chip cookies greeted her as the doors opened automatically. The pleasant woman at the desk surprised her with her familiar greeting. "Good evening, Ms. Dixon."

"Hi."

"We have some cookies fresh out of the oven. Would you like one?"

Jamilla realized she hadn't had dinner and couldn't remember if she'd had lunch. Breakfast was a distant memory, and she struggled with the thought that it may have been yesterday's breakfast that she recalled. She was famished. "Sure." She stepped closer to the desk, her hand extended.

"Did you have a good meeting?"

Taken aback, Jamilla did a double take and stared.

"Oh, I heard you on the cell phone as you walked through the lobby earlier."

Jamilla relaxed slightly and said, "Oh. Yes. I mean, no." She didn't know how to answer the young woman's question. She decided to change the subject. "I'd like a six o'clock wake-up call."

"Are you taking our shuttle to the airport?"

"No." Jamilla turned and walked toward the bank of elevators. She could feel the woman's eyes boring a hole into her back.

When the elevator arrived on the ninth floor, Jamilla was relieved no one had joined her. She walked the fifteen steps to her room, slipped the key card in the electronic lock, turned the knob, and moved into the room as though she were being chased. Without removing her shoes, she climbed onto the bed and curled up into a ball.

She grabbed the thick, soft pillow and buried her face into it. She began crying softly, which gave way to moans. Soon she felt herself screaming. She didn't know how long she'd had her face buried in the pillow when she heard a knock at the door. She quickly sat up and wiped her face. As she opened the door, the housekeeper was inserting the passkey into the lock. They frightened each other.

"Oh, I'm sorry, ma'am," the flustered Hispanic woman said. "Would you care for turn-down service?"

"What time is it?" Jamilla asked, disoriented.

"Just before eight." The woman's accent made it hard to understand her.

What had she been doing for two hours? Had she fallen asleep? "No," Jamilla said sharply, then decided to soften her tone. "I'll do it myself, but thank you."

The woman looked as though no thanks were necessary for her *not* to do work. She left without another word and moved down the hall.

Jamilla decided she needed to call someone—anyone. She set the security lock on the door and returned to the bed. She could see a large, wet spot on the pillow and her sadness turned to anger. How dare she flap around in this quagmire of despair? She hadn't failed; she'd climbed a steep hill, only to find that there was a mountain on the other side of it. But she was that much closer to planting her flag on the summit.

Jamilla picked up the cell phone and entered a speed dial code. Augusta answered on the first ring. "I was wondering if I'd hear from you today." Augusta's voice seemed strained. The pain she felt in her

heart was as real as the arthritic misery she felt in her knees. She
wanted to ask her how it went, but knew she needed to wait until
Jamilla was ready to tell. Something she truly understood.

"It wasn't her," Jamilla blurted.

Augusta was prepared to hear that Clarissa had rejected Jamilla. She
wouldn't even have been surprised to hear that the newfound sibling
was hostile and angry, but that she wasn't even her sister was something she hadn't considered. "What?"

"You heard me," Jamilla continued. "The Clarissa Holmes that I
met today isn't my sister."

"Oh baby, I'm so sorry."

"Sorry for what? It's not your fault," Jamilla said to ease her
mother's conscience, when in her heart she believed the opposite.

As though she could read Jamilla's thoughts, Augusta began, "You
know, there's something your daddy and I never told you."

Oh God, what more can there be? Jamilla held her breath.

Augusta waited three beats before she continued. "Your daddy
made me promise him before he died, God rest his soul, that I'd tell
you the whole story."

"I don't understand. What else can there be to tell?"

"I've been telling myself I was waiting for the right time. But the
truth is, I was hoping that you'd give up the notion that you had to
find your sisters, and I wouldn't have to."

"Mother," Jamilla only called her that when she was upset with her,
which seemed to be more and more of late, "what are you trying to tell
me?"

Slowly the story of their trip to Dale and subsequent adoption unfolded. "So you see, I would have taken all three of you if I'd had the
money. I tried to make arrangements with that old biddy, but she
wouldn't hear of it." Augusta paused, trying to draw strength from her
late husband's presence, which she felt in the room.

"You bought me?" Jamilla stood and began pacing the well-appointed
room. She didn't know whether to be elated that the Dixons had spent
their very last dime for her or angry because they didn't have enough
to get at least one of her sisters.

"When you say it like that, you make it sound like such a disgusting thing." Now Augusta ran hot. "I would think you'd be appreciative instead of annoyed."

"MaDear, I'm sorry. I don't want to seem ungrateful. Actually, it's just the opposite. I'm such a potpourri of emotions."

"Times were different then, not to mention hard," Augusta continued, a little gentler this time. "You almost never heard of black folks adopting babies through normal channels. It was usually when a relative had a baby out of wedlock or was a dope fiend. When I heard about you and your sisters, all I could see was the opportunity to have what I wanted most—a child."

Jamilla returned to the bed and fell heavily onto the ultra-comfortable mattress. She was quiet and reflective as she listened to her mother breathe. She'd never once considered what it must have been like for her parents to want a child so badly they'd get one by any means necessary. "And you chose me."

"I—well, actually, we both did." Augusta chuckled slightly. "We knew there was something special about the three of you, but you were different. You seemed to need us more."

"What do you mean?"

"I can't really explain. It was what the old folks call mother wit. There was just something inside of me that connected with you."

Speaking slowly and more to herself than to her mother, Jamilla said, "And I'm really glad it did."

"What was that, baby?"

For a split second Jamilla thought twice about repeating herself. This time she spoke loud and clear. "I said I'm really glad you saw something special and chose me."

"Me, too, baby girl. Me, too."

Chapter 11

Several minutes passed as Jamilla sat thinking of the conversation with her mother. She didn't know where this emotional journey was going to lead her, but she had to make the trip. Somewhere two women who were a part of her lived and breathed. Hopefully, their lives were full and rewarding like her own, and yet, she wondered if something within them yearned for her.

She hadn't spoken to Maxwell in days, and she silently wondered how much longer he was going to be patient with her and this obsession. She picked up the phone, dialing his number. He answered on the second ring.

"Hey, stranger." His tone was even and cool. "I wondered if you'd ever call me again."

You know, this thing rings just like it dials. "I've just been busy writing." The truth was she hadn't written a paragraph in almost two weeks.

"Ah." Maxwell tried to believe her. "How's it going? Will you make your deadline?"

Hell, no. "If I stick to it daily, everything will be fine." Not a lie.

"Okay, but I don't want you stressing yourself out the way you usually do when you're at deadline, because all of us who love you end up paying the price."

Jamilla blurted, "No, you don't!" and then laughed at herself because she knew Maxwell spoke the truth.

Maxwell paused before he asked, "How did everything go with your meeting? Was your sister receptive?"

"I'd say no, but that wouldn't be quite the truth." Jamilla sighed. "To say it was a letdown is like saying your president is not too bright."

Maxwell laughed. "Why does he have to be *my president*? But really, I don't understand."

"Your boy Fred Brewington sent me on a wild-goose chase." Jamilla relayed the dismal story again without taking a breath, her frustration mounting with every word until she was done.

Maxwell whistled through his teeth and only said, "Wow."

"Is that all you can say? After all, you're the one who recommended this imbecile!" Jamilla's wrath was misplaced, but like a stray bullet had no name, she reasoned, neither did good old-fashioned anger.

"He came highly recommended. But you must admit, based on the information he gave you, we both thought this woman was your sister."

"I know. I know." The wind that blew her angry sail had diminished, leaving her feeling alone and vulnerable.

Maxwell felt helpless and waited in silence for her to say more. When she didn't, he asked, "You think a brotha can pull you away to have dinner?"

Jamilla snapped out of her stupor. "I'd really like that. But you don't have to."

"I know that I don't have to. When do you get back?"

"I'll touch down in Ontario at noon."

"Then how's tomorrow night?"

"Actually, that's perfect." Jamilla sighed slightly. "How about The Yard House in Long Beach?"

"I haven't been there in years." Maxwell smiled. "It's a fun place. I'll pick you up at seven."

"Are you sure you want to drive all the way out there?"

"If I didn't, would I offer?" Maxwell chided.

"No, I guess not. I'll be waiting." With that, they both hung up. Jamilla couldn't stop the butterfly flight in her stomach. Why was she nervous to have a date with a man she'd been seeing for years? It made no sense on any level. She was always afraid she'd say something that would turn him off to the point he'd not want to see her anymore. While she pretended she didn't care, if the truth be known, she did care—more than just a little. She believed he thought he could fill the empty space in her heart, but he was wrong—very wrong.

She wondered out loud, "I bet my sisters aren't putting their lives on hold for me."

Chapter 12

Jamilla tossed her keys on the kitchen counter and kicked off her shoes. The flight back from Atlanta had been late, long, and laborious. Unruly children, sweaty old men, and rude flight attendants grated on any good nerve she thought she had left. Since she'd left little more than forty-eight hours ago, her hopes of finding her sisters seemed all but lost. She glanced at the clock and decided that though it was just before three in the afternoon, it was after five o'clock somewhere, and she went to pour herself a glass of merlot.

As she passed the refrigerator on her way to the cabinet that held the good wineglasses, she caught a glimpse of a picture of her with her parents when she graduated from law school. Her dad smiled so proudly. It made her long for him. After she poured the wine, she decided to retrieve the family album.

She sat looking at pictures from her infancy, and she thought back to how she'd never suspected that her parents hadn't given her life. This newfound information from her mother had rocked her even more. She didn't know what to think about her mother and father *buying* her. Even given her mother's explanation, Jamilla had a hard time wrapping her mind around the concept.

She continued to peruse the pictures, refilling her wineglass until the bottle was empty. When she finally closed the last album, her head was buzzing and her heart ached. Except for the now infamous twelfth-birthday party, not one picture showed her with other little girls. Jamilla Holmes Dixon was always alone or with Augusta and Johnny. She laid her head back and closed her eyes. How was today any different? She really needed a girlfriend, especially today. Someone she could call and have her listen attentively as she poured out her heart.

"I'll call Gloria!" Jamilla went to search for her friend from college's phone number. She couldn't remember the last time they'd spoken, but she knew it hadn't been *that* long ago. She found the number in her BlackBerry and dialed it on the house phone.

The familiar voice picked up on the first ring. "Hello."

"Hi, Gloria, this is Jamilla."

Silence.

"Hello? You there?"

"Yes," Gloria Princeton answered flatly.

"How've you been?"

"I'm doing quite well, thank you."

Jamilla wondered if this had been such a good idea. She'd called her friend to lift her spirits, but she was sure an overdue creditor got a warmer reception. "I've obviously caught you at a bad time. I'll call you later, I guess."

"Don't bother," Gloria snapped.

"What's wrong with you?" Jamilla retorted matching Gloria's tone.

"I can't believe you'd have the nerve to call me after what you did, or should I say didn't do.

"Gloria, what are . . ." Jamilla tried to squeeze her words between Gloria's tirades.

"I thought we were closer than that!"

". . . you talking about?" Jamilla managed to finish her question.

"Oh and now you're going to act like you don't know?" Gloria screamed so loud it was hard to decipher what she was saying exactly.

Jamilla's mind raced as she tried to understand what the woman was talking about. Then Gloria's fury helped Jamilla remember—her wedding! Gloria had married a mutual friend from college a few weeks—or was it months?—before. Gloria had even asked her to be an attendant. "Oh, Glo, I'm so sorry! I've been so wrapped up with finding my sisters, everything else is a blur."

"That's so like you, Jamilla. That's all you ever talk about—you and your missing sisters. Well, you can stick a fork in our friendship because it is done!" Gloria Princeton slammed down the phone.

"That went pretty well, don't you think?" Jamilla said to the purple pillow at the end of the sofa. She considered calling another old friend, but thought better of it. She knew she should be writing, but thoughts of Clarissa Holmes stifled all else. She was about to lay the phone on the end table when it rang.

"Hello." Jamilla didn't bother to check the Caller ID.

"Ms. Holmes. This is Fred, Fred Brewington."

Her first instinct was to hit the OFF button. But something in her refused to allow it. "Yes, Mr. Brewington?" The coolness in her tone chilled even her.

"I've been out of town on a case and just returned to the office a little while ago and got your message." Fred's words rushed forward, as though he knew she wanted to hang up on him. "I'm so sorry that I made such a grave error. But, I'm sure you can see how this might have happened."

"No, actually, Mr. Brewington, I can't understand how you could toy with my emotions this way. I don't understand why you didn't do the job I'm paying you quite handsomely to do by asking this woman some very basic questions that would have proven she isn't my sister!"

"But, Ms. Holmes, I assure you . . ."

Jamilla interrupted him. "You assure me? You assure me that when I looked in this woman's eyes and she thought I was a lunatic that I didn't feel small enough to have to pole vault to get up on a curb? Or perhaps you assure me that my check for ten thousand dollars was money poorly spent?"

"I promise you that I'll continue on the case, and all the time that went into finding the wrong Clarissa Holmes will be credited to your account. Though if you read your contract, it clearly states that I make no promises. Everything I did and all the information I gave you was with the best intentions."

"You know what road is paved with good intentions, don't you?" Jamilla replied angrily.

"I would like very much to continue on the case, but that is clearly up to you."

"I'd like a refund in full."

Fred Brewington's silence resonated through the ether. "I'm sorry, but I don't give refunds. I've already agreed to continue on the case, putting forth as much effort as I did before, but there is no guarantee that your sisters are even alive. They could have changed their names. Moved out of the country, any number of scenarios."

Jamilla refused to listen to such gibberish. "Then I'll see you in court!" Her finger found the OFF button.

Rage suffocated her. She hadn't been able to vent her anger and disappointment until now. She collapsed onto the pillow, with which moments before she'd made cute conversation.

Time seemed to stand still. "Clarissa and Leticia—why can't I find you? Why can't I just open the phone book and you be there?"

Suddenly, Jamilla sat up. The phone book? Why hadn't she thought of that before? It was so simple that it just might work. She wiped her face with her fingertips and moved quickly to her office. She sat on the edge of the seat as she moved her work to the side. Her fingertips lightly glided across the keys before she touched the mouse to open the Web browser. She quickly navigated to the *people search* Web site. Her fingers trembled as she typed in *Clarissa Holmes*. The search resulted in ninety-four hits. None was thirty-three, but six were in Georgia with no age listed. Her heart began to pound as she searched for her credit card to pay for the service. She secretly prayed there'd be more than just the Clarissa Holmes who wasn't her sister.

How simple it had been to locate these women, even if it led nowhere. All the money she'd paid Brewington, and this was probably exactly what he'd done. She quickly entered the credit card information and there before her was the contact information for the six women. Two of the listings were for the Clarissa she'd met. But the other four weren't. There before her were addresses and phone numbers. Though she knew she should have been elated, fear gripped her.

Was she afraid of another failure? Or was it the fear of success? Meeting the wrong Clarissa brought to her mind the reality that she may never find her sisters or that she might find one or both of them, only to be rejected. She didn't know which was worse.

She entered Leticia's name and it yielded seventeen matches. Tears began to stream down her cheeks and the names became distorted in front of her. Finding her sisters couldn't possibly be this easy. If this information is available to her, then surely Fred Brewington had checked into each of these people. But had he? Could she be wasting her time? What else did she have to do? Time had been her best friend and worst enemy simultaneously. She'd had twenty-one years to think of and yearn for her sisters. Making up characteristics in her mind and believing their reunion to be a perfect blending of three bodies with one soul. Then on the other hand thirty-three years had past since they were together. With every moment of every day, they could be moving further and further apart until it would be impossible for them to find one another.

Time was her most precious resource, so she'd better get to using it wisely.

Chapter 13

The grandfather clock bonged softly six times, announcing the evening hour. Jamilla had engrossed herself in the people's search Web sites for hours, and she'd lost track of how much money she'd spent. Maxwell was due to arrive in an hour and he was never late. She'd said seven with the intention of being ready by six-thirty. She reluctantly got up from the desk, stretching. She'd found three women named Clarissa Holmes on four different Web sites who could quite possibly be her sister.

All of the Leticias she'd found weren't the right age. She wanted to take the time now to explore further, but she knew she needed to be at least *almost* ready when Maxwell arrived. As Jamilla ran up the stairs, she hummed the song made famous by Little Orphan Annie, "Tomorrow." Did she consider herself an orphan?

Jamilla stepped into her bedroom and moved to the closet, where she shed the clothes that had brought her across country. She needed to wash the miles off her. She stripped and stepped in the shower. She turned the water as hot as she could stand it and let it pelt her body. She wished she could wash away her woes as easily as the sweat.

Though she wanted to stay under the hot water for hours, she washed and rinsed swiftly. She toweled dry and applied just enough makeup to give her face a little glow. She dressed in yellow slacks and a bright green top. She looked like an ad for a citrus drink.

Just as she suspected, Maxwell rang the bell fifteen minutes early. She darted down the stairs and opened the door without looking through the peephole, something he always chastised her about. Her happiness at the sight of him surprised her. He looked handsome, and his smile invited her to his lips. She kissed him lightly and then said, "It's really good to see you."

Maxwell stepped closer to her and hugged her. "You kinda pleasant on a brotha's eyes yourself."

"Come on in." Jamilla stepped to the side and he entered as his scent tickled her nose. "I'm just about ready to go."

"Good—I'm starving." Maxwell sat deep into the sofa and crossed his legs. "I thought maybe you could stay over tonight."

Jamilla's knee-jerk reaction was to say *hell, no. I don't even want to go now. I've found people who could be my sister.* But instead she said, "I'd love to but I really need to be in my own space tomorrow morning so I can get an early start on writing."

Maxwell raised his left eyebrow and looked at her suspiciously. He knew she never hit a meaningful keystroke before six P.M. He didn't know if she was blowing him off or she had something to do dealing with her sisters. Either way, he was disappointed. He'd thought after their short separation she'd want to *make up* with him. "You're not going to get back out here until really late, then I'll have to drive all the way back home."

Jamilla had been inserting her earrings as she stared in the mirror above the fireplace when she turned so suddenly the gold hoop flew from her ear across the room. "I asked you pointedly if you wanted to drive all the way out here, because I could very easily have met you." Her voice rose with each word. "But how did you put it? *I wouldn't have asked if I minded.*"

"But as I drove here, I thought about it and decided that our time could be better spent if we weren't in the car for four hours."

"I'm not staying at your place tonight," Jamilla said flatly as she went in search of the earring. "Let's just find someplace local."

"Whatever." Maxwell didn't try to hide his frustration or disappointment.

"You know, we don't have to go!" Jamilla snapped. "You asked me, remember?"

"And if my memory serves me correctly, you said you were glad I did. You sure could act like it!"

A shouting match was brewing, and this wasn't what Maxwell wanted. His impotence dealing with Jamilla's problems was getting next to him. He knew he couldn't continue this much longer no matter how much he loved her. He stared at her, seeking the right words, when she spoke.

"Look, I'm sorry." Jamilla moved the few steps to where he sat and knelt at his feet, taking his hands. "The truth is I've started more research. I found a Web site that gave me three potential people who can be Clarissa. I want to be here tomorrow morning so I can start it afresh."

Maxwell looked into her sad eyes and his heart melted. "Then how about I stay here?"

Jamilla didn't answer.

"What, you don't want to be with me at all?"

"No, no. It's not."

"Then what is it?"

Jamilla sat on the floor and turned her back so she was leaning against the arm of the sofa. "I don't know."

"I'm not buying that."

"I do want to be with you, but I just need space right now."

"You want your cake sitting pretty in the crystal-covered cake plate all the while you are chomping down on it with a big, cold glass of milk." Maxwell failed at humor.

"Yeah, I guess I do." Jamilla turned to look at him. "Doesn't work like that?"

Maxwell threw his head back with a belly roll of a laugh before saying, "Not hardly."

"I want you to stay. But let's not go all the way to Long Beach." Jamilla smiled mischievously. "The drive back would be too long."

Maxwell sat up with a huge grin. "You know, we can order in."

Jamilla hit his knee playfully. "No, we can't! I want beer."

"Where do you want to go?"

"BJ's finally opened. Let's go there."

"Then get your purse, woman! What're you waitin' on? There's a lager with my name on it." Maxwell spanked her bottom as she lifted herself off the floor with ease.

Jamilla felt light for the first time in days. She now looked forward to an evening with Maxwell followed by a long overdue night.

As Jamilla grabbed her keys, she caught a glimpse of her reflection in the mirror. For a split second she saw three people. All with her face.

Chapter 14

After three dark beers and a Bloody Mary, Jamilla had finally relaxed. She wasn't thinking of anything or anyone except the here and now. The conversation had been light, and Maxwell made her laugh out loud several times. On the ride home she felt warm and tingly. She wasn't sure if it was the alcohol or the prospects of the remainder of the evening that lay before her.

Maxwell's soft words broke her concentration. "It was so great to hear you laugh like you did tonight."

Jamilla smiled. "You have no idea how good it felt."

"I'm glad."

"Thank you."

"What for?"

Jamilla turned and spoke deliberately. "You're an amazing man—one I'm not really sure I deserve."

Maxwell took his eyes off the road for a moment and met her gaze. "Go on."

"I've been so absorbed in myself and this thing with my sisters that I've shut you out. The best I've offered you was a knife and fork when I came to a fully dressed table." She waited a beat. "I'm really sorry."

"Baby, there's nothing to be sorry for. I admit I'd rather have more of you, but I understand and I can wait. Not forever, but I can wait for a while."

"Maxwell," she hesitated.

"Yes?"

"I love you."

He turned slightly. "I know."

Jamilla wanted to be at home now. The short ride from the restaurant took an eternity. As they turned into the condominium development, she said, "Park in the garage."

Maxwell jerked his head, turning to look at her. She'd never once offered him that option. He wanted to be nonchalant about it and struggled for the right thing to say. "Do you have the opener with you?"

"I can use the keypad."

Maxwell smiled. Had things turned the corner for him? He didn't want to do anything to ruin the moment, but he felt like he was skating on thin ice on a sunny day. "Okay, then the garage it is."

They made the circle and he realized he'd never approached her place from the back before. He wasn't quite sure where to go. "Is it the third one from the end?"

"Yes. Just stop right over there and I'll hop out and open the door."

Maxwell obeyed. Jamilla pressed a few numbers on the lighted keypad and the door began to rise. Maxwell was impressed with the immaculate space before him with the painted floor and shelves lining both sides. Her Honda was parked to the right side, so he pulled in on the left. She met him at the driver's door. As he opened the door, she stepped back so he could exit. As he stood she took his face into her hands and kissed him, long and deep.

The motion surprised both of them. Maxwell leaned back on the car to steady himself. "Wow."

Embarrassed by her forwardness, Jamilla blushed. "I'm sorry, I guess it's the alcohol."

"Girl, do you see me complaining?" Maxwell leaned down to kiss her again.

This time she was a little more reserved. "I guess we should close the garage door before the neighbors start talking."

Maxwell didn't take his eyes off her while she moved near the door that led into the house. "That might not be a bad idea." He couldn't stop smiling. He believed tonight Jamilla would give herself completely to him. Though this wasn't the first time he'd have her body, he was reasonably sure it would be the first time he had her mind, maybe even her soul would come along for the ride. He'd waited for a very long time. This was *their* moment. He was going to relish every second of it.

Jamilla turned and slipped the key into the lock and opened the door. She stepped inside and disabled the alarm. "Are you coming?"

Maxwell stood transfixed. Jamilla's liquid movements mesmerized him. He needed to get a hold of himself. He cleared his throat as he tried to speak. "Ah, yeah."

Maxwell followed her into the house. Jamilla removed her shoes and stepped to the cabinet that held the wineglasses. "Champagne or wine?"

"Are we celebrating?"

Jamilla threw her head back and laughed. "Then I guess it's wine."

"I was just asking. Champagne would be wonderful." Maxwell moved close to her, kissing her neck.

She responded with a soft moan. "Would you get the wine and I'll get us a snack."

"You're all the snack I need," he teased.

Jamilla moved toward him and kissed him with more passion than she'd ever expressed. Something deep inside her seemed to be set free. She couldn't explain why or what was happening, but she decided to flow with it. Their kisses became more passionate with each passing second. The wine forgotten, they moved into the living room and fell onto the couch, never breaking their embrace.

Each kiss was more intense than the last, until the two of them were totally lost in their passion. Jamilla felt famished for love. Maxwell's touch fanned the flames of her desire until she was fully engulfed. He lifted her from the couch and carried her up the stairs, never taking his lips from hers, as though she weighed nothing.

As they fell onto the bed, she begged him to take her. Her request didn't go unanswered. For the next hour and thirty-three minutes, Jamilla Holmes Dixon was taken to a new place—a place where no feelings of loneliness and abandonment dared try to enter. She allowed him to love her, and it felt wonderful.

The two of them lay quietly as he planted small, light kisses on her shoulder. She curled up closer to him as she purred lightly. "Do you still want that wine?" he asked her softly.

"I'd love some." Jamilla reluctantly slid over to her own pillow to allow Maxwell freedom to retrieve the wine. "There's some grapes and cheese in a plastic container on the bottom shelf of the refrigerator."

Maxwell leaned over to kiss her. "I'll be right back. Keep my spot warm for me."

Jamilla only smiled as she watched his tight butt disappear down the stairs. She couldn't remember the last time she'd felt this free. What had happened? Or was something about to happen? She began to chastise herself for allowing Maxwell to distract her. She needed to be spending time on the Web site, searching for Clarissa Holmes. As she drew her fingers to her lips to touch where he had kissed her last, she realized that the information and the people it related to would be there in the morning.

She slipped into the bathroom to freshen up while Maxwell pre-pared a little midnight snack. She decided to shower. She hadn't meant to stay as long as she did, but when she finally turned off the water, fifteen minutes had passed. She quickly toweled her body and smoothed a fresh-scent aromatherapy lotion all over her body. She felt cool and refreshed.

"I'll be out in a minute," she yelled out to Maxwell.

"Take your time, baby. I'm just watching the end of the news." Maxwell sounded content. "Would you like me to bring your wine in to you?"

"No, I'll really be out in a second." Jamilla checked her reflection as she admired her naked, curvy body and smiled.

As she stepped back into the bedroom, wearing only a smile, Maxwell whistled. "Dayum, girl! You going to get a brotha goin' again."

Jamilla slipped between the sheets, which felt cool to her skin. "And the problem with that would be?" She laughed as she kissed him slightly on the lips and reached across him to the wineglass.

"Do you want some strawberries?" He held the huge red fruit in the air above her head.

"Drop it in . . ." Her attention was distracted as David Letterman ended his usual hilariously funny monologue by announcing his lineup of guests.

". . . and tonight it's my pleasure to introduce to you Clarissa Holmes, a premiere jazz vocalist who will be appearing at Radio City tomorrow night." Letterman's words paralyzed Jamilla.

The wineglass fell from her hands and the clear, cold liquid bled all over the sheets and comforter. Maxwell leapt from the bed and ran to the bathroom to grab a towel. "What's wrong with you? Did you see another vision?"

Jamilla was on her feet and standing in front of the television, willing the commercials to end. Maxwell looked up at her, confused, as he mopped up the mess the spilled wine had made.

She turned suddenly and yelled, "Did you hear what he just said?"

"I was kinda into you at the moment." Maxwell tried to make a joke. "I wasn't paying attention. What did he say?"

Jamilla bordered on hysteria. "Oh my God! He said his guest tonight is Clarissa Holmes!"

Maxwell stared at her in disbelief. "Are you sure he said that?"

"Of course I'm sure!"

"Wait a minute. You don't think this is *the* Clarissa, do you?"

"It has to be. That's why I've felt like this all evening."

"What do you mean?"

Jamilla moved to where Maxwell stood and grabbed his hands. "I've felt free all evening. I had no idea what was going on, but I knew something had either just happened or was about to."

"I don't understand."

"I don't, either. I just knew in my heart everything was about to change. Please God, let her be the first act."

"Baby, please don't do this to yourself. I can't stand to see you get all excited only to be disappointed again."

"You act like you don't believe me, and besides, I'm not doing anything to myself." Jamilla pulled away. "I know what I heard."

"Baby, it's not a matter of believing you. Do you know the chances of that Clarissa Holmes being your sister?"

"If you don't believe this with me, then you can just get the hell out of my house. I won't stand for you or anyone else to step on my dreams."

"I'm not stepping on your dreams—I'm just trying to stop you from being hurt."

"You're a little late for that." Tears welled in the corners of her eyes. "I've been hurting for twenty-one years. Hell, my hurt is full grown."

"I'm so sorry, baby. Let's just pull the sheets off the bed and then sit and wait to see who this Clarissa Holmes is. And if she is your sister, then I'll have you on the next plane to New York."

"You promise?"

"Promise."

Chapter 15

"Why is it taking so long for this damn commercial to be over?" Jamilla went into the closet to retrieve a nightshirt. They had removed the soiled sheets and replaced them with fresh ones. Maxwell had refilled their wineglasses and they were now empty. Clarissa Holmes still hadn't made her debut on the David Letterman show.

"You say that during each commercial, you know," Maxwell called after her as he poured more wine in each glass. "It's always this way— the person you want to see is last."

Wearing a hot-pink nightshirt that had *Nightie Night* embroidered across the chest, Jamilla returned to the bench at the foot of the bed next to Maxwell. "Isn't it the star who's usually last?"

"Only if that's who you're waiting to see." He laughed and kissed her on the shoulder.

"What if this is my sister?"

Maxwell pulled back slightly and pondered her question for a moment. "How will you know if it is or isn't?"

"Oh, I'll know."

"Okay, I'm about to say something that might get me hurt or worse, but I gotta say it." Maxwell stood and walked a few steps toward the television. "You thought the other Clarissa was your sister, so do you think that your wanting it to be so will cloud your judgment?"

A very serious look found its way to Jamilla's face. She did want to hit him and would have if he hadn't been correct. She'd wanted the Clarissa she met to be her sister so badly that she'd ignored all the signs that told her otherwise. "I'm hoping I learned something from that experience. And I *feel* differently this time."

"Different how?"

"I can't explain it. But the word that comes to mind is 'free.' I feel free to love. To love you, to even love myself, and that just happened in the past twenty-four hours."

David Letterman appeared on the screen again and Maxwell hit the MUTE button so they could hear. He made jokes about the guest who appeared just before the last commercial break. Jamilla's pulse beat so hard she could feel the blood rushing through her body. Something inside of her told her that she was about to see her sister for the first time.

Maxwell grabbed her hand and gave it a little light squeeze. "It's going to be okay."

"I just want them to get on with it."

David Letterman began talking about the brilliant jazz vocals of the up-and-coming star Clarissa Holmes. He talked about how she'd been a foster child from birth until she graduated from high school. She was known as the singing waitress at a popular national restaurant when a *real* record producer heard her.

"Say her age," Jamilla whispered.

Maxwell held her hand a little tighter.

"Ladies and gentlemen, it is my pleasure to introduce for the first time on national television the jazz stylings of Clarissa Holmes." Thunderous applause rose from the audience as the camera switched to the band.

Jamilla's grip on Maxwell's hand was so tight his fingers grew numb. She began to blink back tears as she stared into her own face on the television screen.

Maxwell softly said, "I'll be damned."

Jamilla began to cry in earnest as Clarissa's smooth, sexy voice filled the air around her. Her dreams of twenty-one years had finally taken wings. Her planets had aligned. "Oh Happy Days" played in her heart.

Her mind quickly calculated the chances of this ever happening. She absolutely never watched David Letterman, and Maxwell had never spent the night at her place. "Is it really her? Is that my sister I'm looking at on the screen?" she asked Maxwell, never taking her eyes off the television.

"Since you're sitting here next to me, that woman could only be your twin, or I guess I should say, your triplet." Maxwell looked at her again and then back at the television. "She even moves her body the way you do."

"Oh my God, it is her, isn't it?" Jamilla was trying to make the rampage of emotion cease.

Maxwell laughed. "Let me say this so you really believe me. That woman looks identical to you."

"I've got to get to New York. You promised me you'd help." Jamilla spoke so fast her words tripped over one another. "Do you think I can get on a flight tonight?"

"Whoa, whoa. Slow down." Maxwell pulled lightly on her arm. "Of course I'll help you, but there's no way we can get on a flight tonight. It's already after midnight."

"Then I want to be on the first flight in the morning." Jamilla ran to her closet to retrieve the overnight bag that she hadn't unpacked from her trip to see the *other* Clarissa. "I'm already packed."

Maxwell laughed as he watched her run around the room frantically. She wasn't doing anything except burning energy. "Come sit down and listen to your sister sing. She's really great."

"I want to be where she is, and that means we need to make preparations. I need a ticket and a hotel room. We have no time to sit and watch television," she yelled.

"Okay, okay, let's get your laptop," Maxwell placated her. "If I make all of the arrangements will you promise you'll sit down and enjoy this?"

"The only promise I can make you right now is that when my sister is on the stage at Radio City Music Hall tomorrow night, I'll be sitting right there watching her."

Chapter 16

Clarissa bowed to booming applause and cheers as the audience appreciated her performance. David stood and walked to meet her center stage. He leaned over and kissed her cheek as he shook her hand. "Ladies and gentlemen," he pulled back as he pointed to her, "Clarissa Holmes." The applause rose again as the screen broke away to commercial.

With both hands on her mouth Jamilla sat staring at a car racing toward her on the screen, but she only saw the beautiful woman with the voice of an angel that had plug the hole in her soul. Maxwell slipped his arm over her shoulder and she spontaneously fell into it. The tears rushed forth, but this time they lightened her heart.

Maxwell search for words to fit the moment, but decided silence would serve them both best. He held her a little tighter as she folded deeper into his arms. He whispered a little prayer of gratitude for the miracle he'd been allowed to witness. The three commercials seemed to drag on for hours when in reality only a minute and half had passed.

Jamilla sat up quickly as David Letterman reappeared.

"We're almost out of time, but I want to ask Clarissa where we can hear more of her wonderfully unique jazz styling?" David said as he smiled admiringly at his grinning guest..

Clarissa beamed as she explained her debut at the Radio City Music

Hall at eight o'clock. She turned to look at the camera when she said, "I promise an unforgettable evening."

She didn't know how true her words were.

"Will you take us out with another number?" David asked as the audience cheered.

"I'd loved to." Clarissa stood and moved fluidly toward the band as they began playing "Get Here," the tune made popular by Oleta Adams.

Jamilla leapt her feet. She couldn't believe the song Clarissa had chosen. It was her favorite tune. She'd played the track so much she'd had to replace the CD. She turned to say something, anything, to Maxwell but there were no words. She only pointed at the screen.

Maxwell gently took her hand and said, "I know baby. Come sit and enjoy it."

As Clarissa began to belt out the words the screen divided and the credits began rolling. Jamilla realized what an amazing talent her sister was. They'd each been blessed with artistic gifts. She wondered what gift Leticia possessed. *Lord, please let me—us—find Leticia.* She stared at the screen willing Clarissa to remain there forever or at least until she left for New York. Her wish didn't come true as the local car dealer proclaiming the end of the month clearance sale.

Maxwell picked up the remote control and hit the power button. The screen faded to black. Jamilla still stared it in silence. He touched her lightly on her left bare left thigh. "If I hadn't been here to witness this, I wouldn't have believed it."

Still staring straight ahead Jamilla quietly asked, "Am I a little less insane to you now?"

"I've never thought you were insane." Maxwell grabbed her hand. "Just real determined, actually the word obsessed comes to mind."

"I knew I'd find her—them—us. I don't know what I'm saying. But we have to get ready." She turned to him with the enthusiasm of a three-year-old with the prospect of going to visit Mickey Mouse. "You promised me you'd help me."

"That I did." Maxwell stood, squeezing her hand said, "Mill, I'm so happy for you."

Jamilla stood throwing her arms around his neck. "Me too."

"I tell you what, you go into that closet of yours and pull out your best concert going outfit and some travel clothes and I'll be back in two seconds." Maxwell kissed her on the forehead before he turned and walked quickly toward the stairs.

Jamilla watched as he disappeared around the corner as he descended the stairs. She wrapped her arms around herself trying to imagine what it was going to feel like when she was face to face with her other third.

Time must have stood still because Maxwell seemed to return instantly as he took the stairs two at a time with laptop in hand. She hadn't moved from the spot where she stood when he'd left. She wasn't quite sure what to do next. He'd left her with instructions but now she couldn't remember what they were.

"Come sit with me." Maxwell rescued her.

With a touch of a button the wireless machine came to life. In silence Maxwell navigated to the Orbitz web site. After he'd entered the origin, destination and date to travel he turned and asked, "How long are you going to stay?"

Jamilla thought for a minute before saying, "I don't know." Panic attached itself to her heart and refused to let go. She hadn't had the time to think about what would happen if Clarissa weren't happy to see her.

Maxwell recognized the fear in her eyes. "Baby, it's going to be fine. We'll give you a couple of days and if you need to extend it you can."

"Okay," was all she could manage.

"You can be on this seven o'clock flight out of LAX. "Maxwell tapped lightly on the screen. "That's the only flight that will get you there so you don't have to rush to make the concert."

Jamilla peeped over his shoulder. "Nothing out of Ontario?"

"Not that would get you there in time."

"Then I need to get ready. I'll have to be at LAX by five." Jamilla stole a glance at the clock on the nightstand. "That's only four hours from now and it takes an hour and change to get there."

"Let me help you pack, so we can get a couple hours sleep."

"Sleep?" Jamilla stood quickly. "I'll never be able to sleep!"

Maxwell knew better than to try to convince her that she'd be much better when she met her sister if she got at least a little rest, so he counted with, "Okay, then we get you packed and you come lay in a brotha's arms for a few minutes before you're off to New York and your long awaited reunion."

Jamilla started to protest, but didn't have a good argument. She moved to the closet and retrieved her suitcase and placed in on the bed. She quickly removed the items from her trip to Atlanta, tossing them into the hamper. She smiled as she thought how quickly the tide had turned. Less than forty-eight hours before she'd stared disappointment and anguish in the face. Now she knew no one would be stopping her from meeting at least one of her sisters.

Maxwell watched her with admiration and awe as she moved about the room gathering things from drawers before she returned to the closet. "How do you think I should dress for the concert?"

"Well, it is New York." Maxwell stood and moved to the closet door. "It not like here, so I'd go more to the dressy."

"You're probably right." Jamilla pulled a white pants suit from the rack. "What about this?"

"Wow that is nice. Is it skirt or pants?

Jamilla lifted the sheer panel on the garment. "It's pants but this makes it look like a floor length skirt. It moves quite elegantly. It's one of my favorite outfits."

"I'd love to see you in it." Maxwell teased. "But yes, it will do quite nicely for your first meeting with your sister. Though I don't think it would really matter if you were a bag lady."

"I hope you're right." Butterflies took up flight in Jamilla's stomach. "There's the possibility she won't want to have anything to do with me, you know."

Maxwell stared wondering if there was a right response. He decided there wasn't. "What are you going to travel in?"

"Why didn't you answer me?" Jamilla wasn't angry—she was exhausted. "You believe it too, don't you?"

"I believe that you've never given up hope and always kept the faith. Now it has paid of." Maxwell moved inside the closet until he was standing directly in front of Jamilla. "Don't be disappointed if it takes some time for the sister thing to kick in. But I can guarantee you when Clarissa gets to know you it will be like you've never been apart."

Jamilla's response was a warm hug that seemed to penetrate every cell in her body. "I think you're right, we should try to rest at least for a few minutes before I go to the airport." She hesitated for a moment, then asked, "Will you drive me?"

Maxwell kissed her lightly on the lips "Nothing would make me happier."

"You know that means you'll have to pick me up too."

"I know." Maxwell stepped back and smiled. "Finally, you're letting me be your man."

Jamilla laughed and it felt so good. She liked the way it felt-*letting Maxwell be her man.* She quickly gathered two pairs of shoes, dress slacks and jeans. As she pulled two shirts from the hangers the last song Clarissa sang replayed in her head. It was as though she'd sent a telepathic message to Jamilla. *Get Here!* Wow.

Just before Jamilla zipped the suitcase she checked the cosmetic bag to make sure everything she needed for her trip was in place. She was ready. Now all she had to do was wait. She'd waited twenty-one years, what was a few more hours—an eternity.

THE JOURNEY

Gwynne Forster

Chapter 1

Clarissa Holmes Medford awoke earlier that usual that Saturday morning, got up, dragged herself through the house to the front porch, and plopped down in the swing. The swing was the one thing in the house that she loved and enjoyed, and that was because it wasn't soiled, cracked, or broken. Practically everything else that she and Josh Medford, her husband, owned was worthless. She went to the back porch, pumped a glass of water, brushed her teeth with most of the baking soda that remained in the box, rinsed her mouth, and went back to the swing.

For fifteen years, Josh Medford had been promising her running water, an indoor toilet, and something other than a tin washtub in which to bathe. As she sat there, pushing the swing with her foot, she wondered for the nth time whether the two sisters she never knew fared better in life that she did. She hadn't learned much in the segregated, ill-equipped, and poorly staffed schools she attended, but she had her high-school diploma, and nobody could take that from her. Hopefully, her two sisters had at least that much.

Clarissa gazed at the breaking sky and the streaks of red creeping through the gray as the sun signaled its awakening. Her second foster mother had loved to watch the sun rise and set and would hold Clarissa in her lap and tell her tales of the sun and its magic. She regarded those as the happiest days of her life, maybe the only truly happy ones. In three of her other five foster homes, she'd had wretched excuses for mothers, and while two of those foster mothers hadn't mistreated her, neither had they spared her a kiss or a hug. Two months after her eighteenth birthday, she married Josh Medford, believing his promise of love, affection, and a better life.

She spat out the taste of baking soda and heaved a long, heavy sigh. She had exchanged a cold and indifferent foster mother for a hot husband, but she had also swapped a bathtub and running water for a tin tub and an old iron pump on the back porch.

"No point in going over all this old stuff," she said aloud and headed for the kitchen to begin her day of drudgery.

Josh stood beside the stove, drinking coffee, and he had begun his morning that way every day for the fifteen years she'd been married to him. Hot days, cold days, windy days, or rainy days. It didn't matter. Josh got up, made coffee, and drank at least two cups of it before he said one word to anybody. As she watched him, he sipped loudly and lazily.

"What day is it?" she asked him, hoping it wasn't the day she went to Miss Elizabeth's house to do the mending.

Josh ran his fingers over his tight curls. "Let's see. It's the nineteenth of June."

"The nineteenth of June, you said?"

He took another sip of coffee. "That's just what I said. June nineteenth. Why?"

Something clicked in her head, and she stared at him, shaken and nearly unnerved by the thought of what she might do, of what she was about to do. Her heart banged against her chest.

"Why?" she asked him with both hands fastened to her hips. "Why? Because it's June nineteenth, the day nearly a century and a half ago when the slaves finally got their freedom, and the day I'm getting mine. I'm gonna pull myself up out of this mire, and I'm going to stay up. You do as you please. Well, I'm going to get some of my own."

He set the cup down forcefully on the ancient Kalamazoo wood cooking range. "What the hell are you talking about, woman?"

Now that she'd started it, she felt bolder and stronger. "I'm talking about this is as good a day as any for you to pack up and hightail it to your eighteen-year-old lover, though I can't imagine what she wants with you."

He frowned and shook his head. For once speechless, and it gave her an urge to laugh aloud, but she didn't. "Well?" she said, turning the screw.

He seemed to recover quickly from the shock, for he shrugged carelessly. "Well, if that's the way you feel about it, I got no reason to hang around here, but sure as you born, you're gonna come crawling back."

This time, she *did* laugh. Laughed until she got the hiccups. "Man, you can't be serious." She laughed again. "Don't forget to take your Viagra with you. You're gonna need it for sure now."

"At the end of the month, you're gonna wish you hadn't been so rash," he threw at her carelessly, as if he didn't believe it himself.

"You're kidding, I hope. Man, I've been hanging on this thread of a rope too long. From now on, I'm getting some of my own."

"You gonna fall flat on your behind, too. How you gonna eat?"

"Don't worry about me. The few pennies I make will take care of me till I can shake the dust of Low Point, North Carolina, off my shoes. You get your things together and go on over there to Vanessa. She can have you."

She strolled to the front porch, sat down in the swing, and very soon, the late-morning breeze, sparse though it was, swept over her shoulders. As the sun climbed, the breeze began to die down, and she started singing. Singing and swinging. And she didn't stop until Josh walked out of their front door with their only suitcase, two plastic shopping bags, and a knapsack. She ran into the house and grabbed the hat that hung on the back of a door.

"Here's your hat," she called after him and tossed it into the dying breeze.

"I thought I saw Josh leaving here this morning with a load like he was going someplace and wasn't coming back," Jessie Mae Woods, her nearest neighbor, said as she walked into Clarissa's kitchen unannounced. "That *was* Josh, wasn't it?"

"You got eyes," Clarissa said, "so why you asking me? I sent him over to that little tart, Vanessa. He's been sniffing around her for months, and I just got sick and tired of it. Good riddance."

Jessie Mae seated herself for a long session of meddling and gossip. "Well, I declare. Girl, you go way from here. Gone, eh? Well, don't let it get to you. He'll be back."

Clarissa stopped ironing and stared at the woman. "Didn't you hear me say I put him out? I don't want him back. I don't know what kind of diseases that little trollop's got. The nasty heifer. Now you go on home, Jessie Mae, and let me get my ironing done. I have to go into town soon as I finish. We can gossip tomorrow morning."

"All right. You come over to my place, and I'll fix breakfast." Clarissa could hear in Jessie Mae's voice the hope for a long and juicy gossip session, but her friend was in for a surprise.

At sundown, Clarissa sat on the top, broken step of her front porch, totally alone for the first time in her life. No brawling, fighting foster sisters and brothers or harsh foster mothers, and no smiling, deceitful husband to crawl into her bed after wearing himself out with a girl half his age. Tears? She didn't have any. As her fingers caressed the strings of her precious guitar that lay across her lap, ideas danced around in her head. Bold and daring ideas.

Darkness set in, but she sat there, quietly immobile like a forgotten statue, occasionally slapping at the flies and mosquitoes and hating the stench of ripening chinaberries and the rotting manure in the freshly fertilized fields across the way, a stench brought to her on the shifting wind. A clear moon slid out from behind a cloud, and she sat there still, thinking about her life. When an owl hooted in the distance, she pulled herself up, went inside, and switched on the naked light bulb that swung from the ceiling in her bedroom. For a long while, she stared up at it and then looked away, sucking her teeth in disgust.

"I deserve more than this," she said aloud, "and God willing, by mid-July, I'll be miles away from Low Point, North Carolina. I've got talent, and I'm going to find a way to use it."

Early Monday morning, Clarissa stuffed her guitar into its case, closed it, locked her front door, and set out on foot for the bus station about a mile from where she lived. During the two-hour ride to

Raleigh, the state capital, she tossed ideas around in her head, couldn't make up her mind, and finally decided to be herself—a country woman trying to make a living.

She walked into Helbrose Studios and spoke to the receptionist. "Good morning, Miss. I came here to see Mr. Helbrosé. Would you please tell him that Clarissa Holmes is here."

The woman stared at her. "I don't have you on my list of appointments for today."

"That's all right," Clarissa said. "Nobody's perfect. I forget things myself."

A helpless, flustered look came over the woman, who appeared to be around sixty. "Have a seat, Miss. I'll . . . I'll be right back. She reappeared, seemingly more nonplussed than when she left the room.

"Uh . . . Mr. Helbrose said he can give you fifteen minutes of his time, and you'd better not waste it."

Clarissa removed her guitar from its case and followed the woman. "I don't know what you told him, but the Lord will certainly bless you."

When she entered Helbrose's office, the odor of stale cigarette smoke assaulted her nostrils, and the fumes caused her eyes to smart. Helbrose sat behind a huge, well-worn mahogany desk, a cigarette dangling from the corner of his mouth.

"Who are you and what do you want?" he asked, his manner brusque and uninviting.

Clarissa didn't answer, but ran her fingers over the strings of her guitar and let her rich alto voice pour forth "Stormy Weather."

The cigarette slid from Helbrose's lips, and he braced his hands on the desk as he half stood, leaning forward, his mouth a gaping hole. "Do you know 'Help Me Make It Through the Night'?" he asked when she finished.

She had sung it a hundred times, and she sang it then as if she'd just learned about Josh's affair with Vanessa Hobbs, as if she hadn't a friend in the world, as if she were trying to climb up from a deep, dark pit. She sang it without realizing that tears cascaded down her face.

"Where'd you come from?" he asked in a tone of wonder.

"Low Point."

"You under contract to anybody?"

She shook her head. "I just want to make a tape and get three or four copies to send out so I can get a job."

"All right. And I'll give you some references. If you want a manager or an agent, I'll be glad to take you on."

She didn't know how good she was, although she knew she had a voice, but he seemed a little too anxious.

"Thank you, sir. I appreciate the encouragement, and I sure do need those references. How much do you charge to make the tapes?"

"For what you want, a couple hundred bucks."

She nearly sat on the floor. "Mr. Helbrose, I don't have no two hundred dollars."

"All right. All right. I'll make you a demo plus two copies of those two songs, but I want a hundred bucks up front and another hundred within three months. He took a form from his desk drawer, crossed out a line, and handed it to her.

"You're going to be famous, and don't forget who got you started. Sign this."

"Can't you give me at least four copies?"

He shrugged and lit another cigarette. "With business as slow as it is, why not? Time was when the kids wanted to be singers—now, they just want to rap, and I'm damned if I'll sink to making rap demos. Go on in the studio across the hall. Edgar will get you started." She read the contract, signed it, and went to find Edgar.

Three hours later, with the demo tapes in her pocketbook, Clarissa stopped at the receptionist's desk. "You got a phone book?" she asked, then stood there and copied the phone numbers of every person whose last name was Holmes. In the lobby of the building, she found a pay phone and called each one of them but, as usual, none was a female triplet or knew of a woman who was one.

Near the entrance to the lobby, a man stood behind a desk marked INFORMATION, so she walked over to him. "How are you today, sir? I hope you can help me out."

His raised eyebrow failed to intimidate her, and she produced for him the broadest smile she could muster. "Where's a public library, sir? I have to walk to get there, so I'd appreciate directions to the nearest one."

He walked with her to the front door and pointed. "About seven blocks straight down there. You can't miss it."

"I sure do thank you, sir. I'm hoping this is going to change my life."

"You'll need more than hope, I expect," the man replied. "Anyhow, I wish you the best."

She hadn't spent much time in libraries, and about the only thing she knew about them was that they contained all kinds of information. She went to the first person she saw behind a desk.

"I need help, ma'am," she said in a strong voice, hoping that help wasn't restricted to people with white faces.

"That's what I'm here for," the woman said. "What are you looking for?"

With the librarian's help, Clarissa located jazz clubs in Washington, D.C., Kansas City, Missouri, Chicago, and New York City. Later, she sent a demo tape to each along with a letter requesting a two-week singing engagement in exchange for food, rent money, and transportation to and from work. She received immediate offers from three clubs, chose The Limelight in Washington, D.C., left her house in Low Point behind, and headed for her future.

"You sound great on those tapes," Buck Ryan said to Clarissa when she arrived at The Limelight and introduced herself. "But these recordings can be faked. Let me hear you."

Exhausted from the seven-hour bus ride and dry-mouthed, she knew it was then or nothing, so she asked for a glass of water, drank it, and cleared her throat a few times. "Anything special you want to hear, Mr. Ryan?"

He leaned back in his chair and regarded her suspiciously. "Anything? Pretty sure of yourself, aren't you? Sing me some Billie Holiday."

Nothing could have pleased her more. She sang four songs popularized by the famous singer, and ended with "God Bless the Child."

"It's a deal," he told her. "I got you a room and breakfast at the Phyllis Wheatley YWCA. Here's your weekly bus pass, and you ought to be able to eat lunch for a hundred dollars a week. You can eat dinner here. What kinda clothes did you bring with you? My entertainers look good."

"I'm a poor woman, Mr. Ryan. I don't have no fancy clothes."

"Hmm." He rubbed his chin. "We'll see. Be ready to start tomorrow night. Jimmy will take you over there. It's not far, about six blocks."

She checked into the room, hung her clothes in the closet, and opened the only other door that didn't lead to the hall. *A bathroom with a tub and a toilet. Her very own bathroom.* She raised her eyes toward the heavens and spoke aloud. "From now on, every time I move, I'm gonna better myself. Every step I take is gon' be a step up."

She went downstairs to the first-floor lounge, got a telephone book, wrote down the telephone number of every person listed as Holmes, and telephoned each one, but the trail to her sisters proved as elusive as ever.

"How long've you been here?" a tall, dark, and handsome woman who she estimated to be around her age asked her.

"I came today. You know where I can buy some lightweight black cloth? I need a long skirt, and I can't afford to buy one." After explaining why she needed it, she added, "I have a pretty black crocheted top that I can wear with it."

The woman seemed to think for a minute, and then her face brightened. "I'm not much with a needle and thread—I teach eighth-grade humanities. Let's run up to U Street and see what we can find. My name is Cindy Ross. Let's go."

By midnight, Clarissa had made a long, slim black-jersey skirt that suited both her five-feet-nine-inch svelte figure and the black top she had crocheted years earlier.

"Not bad," Buck Ryan said of her attire when she arrived for work at six o'clock the next evening. "How you gonna do this? Did you bring any music?" When she shook her head, he said, "I reckon you play the piano as well as that guitar."

"No, sir. I can play a little by ear, but truth is, I'm just gonna sit and sing. All I need is my guitar and a stool, the highest you got."

He stared at her, all the while drawing on his cigarette and blowing the smoke over his shoulder and away from her. "Okay, we'll try it your way. Ever use a mike?"

"Only when I made the demo tapes."

He handed her a microphone and went to the back of the club. "Sing something."

She sang a few lines of "Back In Your Own Back Yard."

"Right on, babe! From now on, you use a mike. It puts a nice, sexy come-on in your voice. Eat your dinner, and you can get a sandwich, pie or ice cream, and something to drink after your last show. Be ready to sing at eight o'clock."

I've got two other offers if this doesn't work out, Clarissa told herself when she walked out on the stage and looked at the noisy crowd. "Thank y'all for coming," she said into the microphone, mostly to assure herself that when she opened her mouth a sound would come out. She plucked a few notes on her guitar, hammered in syncopation, and wrapped her sultry alto around the words and music of "Early One Morning." Within seconds, a hush swept over the room and, by the song's end, the patrons were standing, applauding and yelling for more. Her second and last show ended at midnight, an hour and a half after the scheduled time.

"Here's a couple hundred," Buck Ryan said to her when she went to her tiny dressing room. "Get yourself a couple of sexy evening blouses and another skirt. And from now on, you supposed to sing an hour, you sing an hour. Not a minute longer if they clap till they burn up their hands."

She frowned at him. "But I thought—"

"You do like I say, unless you want to wear out your voice. Two hours of singing six nights a week is more than enough. Get something to eat. Jimmy will drive you to the Y."

She tried to fathom his attitude toward her, but how could she read a man she didn't know? "I guess I did pretty good, huh?"

He lit a cigarette, inhaled deeply, and turned away from her to expel the smoke. "You saw how the people reacted, didn't you? Eat something, go home, and get some rest."

The crowd at The Limelight grew larger with each succeeding night, and by the end of the week, Clarissa could hardly believe her eyes when patrons stood along the wall as the club overflowed with them, and Ryan had to turn them away.

"You got a couple of television appearances," Buck told her one evening when she arrived to work." I told 'em, you charge twelve hundred, but you gotta join the union. Fill out this form, and I'll get you your union card."

"Twelve hundred what?"

For the first time since she'd met him, she saw him laugh. "Dollars, babe. Dollars. TV pays good money."

"But I have another week working with you."

"Yeah. I'm getting a lot for nothing. You sign a contract with me, and I'll pay you a thousand a week."

So much so fast. She'd better watch it. "Thanks, Mr. Ryan. I'll think about it."

"*You'll what?*" he shouted. "I just want you to sign something that says you won't sing in any D.C. club but mine."

"Suppose somebody offers me more?"

"Make it six weeks at twelve hundred a week. Okay? By that time, the whole country will know who you are." It wasn't enough, she knew, but it was her first job and, to her mind, she owed the man.

She agreed, finished her snack, got into the car with Jimmy, and hummed "Amazing Grace" all the way to the YWCA.

"How's it going, girl?" Cindy asked her at breakfast the next morning. "I see you made *The Herald*. Nice little piece they had on you."

Clarissa buttered a piece of toast and smeared it with grape jelly. She missed the buttermilk biscuits, sage sausage, grits, and scrambled eggs that she always had for breakfast back in Low Point, but people in Washington said sausage and biscuits—made with hog lard—were unhealthy, so she ate the toast and poached eggs and made herself like it.

"I know I'm blessed, Cindy, but my head is swimming with all this commotion. Would you believe that two weeks ago I'd never sung anywhere except second row of the Mt. Pisgah Baptist Church choir in Low Point, North Carolina?"

Cindy's laugh came out in spurts. "Yeah, I'd believe it. I can tell you're as straight as the crow flies, as my grandfather always said about my grandmother."

Clarissa completed her two payless weeks at The Limelight and the first two weeks of her new contract and managed to save half of what she made. But working night hours meant that she couldn't go to the movies and shopping with Cindy and, to Clarissa's disappointment, their friendship failed to develop as she would have liked. She knew Buck Ryan was making money, thanks to her singing, because he began

taxing the overflow crowd with a cover charge and a two-drink mini-
mum per show.

"Why don't you ask for more money?" Cindy urged.

"No, a deal is a deal. People are learning about me, so I'm getting
something out of this, too. In another month, I should have some really
good clippings, and I'll be able to demand more." She didn't say that
she was biding her time until she could present herself as a polished
person, but she read newspapers, books, magazines, and anything that
she thought would help her to speak better and with more self-assurance.

However, all that changed when she went into the lounge before
breakfast the next morning and picked up the morning paper. Her
lower lip dropped as she groped for a chair. Her bubble had burst.
Shortly after she'd left the club just before midnight, the police arrested Buck Ryan for trafficking in drugs and closed The Limelight.
She had to find a job.

Chapter 2

A month later, having applied for a job singing in every nightclub and supper club in the city, Clarissa knocked on office doors with a heavy heart, knowing what to expect. *Come back after this thing with Buck Ryan blows over—you're too closely identified with him,* club managers told her. Her talent meant nothing now, and she was just another woman looking for work.

Clarissa had always been a practical person, and she was no less so now. She had to eat and pay for her room, and she was not afraid of work. When Cindy asked her what she planned to do, she replied, "Any honest work."

"Well, if I can help, let me know. I'm not one to see a friend falter and not give her a hand."

"I'll remember that, but I managed to save a little, and I'll be all right."

She registered at the D.C. Employment Agency and, for the next two months, worked as a baby-sitter, cleaning woman, temporary caretaker for an invalid man, and at many other assorted jobs. Every morning, she found it harder to get out of bed. She walked with slower steps, and laughter no longer came easily. But she couldn't go back to Low Point to do Mr. Amos's laundry for fifty cents a shirt and Miss Elizabeth's mending for eight dollars a day. She dragged herself to church that Sunday morning and sat in the last row, uncertain as to why she'd gone there in the first place.

After the sermon, a clerk read announcements, and then she heard the preacher say, "If any of you ladies wants to be a live-in companion to an older woman, see me after service. The pay's good. You get to go to the movies, opera, theater, and travel. No housework. You must be single and have a high-school diploma, and you can't have any of the brothers hanging around you."

"I could save some money," Clarissa said to herself, "and maybe study music. Going to the opera and things like that, I could learn a lot."

Three days later, Clarissa moved into the home of Lydia Stanton, a wealthy, wheelchair-bound septuagenarian. "My own room, sitting room, and bath," she marveled, as her gaze took in the elegant setting in a beautiful, four-bedroom modern house on upper Sixteenth Street.

"Lord, just look at this," she said, blinking back the tears as she swung around and hugged herself, "and I don't even have to wear a uniform." She sank to her knees and thanked the Lord. "If I can just stay here a year, I can save my money and never be dirt poor again."

She answered the knock on her door, opened it, and looked into the face of the uniformed housekeeper. "Lunch will be served in fifteen minutes, Miss Holmes."

Clarissa gulped, momentarily speechless. "Uh . . . thanks. What is your name?"

"Lorraine, ma'am. If you need anything, just press that green button on your phone."

Hoping that her bottom lip didn't betray her, Clarissa forced what she hoped passed for a smile. "Thanks. I hope you'll have time to show me around."

The woman stared at her. "I . . . uh . . . guess Mrs. Stanton will do that. She uses the elevator to get from floor to floor."

"Oh." Clarissa recovered, aware that she had made an error. "I didn't realize there was an elevator. Thanks."

Clarissa went to her bedroom window and looked out on Sixteenth Street at the trees, shrubs, and elegant homes that surrounded her. A house with an elevator, ceilings that she wouldn't be able to reach with a broomstick, a maid who called her Miss Holmes and who she was supposed to call Lorraine and summon by pushing a green button on a telephone. She laughed. Laughed until her shoulders shook. Laughed until tears drenched her face.

A short time later, she joined Lydia Stanton in the breakfast room, where her new employer sat at the table, her wheelchair stationed beside the door. "I hope you and I are going to be good friends," Lydia said. "I got tired of staying home alone and missing the things that I enjoy just because I don't have anyone to enjoy them with. Do you play bridge?"

"No, ma'am, but if you're willing to teach me, I'm eager to learn. I've never been to any kind of concert, because I always had to use my little money just to stay alive. I love music, though—any kind of music."

"Then we'll get along just fine. I'll get us season tickets to the ballet and the symphony concerts."

The only dressy clothes she owned were the ones she wore while singing at The Limelight, and they probably wouldn't suffice. "I'll need a salary advance to get some clothes if you want me to dress up. I don't suppose my two long black skirts and three black blouses will be suitable."

"Probably not. By the way, if there's anything special you like to eat or that you dislike, tell Lorraine. I don't bother about the food. She plans the menus."

I hope I don't have to spend too much on clothes, Clarissa said to herself, mindful of her plan to save practically all of her salary. She sipped the cucumber soup—whoever cooked a cucumber had to be crazy.

"After lunch, have a look at those Saks Fifth Avenue catalogs on the table in the den. If you see anything you like, I'll call the store and have them sent out for you to try on." Clarissa nearly choked on the broiled lamb chop. She couldn't afford a Saks Fifth Avenue handkerchief. "I'll put them on my account."

Clarissa couldn't help gaping at Lydia Stanton. "You mean you're going to pay for my clothes?"

Lydia laughed. "Yes, I am. I've been in this wheelchair ever since I was in an automobile accident seven years ago, feeling sorry for myself, being bored, plain wretched, and letting life pass me by. I am going to enjoy introducing you to another way of life. Did you read Pygmalion?"

"No, ma'am."

"There's a copy in my library. Or we can rent the movie, *My Fair Lady*. Same story."

"I'd love to read it. Reading is something I never had time to do, but I'm going to use some of my free time reading. I want to learn to speak better and to carry myself well."

Lydia's face seemed to glow with pleasure. "Yes, Clarissa, you and I will get along very well."

Thrilled at the thought of what was in store for her, Clarissa telephoned the woman who was her foster mother from her fifth through her ninth year, the only one of her five foster mothers who gave her love and affection along with the required food and shelter. She made certain that Eunice Jenkins always knew where she was.

Chapter 3

A week later, Clarissa sat in the auditorium at the Kennedy Center, fascinated by the glitter, and bewitched as members of the Danish Royal Ballet Company danced *Swan Lake*. She didn't want it to end.

"Is this all?" she asked Lydia as the dancers took their final bows. "Isn't there any more?"

"The comedians have a saying, 'Always leave 'em laughing'." Lydia said. "It's better to leave wanting more than to leave thinking we wasted our money."

Clarissa buttoned her new camel-hair coat and hooked its fox-fur collar, gifts from Mrs. Stanton, then helped her employer into her coat, pushed the wheelchair to the lobby, and waited for Lydia's chauffeur.

"If our relationship ended this minute," she told Lydia, "you would have a special spot in my heart for as long as I live. I never dreamed of coming to a place like this one." Without thinking, she began humming the tune, "For Once In My Life."

"Do you know the words to that tune?" Lydia asked Clarissa after Sam, the chauffeur, lifted her into the car, stored her wheelchair in the trunk, and headed toward Sixteenth Street.

"Yes, ma'am. I sure do."

"My dear husband used to sing that to me. He had a wonderfully rich baritone voice, and I loved to hear him sing. Seven long years. Lord, how I miss him! And how I loved that song!"

Clarissa didn't hesitate. "*For once in my life, I have someone who loves me*," she sang, caressing each word in her haunting, smoky alto.

Lydia Stanton turned sidewise to look at Clarissa. "With a voice like yours, you should be rich."

Clarissa spoke in a voice tinged with resignation. "Not in this town." She related the story of her short-lived success as a jazz singer. "Nobody in this town will hire me."

Lydia folded her arms and leaned back into the soft-leather comfort of the Lincoln Town Car. "Time heals a lot of things."

Within less than a month, Lydia managed to expose her to opera, a symphony, several ballet performances, and a production of *Porgy and Bess*, Gershwin's tribute to the many musical idioms of the African-American subculture.

I'm living in a dream world. Most people in this country don't live like this. I ought to think more kindly of Vanessa. If it hadn't been for that little slut, I wouldn't know these places existed."

Tonight, we're going to Blues Alley to hear some first-class jazz," Lydia said that Friday night, "and you pay careful attention. People say the woman singing tonight is a cross between Billie Holiday and Ella Fitzgerald."

Their table was at the edge of the stage, and Clarissa took in the woman's every gesture, the way she wooed the patrons and drew them to her. *I did that, too. I had them with me all the way, and I can do it again.* By chance, she glanced toward the next table, and her gaze caught that of a man who had obviously been looking at her, for he raised his glass and smiled. Stunned by the unexpected and unaccustomed attention, she looked at Lydia, hoping that her employer's expression would not be one of disapproval.

"I see you have an admirer."

Clarissa folded and unfolded her hands and rubbed her fingers together. "I didn't do anything to encourage him."

"I know," Lydia said. "All the better when you do nothing to invite it. He's been looking at you ever since we've been sitting here."

"I can't do anything about that, Mrs. Stanton. I don't have my divorce yet. Too bad. He looks like a very important person, and he sure is good-looking."

The waiter handed Clarissa a note. She didn't read it, but accepted a pencil from the waiter and wrote on the back of the note: "*Since I'm married, I don't consider myself free to read your note, but thank you.*" She didn't sign it.

"You're a wise woman," Lydia said. "I'm not sure I would have been able to resist reading it."

Wisdom had nothing to do with it; she was protecting herself from her libido. "I haven't had a loving marriage, so I'm more likely than you to fall for sweet talk."

"A lonely woman is always vulnerable," Lydia said. "Let's go after the end of this set. As much as I'm enjoying this, I'm getting sleepy."

"She doesn't sing as well as you do," Lydia said of the renowned jazz singer, as they rode home. "What you need is a chance, and I'm going to see that you get it. I've got friends in the music business, and a few of them owe me."

Clarissa could hardly contain herself as her heartbeat accelerated to a rapid pace and she thought the bottom had fallen out of her belly. "You would do that? Nobody's ever opened doors for me, Mrs. Stanton. God bless you."

The following afternoon as Lydia and Clarissa stuffed pre-addressed envelopes for a YWCA fund-raiser, Lydia said, "Allen Harkens will be here tomorrow morning at eleven. He's a man who can make you famous. I want you to sing something for him."

"I'll do my best, ma'am. I don't know how to thank you."

"Don't thank me, Clarissa. Just sing your heart out. Allen is a self-important jackass, but he knows the music business."

"Where's your ingénue?" Harkens asked Lydia when he entered the living room that morning.

"This is Miss Holmes, and she's anything *but* an ingénue."

Clarissa decided at once that she did not like Allen Harkens. When introduced, she extended her hand, but he ignored it, put a hand on her waist, and kissed her. Nonetheless, knowing that she shouldn't offend him, she forced a smile to her face, stepped back, and let her voice fill the room with the song, "Rocks In My Bed." Harkens stared at her with a stunned expression on his face, and at the song's end, he bowed to her.

"If you've got a demo, I can book you into any club in this country."

"I have one," she told him, "but I don't have a copy."

He patted her back. "No problem. I can make all the copies we need." To Lydia, he said, "The gal's got enough talent for a dozen singers."

"If I'm leaving here, I want to give Mrs. Stanton ample notice."

Lydia waved her right hand in a motion suggesting that the thought was ridiculous. "You start singing as soon as you sign a contract. Allen, get her a decent contract."

"Sure thing, Lydia."

"This is your chance," Lydia told Clarissa after Harkens left them. "Maybe your only chance." Her gaze bore into Clarissa. "You didn't like Allen. Why?"

"I don't want no strange man putting his hands all over me. He acted like he had some right to paw me."

An expression of sadness clouded Lydia's face, and she looked away. "You're going into the entertainment business, so get used to it. He doesn't even know he did it. Just make sure you never spread your legs in order to get a job or to keep one."

Clarissa sat down and nearly missed the chair. "You mean some man will expect me to prostitute myself just so I can sing?"

Lydia rolled her eyes toward the ceiling. "You wouldn't be the first woman to do it, but with your voice, you won't have to stoop to that. I didn't have half of your talent, and I made it the best way I could. Thank God I met my husband before I got dragged into the ugly end of the business.

"He worked in real estate, and after we married, we worked together building, managing, and renting property." She wiped her eyes. "He enriched my life in so many ways, and just like that"—she snapped her fingers—"a drunken driver took his life and left me a cripple."

Clarissa draped an arm around Lydia's shoulders. "Saying I'm sorry won't help, but I am. I hurt for you."

"I've quit living in the past, Clarissa, and since you've been here, I've been able to enjoy things that Larry and I did together. Now, let's get busy. What we need is a good pianist who can score some songs for you, and it'll do you a lot of good to take courses in grammar and vocabulary building. I want you to present yourself as a refined and elegant lady, not as a singer with nothing else to offer. You're a fine person, and I want it to show."

One week later, Lydia received a phone call from Allen Harkens. "I got four gigs for your girl, Lydia, but get some of that hayseed out of her. These are high-class joints. She starts at After Hours in St. Louis two weeks from Friday."

"Good. Clarissa's got polish enough, and don't you start anything with her."

"Not to worry, babe, I go to church these days."

"Yeah. Right," Lydia said. "The first man to squeeze my twelve-year-old breasts was a deacon in my parents' church. So you bet I'm impressed with your new sanctity."

Clarissa's euphoria at the news that she would resume her singing career proved short-lived. She phoned Eunice Jenkins to tell her that she would be at the YWCA in St. Louis, and learned that her beloved foster mother had suffered a stroke.

"I hate to disappoint you," she told Lydia. "I had five foster mothers, and Mom was the only one of them who treated me as if I were her own child, one that she loved. I cried for months when they took me away from her. Her husband died, and foster mothers had to be married."

"But she would want you to have this chance."

"I know, ma'am, but she needs me. One of her daughters is in the army, one has young children, and the other is not dependable. I appreciate all you've done for me, but this is the only mother I ever had."

"All right. You're giving up a lot, but I respect you for it. If you need me for anything—I mean anything—you know how to reach me."

Without thought as to what she did, Clarissa leaned down and hugged Lydia. "I'll be there for you, too, if you need me."

Chapter 4

A month later, with three thousand of the thirty-eight-thousand dollars she'd managed to save, Clarissa buried Eunice Jenkins in a silver, satin-tufted casket on a hill in Goldsboro, North Carolina. Her foster mother had died smiling while Clarissa held her hand and sang, "In the Sweet Bye and Bye." She dragged herself away from the grave, oblivious to the sleet, rain, and the tears that turned to icicles on her cheeks.

The next day, after assuring herself again that the seven Holmeses listed in the Goldsboro telephone book were not the ones she sought, she packed her bags, phoned the YWCA for a room, and headed back to Washington, D.C.

"I'm still here," Cindy told her. "I could get my own apartment, but as long as I stay at the YWCA, my dad doesn't gripe about my being alone in this big, wicked city." A low, sexy laugh streamed out of her. "You're a southerner, so you may imagine how he is."

"I sure can," Clarissa said, unwilling to indicate that she had no idea as to the attitudes of one's biological father. She didn't know who or where hers was.

She didn't expect Lydia Stanton to rehire her, but she called to tell her what had happened.

"Where are you, Clarissa?"

"I'm here at the Y."

"What are you doing there? Come on back home here where you belong."

"Yes, ma'am," was all she could manage to say. "I haven't had a lot of luck in life, but . . . well, here lately . . . I guess I'd better get my stuff together." When she got downstairs to the lounge, Sam stood. "Welcome back, Miss Holmes."

She followed him to Lydia's limousine, thinking how typical of the woman to treat her as if she were a guest rather than a servant. *I won't mention singing to Allen Harkens*, she said to herself. She had chosen to forego the opportunity in order to be with her foster mother, and she was glad; if she hadn't, Eunice Jenkins would have died alone.

"Well, you look the same," Lydia said, "except for that soul food around your middle. I hope you'll soon get rid of that. We're going to a reception at the MLK Library tonight. I hadn't planned to attend, but since you're here, I'm anxious to go. I hope you can fit into one of your nice evening dresses."

Clarissa dressed in a black sheath that sparkled with polished ebony beads—a gift from Lydia—and black patent leather slippers and carried a small black beaded bag. "You need a nice black dressy coat," Lydia said. "Here, wear this velvet cape. It doesn't suit anybody in a wheelchair." Clarissa looked at the mink-lined cape. "Ma'am, I can't accept this. I won't even know how to walk in it."

"Then I'll tell you. You put one foot in front of the other and keep repeating it till you get where you're going. That cape's been deteriorating in my closet for seven years. I'd just about forgotten it was there."

"You do yourself proud tonight, ma'am," Sam said to Clarissa as he helped her into the limousine.

"Thank you, Sam. I'm not proud, though. I'm just giving thanks." *I may not be Connecticut Avenue*, she said to herself, standing beside Lydia's chair in the receiving line, *but upper Sixteenth Street ain't bad.*

"Well, well, Lydia, good to see you back among us," a man of some girth and ego said. "Where'd you get such a stunning nursing attendant? Wish I had her for my father. She might put some life in the old man."

You can always count on some self-important jerk to remind you of your origins, Clarissa said to herself and held her head a little higher.

Lydia leaned back in her wheelchair and narrowed her eyes. "You're still putting your foot in your mouth every time you open it. Representative Montague, this is Clarissa Holmes, one of the great jazz singers of our time."

"Did you say Clarissa Holmes?" a male voice said. A slim man of indeterminate age introduced himself. "I heard you several times at The Limelight, and I've wondered what happened to you."

He took a card from his pocket and handed it to Clarissa. "Would you please call me tomorrow? Where do you live?"

"Miss Holmes is my guest, Mr. Roth. I'm in the phone book."

"I'll call tomorrow, Mrs. Stanton, and to think I almost didn't come here tonight. What a piece of luck!"

"My apology, Miss Holmes," the congressman said in a whispered aside to Clarissa, his southern drawl thick and syrupy.

She whirled around and glared at him. Insult her in public and apologize in private, would he? "Take your apology and shove it," she told him, madder than she'd been since the morning she walked in on Josh slamming himself into Vanessa Hobbs, and in her bed at that. She let her gaze pierce the congressman until he blinked. Then, she turned her back to him.

"That's one reason why I hate these fund-raising receptions," Lydia said, letting Clarissa know she heard the exchange. "You brought him down to size, something I've wanted to do for years."

Chapter 5

Clarissa was unprepared to talk business when Roth called the following morning, because she hadn't taken his interest in her seriously. "I'm not prepping myself for another big disappointment," she told Lydia.

"You want me to try out for a Broadway play? Mr. Roth, I've never been near Broadway, and until six months ago, every play I'd seen had been on a television in somebody's house other than mine. You don't want me to act silly like those TV people, do you?"

"No indeed. You'll be a maid in a wealthy family, watching that family rip at the seams, and you'll sing the blues as a way of commenting on what's going on. With that voice of yours, you'll be perfect."

"Well, I'll do my best."

She won the part, and after tryouts in Washington, D.C., and Philadelphia, *Another Kind of Blues* opened in New York. Clarissa was not the lead actress, but a minor member of the supporting cast. Yet, the audience cheered her longest and loudest.

Clarissa Holmes is a genuine original with a spectacular voice, the *Daily News* critic wrote, and *The Herald* critic proclaimed, *It's been many years since I heard a voice like that of Clarissa Holmes. Don't miss her.*

Late in the day on which those notices appeared, Clarissa entered the theater with nimble steps, humming her opening song, smiling and greeting stagehands. Her world had finally taken shape, and she had a niche in it. Little did she know that that sense of well-being would be short-lived.

"If I don't watch her, Miss Collard Greens will be moving right into my dressing room," Clarissa heard the show's star say. "No actor with sense tries to upstage the star. She'd better watch it."

"Tell me about it!" another woman said. "What do you expect from somebody who didn't know the curtain from the set? Where the hell did Roth find her?"

"How y'all doing?" Clarissa said, walking between them as if she hadn't heard what they said. Neither spoke.

I don't care, she told herself. *I'm gonna sing to the best of my ability, and if the audience applauds me and not them, too bad.*

Nothing prepared her for the coming trouble. On stage, she was supposed to sing while ironing, but there was no ironing board, although she'd seen it where it was supposed to be minutes earlier. Not to be outdone, she looked at the audience and grinned. "I'm supposed to be ironing, but the ironing board walked off the stage, so I guess I'll polish the furniture." The comment brought an explosive applause from the audience, which had witnessed the act of sabotage before Clarissa came on stage. Each night, the snide remarks and cast members' interferences with her performance grew worse, more blatant and more intolerable.

"I'm starting to hate this work," Clarissa told Lydia by phone one evening. "It was not an accident that a pot of flowers dropped down from a window and almost hit me on the head as I was about to enter the theater yesterday. During the show, they throw me miscues, and do everything they can to make me look stupid. So I am going to leave at the end of this contract. Mr. Roth asked me to sign on for the run of the show, but I'm going to tell him no, thank you."

"Show people can be vicious if they put their minds to it. If you're not happy, you shouldn't stay. Life is too short."

"From now on, I'll stick to singing. No more acting for me. At first, I loved it. Oh, well . . ."

"But you can't leave—you're the whole show," Roth told her. "We didn't plan it that way, but you're the person people come to see."

"I'm sorry," she said, and she was, because he took a chance on her, and she appreciated it. "I don't wish the other cast members any harm, but I don't care if I never see any of them again."

After the show that night, Roth assembled the entire cast. "You've made Clarissa's life miserable, so she's leaving us." He didn't respond to the chorus of gasps. "If next week's take falls off significantly, I'm closing the show, and you can all look for another job. If Clarissa had stayed, the show would have run for at least a couple of years. I hope you're pleased with yourselves."

He clasped Clarissa in an embrace. "You're a real pro. Next time, you'll be the show's star. Get a good agent, and you'll go places."

Clarissa thanked him, but didn't tell him that she didn't care to have another foray into acting.

Now I have to make it myself, Clarissa said to herself the next morning when she awoke, once more without a job. *At least I'm not broke.* She answered the phone, thinking that Lydia was her caller.

"I'm Morton Chase. Roth told me you need a good agent. I heard you in *Another Kind of Blues*, and I can promise you that if you want to work in clubs, festivals, and TV, I can keep you busy."

Wary of the machinations of entertainment people, she called Roth and asked him whether he recommended her to Morton Chase and, informed that he had, she called the agent and hired him. That Thursday, she headed for St. Louis, settled in the hotel room that her agent reserved for her, got the telephone book, and began checking off entries with the last name of Holmes When she'd called most of them to no avail, her spirits began to droop. With shaking fingers, she dialed the last one.

"Hello," she said to the man who answered, "I'm trying to find my sisters."

"Why you calling here, lady?"

"Please, sir. My mother gave birth to three girls, triplets, and we were separated right away. My first foster mother said the woman who gave me to her wasn't my mother, but somebody else. All I know is that there were three baby girls named Holmes, and we're now thirty-three years old. I want to find my sisters. If you know anything, please tell me."

"That's rough, lady. I sure am sorry, but I don't know anybody who would fit that picture. I wish you luck."

At least he hadn't hung up on her as so many had done. "Thanks for your patience, sir."

"No sweat. Hang in there." He hung up, and she slumped in her chair. Maybe they weren't alive. But they had to be, and she meant to keep on looking for them until she found them.

The following evening, she performed to a packed house at BB's, with only her acoustic guitar. *This is where I belong*, she realized, *on the stage singing to my people.*

"You need some private life," Chase told her at their first meeting when he went to St. Louis to hear her sing. "I got two daughters almost your age, and I want to see them happily married and giving me some grandchildren."

"Been there and done that. Well, most of that. I don't have any children, but I've got a philandering husband in North Carolina shacking up with an eighteen-year-old whore."

Chase's eyebrows shot up. "Then you'd better get a divorce, because he can claim half of what you earn. In most states, the law says that what a spouse earns is community property."

"Don't make me laugh. He's lucky I didn't skewer him."

"Yeah, but you'd better protect your flank. As soon as he knows you're making money, he'll be back."

Chapter 6

After a successful five-week run in St. Louis, she opened at Pilot III in Kansas City, Missouri, with her own three-piece band that consisted of guitar, bass, and piano. For the first time, when she walked out on the stage, the patrons stood and applauded, and her nerves rioted throughout her body. She opened her mouth, and not a sound escaped. Her gaze drifted to the front row, and a man who sat alone gave her the thumbs-up sign. She turned around, signaled the band to start again, opened her mouth, and out poured "St. Louis Blues." She glanced back at the stranger, who made the sign again, but neither smiled nor showed any other kind of emotion. She tried to ignore the quivers racing around in her body, forced a smile, and bowed in appreciation for the applause.

"Who was that guy?" Raymond, her guitar player, asked her after the show.

"Never saw him before, but I had a strange feeling about him, like I'm supposed to know him."

"Maybe that's because the cat looks like money," Oscar, the pianist, suggested. "I'll bet a lot of women have thought they oughta know him. He's one cool-looking dude."

"No," she said. "It's more than that. Almost a premonition. He didn't hang around, though. Thank God."

"I hope to hell he's not a stalker," Raymond said, articulating her second thoughts. "Never can tell about these three-piece-suit types."

She thought Konny, her bass player, winced at that remark, but she wasn't sure. Besides, why should he? She'd never seen him wear anything but chinos, a plaid shirt, tweed jacket, and hat at work, and baggy jeans during their rehearsals.

The four of them sat in a small upstairs bistro a few doors from the Charlie Parker Memorial that stood near the corner of Eighteenth and Vine. Jazzmen loved to frequent the place because they were unlikely to encounter groupies and fans, and the owner didn't expect to sell them more than coffee and a light supper.

Sipping on his third cup of black coffee, Konny looked at the others. "Wanna go jamming over at the Key Note? It's too early to go home."

"Man, you never want to sleep," Oscar said. "Sorry, but my old lady looked like she had some plans for tonight, and I'm going home. If I don't, tomorrow night I'll have to beg." The other two men gave each other knowing looks.

Raymond's laugh amounted to an innuendo. "Right on, man. Sometimes I forget you're only thirty. Go do your thing."

"What's he talking about?" Clarissa asked.

Konny flipped back the hat that he wore everywhere and lit a cigarette. "Sex. What else does Raymond talk about?"

Raymond, who was twice Oscar's age, lifted his glass in a salute to the group. "At least I can talk about it." He looked at Oscar. "When I was your age, I took care of business, man, like it was going out of style. And speaking of business, Clarissa, a good-looking and talented woman like you got no business being by herself."

"I'm married."

She knew Raymond wouldn't drop the subject; he never did until he had exhausted it. "Yeah. In name only. Somebody needs to take a stick to that husband of yours."

Konny drew on his cigarette. "Leave him to heaven, girl, and get yourself a man."

Clarissa didn't want to think about Josh, but she knew she would have to, for one day he'd come crawling back to make her more miserable than when they lived together in Low Point. And she didn't feel like jamming. Besides, Buck Ryan had warned her to conserve her voice.

"I'm turning in," she told them. "See you tomorrow morning at Konny's place."

She eased into a Tuesday-through-Saturday-evening work routine and adjusted herself to the constant companionship of three men who quickly filled the void of father and brother in her life. After a month, she moved out of the YWCA and into a furnished apartment near the club.

"I'll never get used to living up this high," she said to herself, looking down from her thirty-second-floor balcony at the square below and the ant-like shapes that moved to and fro, here and there, across its plain. A blue, red, and gray streaked sky cushioned the descent of the setting sun, and she gasped in awe. And to think that she had lived thirty-three years without seeing that particular scene and feeling the spiritual healing that it evoked in her.

I guess poor people are so busy grubbing for something to eat and a place to stay that they don't have time to appreciate nature. People working hard out in the cold, in the hot sun, sometimes two and three jobs, don't feel like making love the way they ought to, either. Where's a man who's been splitting logs or working at a sawmill all day going to get the energy to satisfy a woman? Life is not fair. Josh and I didn't stand a chance.

Each night, she sang to sellout crowds, and each night when she walked out on the stage, she glanced down to see the stranger whom she and her band referred to as Mr. X. And he was always there, a part of the scenery, manifesting no more emotion than did the tables and chairs around him, but night by night, he seeped into her.

One Monday afternoon she and the band members sat in her apartment, working out a new arrangement. "The dude just sits there looking at Clarissa while she sings, and when the show's over, he gets up and leaves. He's either smitten or he's a kook," Oscar said.

Konny disagreed. "Did it occur to you that the man may love great jazz? If he was after Clarissa, he'd have made a move long ago. The man loves to hear her sing."

"He used to give me the willies," Clarissa said, "but you know, he's comforting. I've gotten used to him. He's like an old friend who welcomes me every night."

Raymond's eyebrow shot up. "Don't get careless. He could be a weirdo."

She made buttermilk biscuits while Oscar revised the arrangement. "All you're getting today is biscuits, ham, and apple pie. If I'm not careful, you fellas will move in with me just so you can eat."

"Yeah," Raymond said under his breath. "Oscar's subject to give up that deal he's got at home so he can fill up on your biscuits. Man, ain't no biscuits on earth *that* good."

She enjoyed their camaraderie and, working with them, she learned much about men. *If I'd known then what I know now, I wouldn't have wasted fifteen years of my life on Josh Medford, a loser even before he left his mother's womb.*

That night, after the band played "'Round Midnight," it's third and last warmup number, Clarissa walked out on the stage to the microphone, let her gaze sweep the audience as she usually did, and stopped. Mr. X was not in his usual seat. She scanned the place again as a hush settled over the patrons. He was not in the house. She gathered her aplomb and, after a minute, signaled Oscar to begin. But for the first time since she'd become a professional singer, she could hardly focus on her work.

At the intermission, the band members gathered around her. "He'll be back tomorrow night," Oscar said.

"Right." Konny tugged at her hand. "He probably went out of town on business and couldn't make it back. Not to worry."

But their words didn't placate her. "I wish I'd sent him a note thanking him for his support."

"Naah," Raymond said. "Wouldn't a been proper. He was probably a businessman away from home, and his work here is finished. Forget about him."

She didn't think she would, for a second sense told her that he was unfinished business. However, the next morning brought a situation that forced her attention on Josh Medford. She answered her telephone at eight-thirty that morning.

"Hello, Clarissa Mae. When you coming back home?"

She grabbed the nearest chair when she almost fell to the floor. "Josh? For the Lord's sake, where'd you come from?"

"I'm home here in Low Point where you ought to be."

Anger furled up in her, slow and suffocating, like smoke from a bed of damp leaves. "What did you do with your little whore?"

"Watch your mouth, woman. Just because you're in the big-time doesn't mean I'll take any flak off you. I'm suing you for desertion."

Her bottom lip dropped, and her eyes narrowed to slits. "Is that so? Aren't you in for a surprise?"

"You the one," he spat out. "I'm suing you for a divorce, damages, and spousal support, and my lawyer says I can get it."

She ground her teeth. "Yeah. If I know you, you got some chicken-shit lawyer who doesn't know what side is up. You're an adulterer, and you're planning to sue *me* for divorce? See you in court."

She hung up and called Raymond. "I have to leave," she said after apprising him of Josh's threats.

"Too bad. Finish the week, and the band will work out the rest of the contract. The boss'll be happy as long as he has a good jazz program."

Chapter 7

She flew to Raleigh, rented a car, and drove to her friend Jessie Mae's house in Low Point. As she traveled along the dirt road beside Gospel Creek—so called because the local Baptist ministers baptized their converts there—she couldn't help wondering how the people who lived there tolerated their poverty. On the other side of the creek, a lot of people had big cars, nice houses, paved sidewalks, and white faces. When she lived in Low Point, she accepted it, though she knew it wasn't right, but now, she just wanted to get away from there as quickly as possible.

She parked in front of Jessie Mae's unpainted, L-shaped house, a replica of the one she'd once called home, got out, and knocked on the back door.

"Come on in, Clarissa," Jessie Mae said. "I'm just getting together a little dinner." In Low Point, people referred to the midday meal as dinner.

"If I go to that old house, Jessie Mae, he'll swear in court that I never left him."

"Girl, he ain't spent a single night there since you left. Everybody knows he's staying over there with Vanessa Hobbs and her low-life mama."

"Don't I know it! And I have to put my life on hold to deal with his stupidity."

Jessie Mae looked hard at Clarissa. "Girl, you changed. He gon' be surprised at how good you look, and you don't sound like you gon' take no mess, neither. Things going good with you?"

"Yes, indeed. Thank the Lord. I should have trucked out of here the minute I caught that little strumpet in my bed."

The next morning, after an hour with Claude Hollinger, the local white—and only—lawyer, Clarissa drove back to Jessie Mae's house, wondering how she had ever been satisfied to exist—she wouldn't call it living—in Low Point.

"If I was white," she said later to Jessie Mae, "old man Hollinger would expect me to abide by the law, but since I'm black, he didn't hesitate to skirt the law and get me a hearing day after tomorrow instead of the prescribed six weeks.

"*You got some extenuating circumstances you can prove, ain't you?*" he said, "and wrote that on the papers without waiting for my answer."

Two days later, she faced Josh in court, accused him of adultery with Vanessa Hobbs when the girl was only seventeen, and presented Jessie Mae and two other witnesses to support her accusation.

"Divorce granted to Clarissa Holmes Medford," the judge said at the end of the hearing. "Defendant's petition for spousal support denied."

"It doesn't pay to be a smartass, Josh," Clarissa said to her ex-husband. "You got the short end of the stick. Nothing. Nada. How'd you find me?"

His shrug said he'd tried and lost, and the result didn't bother him. "Easy. You're a bigshot now. Vanessa found where you were working in half an hour, told the man she was a neighbor, that your mother was dying and she needed your phone number. Piece of cake."

"How could you? My mother died when I was born."

"It didn't hurt nobody. Dead is dead. You sure looking good."

She let a grin slide over her face. "I know. And the more money I make, the better I'm gonna look. Have a good life." She walked out of the county courthouse, barely able to suppress a laugh. She would remember him standing in the open door, his hands on his hips, a frown on his face, and his mouth a gaping hole. Oh, how sweet it was!

* * *

Clarissa broke her flight back to Kansas City with a stop in Washington. "I'm always starting over," she told Lydia. "It seems like every time I get a good, strong following on a job, I have to leave it."

"You're going back to Kansas City, aren't you?"

"Yes, but I don't know whether my agent can book me in my old spot, and I don't want to tour from city to city sleeping on a bus."

"Tell your agent that, and take charge of your life. You put Josh right where he belongs—out of your life. There are two things a woman doesn't need: a limp penis, and a man who's always somewhere else when he gets hard." She didn't think she would ever get used to hearing Lydia say things like that. For all her seeming primness, Lydia could spit out some earthy comments.

A reply was in order, so she said, "Well, Josh walks like a man, talks heavy like a man, and sure looks like a man, but his similarity to one ends right there. I'm hoping eventually to find one who has *all* the attributes of a man, if you get my meaning."

"I get it, all right. He found himself a seventeen-year-old who probably didn't know he was useless in bed. Good riddance!"

Chapter 8

A call to her agent resulted in Clarissa's immediate return to Kansas City. "You're expected back at Pilot III," he told her.

Raymond and Konny met her at the airport. "Where's Oscar?" She could hardly breathe as she waited for their answer. She couldn't sing those new songs without a piano player.

Raymond draped an arm around her shoulder and hugged her. He was the only one of the three who took such liberties with her, claiming the obvious, that he was old enough to be her father. Indeed, she looked to Raymond for advice and comfort as one would to a father.

"We've been working on a new song for you with my guitar rather than the piano backing you. Oscar's at home scoring it, 'cause he writes a hell of a lot better than I do. You'll love it. Say, what's with your old man?" He picked up one of her bags, and Konny took the other one.

"Josh Medford is history. My divorce papers are in my suitcase." She wanted to ask them if Mr. X had visited the club during her absence, but she didn't. He was a ship that passed her in the night, that slipped through her life without making a sound.

"I wish I could find a good woman like you, Clarissa," Konny said. "You don't drink, don't do drugs, and don't sleep around. Something tells me you actually say your prayers. You got any real nice, single girl-friends?"

"One. But she's in Washington, D.C. She was kind to me when I first left that hick town I'd lived in all my life. Hmm. She's nice-looking, too."

Konny ran his fingers over his hair. "No kidding, Clarissa. I'm tired of these women who're out for a good time and don't care which man they're with. It's getting to the place where I feel like running when one of 'em approaches me. Invite your friend to visit you for a weekend. I promise I'll treat her the way I would my sister."

Raymond fastened Clarissa's seat belt, ignited the Crown Victoria's engine, and headed out of the parking lot. A chuckle escaped him. "That sounds good, Konny, but I bet you don't even have a sister."

"I have three sisters, all younger that I am. I'm serious. When we got together with Clarissa, I was thinking of quitting clubs, settling somewhere and teaching music, but once we four got together, I knew we had something, and I couldn't quit."

She thought of Cindy Ross, a woman who had befriended her, a woman alone in a town known to contain four women for every man, including the men with HIV, AIDS, various antisocial traits, and a different sexual preference.

"Okay. I'll invite her, and you'd better not let me down. I'll send you to meet her and bring her to my house."

Konny's white teeth sparkled in his broad smile that she recognized as a testament to his hope. *I never guessed he was so lonely*, she said to herself, turned and regarded him slumped in the backseat. "She's a fine person, Konny, I hope the two of you like each other."

"If she's got both feet and all of her front teeth, he'll love her," Raymond said. "This is no life for a single person, Clarissa, and you'll soon realize that. Oscar wants us to rehearse tomorrow morning at his place." She said she'd be there at eleven, their usual rehearsal time.

To celebrate her freedom, she bought a new evening gown, a strapless red sheath that won high praise from her band members and gave her the confidence to wear dangling earrings and her hair combed down rather than up in a knot, Billie Holiday style. An unusually clamorous ovation greeted her when she stepped out on the stage. She bowed and, with her heart in her throat, glanced toward the table where Mr. X usually sat and froze when she saw him.

Her heart began a wild gallop, and she didn't try to inhibit the smile that spread over her face. She waved to him and, to her surprise and delight, he smiled and waved back. Without giving thought to why she did it or to anyone's reaction, she walked over to Oscar and said, "I want to sing `Solitude.' I know it's not on the program, but—"

"Okay," he said. "Key of G," and riffed off a few bars. She walked back to the microphone, waited for her cue, and lent her voice to Duke Ellington's famous song. Even as she sang it, trying not to look at the man to whom she sang, she knew he would recall never having heard her sing it before and that he would realize the band hadn't rehearsed it, for only the pianist accompanied her.

"I'm brazen," she admitted to herself at the end of the song, when Mr. X stood and applauded, telling her without words that he knew she sang it to him.

"What's with this dude?" Oscar said as they sat in their favorite bistro drinking coffee after the show. "You sang a love song to that guy, and he damned well knew it because he stood and applauded. Then, he high-asses it outta there without a word. I was sure he'd go back-stage to see you. Man, that's weird."

"Yeah," Konny said. "That cat's been freaky from day one. He's either married and doesn't fool around, or he's gay."

"In either case, he's acting like a gentleman," Raymond said, "though I'm beginning to suspect that ain't what Clarissa wants out of him right now."

"I'm not here, so you can talk about me all you want to." A long sigh eased out of her. "I'd love to talk with him, so I'll know what kind of person he is. He's revved up my curiosity."

"Yeah," Oscar muttered. "That ain't all he's revved up."

"I got you a recording contract with MCA," Morton Chase, her agent, told her by phone the next morning, "and you're in good com-pany. It only records the top performers. You've gone as far as you can go without putting out some CDs."

In her excitement, she shoved the enigma that was Mr. X to the back burner of her mind, called her band members, and began the job of choosing the music for her first recording. She had never aspired to national recognition, but she seemed headed that way, and as long as her flag was waving, she wasn't going to complain about the breeze.

"I was hoping you would join us for Christmas," Lydia said when they spoke the next day. "You haven't met my son yet, and he'll be home for the Christmas holidays. Well, he no longer calls this home, but I suppose I'll always consider my home as his."

"I had hoped to be there, but I have to be in New York. My agent got me a record deal, and as their most recently signed singer, they didn't take into account my convenience when they set the recording date. I'll see you before the year is out, though."

She'd promised Konny to introduce him to Cindy, and she hoped she wouldn't regret it for either of their sakes. Deciding to be straight with her friend, she phoned Cindy before leaving home for work that evening. "He's real nice, Cindy, but I didn't realize he was so lonely."

"If a guy has a hard time getting a girl, something must be wrong with him."

"Cindy, musicians attract a certain kind of woman, and if they want a different, more conservative type of woman, they have to look for her. I wouldn't mislead you. They'd be all over him, if he encouraged them. Konny is tall, nice-looking, and clean cut."

"Okay. All I can lose is one weekend, and I'll at least get to see you. Tell me when and where."

Chapter 9

Counsel Patterson, Jr., or Konny, as he was known in the music business, grew up as the only son of a university professor and a mother who enjoyed wide recognition as a journalist. His family gathered in the dining room for family prayer on Sunday morning, went to church, the theater, the movies, jazz concerts, opera, and football games together and hadn't owned a television until Konny was a senior in high school. He smoked his first weed at Harvard, lost his supper, and lay stretched out on his bed, drunk, for the next twenty hours. He hadn't touched the stuff since. He didn't tell people in the entertainment business about his background, that he was a classical musician with an advanced degree in the organ and certain string instruments. Not even Clarissa, Raymond, and Oscar were privy to that information. He'd tried for years to be "one of the boys," but he'd only made himself miserable. Clarissa was his type, but she was also his boss. In any case, she looked straight at him on a regular basis and didn't see a man, but a bass player. If she had shown even the slightest interest in him as a man, he'd have heated her up plenty.

He called a halt to his ruminations, put on his overcoat, and headed for the Kansas City International Airport. Hopefully, nobody he knew would discover the gray pinstripe suit, light gray shirt, and red tie that he had on beneath his coat. He wore his one suit only when he was going to see his mother and father. They didn't mind his pursuing a career in jazz rather than in the classical music for which he'd been trained, but they didn't want to see him wearing what they called "prison clothes." Halfway to the airport, he checked the glove compartment of his Chrysler New Yorker—Raymond and Oscar made jokes about his sedate car, but it suited him—to be sure he had the sign that read "CINDY ROSS." He called the airline for the tenth time to determine whether the plane would arrive on time and then flipped on the classical music station. Damn! If he could just steady his nerves. She was only one out of a hundred and ten million American women over eighteen and under sixty. What was he so excited about?

Holding the sign well out in front of him, he stared at every woman who walked through the door leading from the security area, and ninety percent of the time, he released a breath of gratitude when the woman walked past him. Suddenly, his heart battered the walls of his chest as a tall, dark, and pretty woman walked toward him, her face beaming with a smile.

"Hi, I'm Cindy Ross, and you do not look like a jazz fiddler, thank God." She held out her hand, but he ignored it and hugged her. *What a relief*!

"I'll look like one Tuesday night," he said, unable to stop laughing, so great was his sudden sense of well-being. "I'm Counsel Patterson, Jr., but everyone calls me Konny, and you'd better do the same."

She looked up at him, searching his face. "You are not what I expected, and I'm glad. Clarissa said such nice things about you that I thought she had exaggerated out of necessity. I didn't believe her."

He smiled, partly because it was what he felt and partly because he wanted her to be at ease with him .He didn't want to share her with the others until he got to know her, until he knew whether he was interested or merely attracted to her. "If you aren't tired, we could get something to eat and I could show you Kansas City. We have some interesting museums and monuments."

"I'm not tired, I refused the airline's gourmet pretzels, and I'd love to see the city."

He picked up her bag with one hand and took hers with his other one. "Girl after my own heart. I'll phone Clarissa and let her know you're here."

*   *   *

"Well," Clarissa said when Cindy and Konny arrived at her house at about eleven o'clock that night, "I thought you got lost."

"I'll see you tomorrow, Cindy," Konny said, taking her hand and smiling as he gazed intently into her face. "Good night, Clarissa."

"Don't you want to come in?" she asked him.

"Thanks, but I'll let you two enjoy being together."

"Thank you, Konny. I appreciate your meeting Cindy for me."

"Not half as much as I do," he said. "See you."

"If I know Konny, you two hit if off just fine, or he would have brought you home immediately. Say, was that a business suit he had on under that overcoat? I thought I saw gray pinstripes."

"You did, indeed. Thank you for introducing me to him. I like him a lot."

"*Gray pinstripes.* Next, I'll see rabbits hopping on my ceiling. Well . . . we rehearse tomorrow from eleven until one, and—"

"I know. Konny told me. After the rehearsal, he's going to take me to explore Union Station. I've heard it's like a little city."

"Nobody ever heard of Konny doing anything but working, going jamming at clubs, and going home. Something tells me I don't know Konny."

Cindy looked at her and grinned. "Your description of him didn't exactly fit, and I liked the difference."

Sleep didn't come easily for Clarissa that night. For the first time since she left Lydia's employment, she had an acute sense of loneliness. "I'll see you tomorrow," Konny had said to Cindy. Four words, but his smile and the intimacy those words conveyed sent shivers through Clarissa. She could feel, almost taste and smell, the simmering emotion in that seemingly innocent scene.

"Everybody but me," she said aloud. She needed the arms of a man she cared for, the sweetness of a man's strength and tenderness, the joy of belonging to that man, and knowing there was little likelihood that she'd have that feeling any time soon brought tears to her eyes. For the first time in her life, she wanted a nameless, faceless *any-man* to make love to her and cool the fire of her libido, a fire that Josh Medford had never been able to quench.

"I'm not jealous of Cindy or of any other woman who has a good man," she said aloud, sitting up in bed when sleep still hadn't come at three o'clock. "I just want what's due me."

After her show that night, Clarissa gave Cindy a key to her apartment. "Konny will look after you. I'll see you later."

"Where you headed to?" Raymond asked her.

"You said I needed a life, didn't you? See you tomorrow at eleven."

She got a taxi in front of the club and settled into the backseat. Calm and peaceful. *I ought to be scared.* The taxi soon turned into Twelfth Street and stopped at the door of the Marriott Downtown Hotel. She paid the fare, got out, and strolled into the spacious and grand lobby. After letting her glance sweep the place, she took a seat in a dark-blue lounge chair near the entrance to the bar, removed her coat to expose her red sheath evening gown, and crossed her knees. She wished she smoked, because that would give her something to do with her hands. *How did women get the nerve to go into a bar alone and sit there comfortably, as if they belonged there?*

Very soon, a man passed, turned back and looked at her, but she refused eye contact, and he went on into the bar. About forty, she surmised, well dressed, decent-looking, and on the make. She wondered if his wife knew he picked up women who sat near the entrance to bars in big, high-rise hotels. *Am I any better? Maybe he's like me. Lonely.*

Deciding that she didn't have the stomach for it, she uncrossed her knees and rose to go. "Would you share a drink with me?" the man who'd gone into the bar minutes earlier said as he came out and walked directly to her.

"Thanks, but I'm leaving."

"Too bad. I see you don't care for this sort of thing any more than I do." He extended his hand for a handshake. "My name is Lawrence Bishop, and I'm from Shreveport, Louisiana. I'm here for a merchants' meeting, and I've had a rotten day. I just want somebody to talk with, somebody who's not interested in merchandising."

She didn't know why, but she believed him. "All right. We can talk for a few minutes."

He put her coat across his arm. "It's noisy in the bar, but they'll serve us in that section over there." He pointed to a cluster of tables amidst a group of artificial trees strung with lights for the coming Christmas holiday.

"I won't ask why you're here alone," he began, "because it's none of my business. Do you mind telling me your name and what you do for a living?"

"You may call me Clarissa Mae. Just so you don't get the wrong idea, I'm not a prostitute. If I had a mother, I'd be happy for her to know what I do and to watch me do it."

His laugh had a merry, infectious ring. "In other words, you're famous and you're keeping your identity from me. Fair enough. What do you do when you get lonely?"

It was her turn to laugh. "I consider doing things that are out of character."

"Me, too. I walked in here looking for a woman to take upstairs to my room. It's a good thing I ran into you or I'd probably have been an adulterer for the first time in my life." He shook his head. "I was so damned miserable. I just needed to lose myself in a loving woman."

"What did I do that caused you to change your mind?"

"Body language. When I walked up to you, you stepped back from me, increasing the space between us, and your handshake was brief. A teenager could have read that. Why did you sit near the bar?"

She lifted her shoulder in a quick shrug. "Same reason why you went in there and, like you, I don't have the stomach for it."

"But you're young, elegant, and so beautiful. Why should you be lonely?"

"I could say those exact words to you. I'm a relatively recent divorcee, and I haven't yet tested the waters, mostly because I'm not eager to get back into that quagmire."

The waiter took their orders, bourbon and water for him, white wine for her. "Marriage can be bliss if you're lucky enough to get the one who's right for you," he said.

"Did you?"

He nodded. "Yes, and I hope I'm never tempted to violate it again."

"That's a naïve hope. You'll be tempted aplenty, but when you see trouble coming, walk the other way. My ex-husband walked right into it and wallowed in it."

"I'm sorry."

"Trust me, Mr. Bishop, I'm happier now than I was during those fifteen years I was married to him. Loneliness is better than living in a futile relationship. Maybe I didn't meet his needs, just as he didn't meet mine. I wish him well."

Bishop raised his glass and sipped the bourbon a little at a time. "The sad thing about our encounter is that I'm positive I would have enjoyed making love with you. You're sensitive, and you're very tender. I could use some of that." He let the contents of his glass stream down his throat. "Thanks so much for your company, Clarissa Mae. We'd better separate before I do something stupid like asking you to spend the night with me."

She rose and reached for her coat. "Thank you for the compliment. Have a good life. Good-bye." She refused his assistance getting into her coat and headed for the door.

"May I get a taxi for you?" she heard him call after her. But she didn't respond. Talk about sensitive and tender! She needed him as badly as he needed her, and if she had remained with him much longer, she might have gone with him to his room, and guilt would have plagued her for the rest of her life. She got into a taxi at the hotel's door and headed home.

She had no pride in the fact that she didn't follow through with her plan to find someone to sleep with. God was answering prayers she'd stored up over the years when he led Lawrence Bishop into the lounge. Maybe what his wife didn't know wouldn't hurt her, but if he'd bedded another woman, he would behave differently toward her thereafter, and she'd feel it. It might be barely noticeable, but he would lose something of his feelings for her and she'd catch it in a minute. She knew, because she'd been there. She'd nearly gone berserk when she'd found out Josh was screwing around. Damn him! From then on, she'd felt nothing for him.

Cindy had gone to bed when Clarissa got home. She sat in the darkened living room, musing over the evening. Would she have made love with that stranger if he had encouraged it and if he hadn't been married? And what about the next time? She went into her room, undressed in the dark, and went to bed. *I need to find someone I can care for*, she said to herself and turned out the light.

Chapter 10

On December the twentieth, Clarissa and her band checked into the W Hotel on Lexington Avenue in New York City and went directly to the recording studio in Long Island City, a helter-skelter, industrial-type area that bore no resemblance to sleek mid-Manhattan. Yet, it was only a short drive across the Fifty-ninth Street Bridge.

"Lord, I never saw so many rude people in my entire life," she told Raymond. "They knock you down if you don't jump out of the way. What's their hurry?"

"Don't ask me. I lived here for nearly twenty years, and I soon discovered that the way to make it in this city is to act just like the New Yorkers act. Don't let grass grow under your feet. If you stay here longer than a week, you'll have to take antistress pills."

She looked at him much as a mother does when indulging a recalcitrant child. "Raymond, if you think I should take stress pills, I'm getting out of here tomorrow morning. Some of that stuff makes people forget who they are."

"Yeah? I can think of a few people I'd like to keep supplied with it. Maybe they'd get their behinds off their shoulders. I hope these recording sessions will be over by Christmas Eve."

"Don't even think it," Oscar said. "We get Christmas Day off and we have to go back into the studio on the twenty-sixth. I told my old lady to forget about the tree and presents, and we'll have Christmas here in New York. This place jumps during Christmas."

"Are you planning anything for Christmas Day?" Raymond asked Clarissa.

She was, but it wasn't anything she could share with Raymond, dear as he was. "I'm going to ride through Central Park in a hansom carriage, if I have to do it all by myself."

"I hate to think of you by yourself on Christmas Day—if I didn't think we'd freeze to death, I'd go with you. I'll be with my brother and his family. What you doing, Konny?"

"I'm getting a train to Washington at four o'clock Christmas Eve, and I plan to be back around noon on the twenty-sixth."

Clarissa eyed Konny with an appraising look. "She's a lucky girl. What about your parents? Won't they expect you?"

"They're not stupid. I'll call 'em."

"Yeah, man," Oscar said. "Your dad will definitely understand the call of the wild. But don't count on your mother. She'll think you should go home to mama. Getting my mother to understand that I needed to be with my girl was like trying to teach a tone-deaf person how to sing. Go do your thing, Konny."

Clarissa didn't want to be with her band members Christmas Day, for she saw it as her one chance to be alone long enough to call every Holmes entry in the five New York City telephone books. She got up early Christmas morning, ate breakfast in her room, called the reception desk and requested the telephone books. By lunchtime, she'd gone through the two hundred and fifty-five entries in the Manhattan directory.

Why can't people be more loving? she thought. Very few of those she called sympathized with her plight. She telephoned Lydia, wished her a pleasant day, dressed, and went downstairs to lunch.

"Somebody ought to teach these Yankees how to roast a turkey and how to make decent gravy," she said to the person at the table next to her.

The woman pressed her napkin to the corners of her mouth and looked sheepish. "I've been thinking how good it is, but of course it's well known in my family that I can't cook. I take it you can."

"Yes, indeed," Clarissa said. They exchanged pleasant small talk for a few minutes. She rose to leave. "Well, Merry Christmas. I have to make some calls." Back in her room, she continued her search in the Brooklyn directory until pangs in her stomach told her that it was time to eat.

Her phone rang. "Hello. Hi, Raymond. How're things at your brother's house?"

"Great. We're thinking of going to the Vanguard to take in some jazz. Want us to pick you up?"

"Thanks, Raymond, but I'm going to stay right here where it's warm. You go, and have a good time."

"All right, but don't say I didn't ask you."

She hadn't even started on the Queens Borough. If Louis Armstrong and other black notables had lived in that area, she was sure many other African-Americans lived there. Around midnight, exhausted and aching with the pain of failure, she closed the last book and flung herself into bed. Maybe they had married, as she had, and used their married names. Maybe . . . Anything was possible, but she would find them. When she made enough money, she would be able to afford newspaper and television ads. Comforted with that thought, she dozed off and was soon trying to climb a barbed wire fence that separated her from two women whose faces she couldn't see.

She slept fitfully and awakened exhausted when she received a call from Morton Chase at nine the next morning. "What's the matter, Clarissa? You sound groggy."

"Hi, Morton. Hard time getting to sleep last night. What's up?"

"I got you booked into Toronto. That town's big on jazz."

She got out of bed, stretched and yawned. "Morton, don't butter me up. It's cold as the devil up there right now. That place will make Kansas City seem like a boiler room. When?"

"It's a New Year's Eve gig."

"I've never asked the guys to work on a major holiday."

"Tell 'em they'll each get a five-hundred-dollar bonus. They're paying you twice your usual fee."

"Tell those Canadians to make the bonus a thousand each for the band members, and we'll take it."

"A thousand-dollar bonus for one night on top of my regular salary?" Oscar asked her. "Damned right, we're going."

She couldn't understand her eagerness to get back to Kansas City. It wasn't home, and she would never regard it as such, but she was drawn to it. "When we leave Toronto, I hope we're headed for Kansas City," she told her agent when she called him.

"Right. You got a two-week stand there."

She hung up and began to pack. She'd promised to see Lydia before the end of the year. "I'm going to Washington, and I'll meet you in Toronto December thirtieth," she told her band members later when they met.

"I'm doing the same," Konny said. "See you guys in Toronto."

"You really like Cindy, I take it," Clarissa said to Konny, as they sat together on Amtrak's Acela Express to Washington, D.C.

"From the minute I first saw her. She's wonderful."

"I'm happy for you," she said, feeling the emptiness, the loneliness begin to seep back into her. "I'd give anything to feel what you're feeling."

He propped his left foot on the footrest in front of him, leaned back and closed his eyes. "Didn't you feel it when you fell in love with your husband?"

She shook her head. "Konny, I've never felt it. I realized long ago that I married to escape the situation I lived in. Out of the frying pan and into the fire. I was eighteen. What a mistake I made!"

"Put it behind you, Clarissa. You have a great career before you, and you're one of the finest women I've ever met. Decent to the bone. Warm and giving. You're in for some happiness, lady."

A frown eclipsed her face. Konny didn't speak that way around Raymond and Oscar. "Thank you. That's one of the nicest things anyone has ever said to me."

"Don't thank me. It's true. If you'd given me the slightest encouragement, I'd have gone after you like the FBI after a counterspy."

She swung around and stared at him. "You're making this up."

He laughed, but the laugh held no merriment, only a hollow sound. "I can laugh about it now, because I'm over it, and I have Cindy. Don't you know how a woman's simple kindness and gentleness affects a man, and especially if she looks like you?"

She wanted to get off that subject. "What is it about Cindy that attracts you?"

"Everything. She began smiling the minute she saw me with that sign. And you know, she's the same kind of woman that you are. Independent, feminine, decent, honest, and tender. And she's a straight shooter. I hope we can make it."

"So do I. Give her my love. By the way, when do you think our CD will get to the radio stations?"

"Raymond said the first recording we did has been packaged as a single, and the studio shipped it to disk jockeys yesterday."

"Good, that means our New Year's Eve program should have 'Another Kind of Blues' in the second spot. I don't mind. I love to sing it."

"Thanks, Clarissa. I think it's the best pop song I've written."

They separated at Union Station in Washington, and he left her with much to think about. For instance, what had he written that wasn't a pop song? And if she had encouraged him, he'd have gone after her. Whew! That had never occurred to her. She breathed deeply with relief as she settled into a Capitol Cab. He wouldn't have told her if he hadn't already gotten over it. Thank God for Cindy.

Chapter 11

Warmth and a sense of well-being stole over Clarissa as she rang the bell of the elegant beige-and-brown Tudor-style house on upper Sixteenth Street. It struck her forcibly that Lydia Stanton's house was the place she called home, and she didn't know when she began to feel that way.

"Well, well. Miss Holmes. Come right on in. Merry Christmas," Lorraine, the housekeeper said, gushing as if she were welcoming Lydia Stanton's daughter. "Mrs. Stanton is in the living room."

She handed her suitcase to Lorraine, hurried to the living room, and came to an abrupt halt at the door. So this was how the wealthy celebrated Christmas. Near the fire that crackled in the marble-framed hearth stood a ceiling-high Douglas fir decorated with hundreds of twinkling lights and trinkets of all kinds. Colorful Christmas stockings hung from the mantel, and the odor of fresh green pine branches and bayberry delighted her olfactory sense. She looked at Lydia's wheel-chair-bound figure, alone amid the beauty and wealth, and experienced a pang of guilt. *I owe her everything, every opportunity and every applause, and I should have come here to be with her at Christmas.*

Troubled as to how she would let Lydia know she was there, she sang "Silent Night" as she walked toward her.

"Clarissa. Clarissa. I knew you had to come either today or tomorrow, because you said you'd see me before the end of the year. Come give me a hug." They held each other for a long while. "I'm so glad to see you."

"I'm sorry I didn't come here Christmas, ma'am. The recording was important, but maybe if I had insisted, the company would have let us do it after New Year's."

"Oh, for goodness sake! You're here now, and that's what counts. My regret is that you didn't get to meet my son, but you will. I hear that your career is skyrocketing, and I'm delighted. The next time you perform here in D.C., I am going to be in the audience."

Clarissa told her about the recording venture and her date for a televised New Year's Eve performance in the largest hotel in Toronto. "I've always known that you will be famous. It's just beginning. You can't imagine how pleased I am."

"Any place you want me to go with you tonight, or have you hired another aide?"

I've interviewed a lot of women, but I haven't lucked out yet. I don't suppose I'll find anyone like you, though. How'd you like to go with me to see Diane Reeves? I can send Sam for tickets. Just what you're wearing will be fine. I'd love to hear her."

It was a plea, and she lowered her gaze so as not to display her humility that this woman to whom she owed so much would beg her to do something. "I'm trying to think of something you could ask of me that I wouldn't do, and nothing comes to mind," Clarissa said, forcing joviality. "I have a dress in my suitcase that tops this one. What time do you want us to leave?"

The woman's eyes shone with pleasure. "Wonderful. A quarter of eight. Sam will be happy to see you."

At the concert that night, she absorbed the great diva's performance into every pore of her body. *I've got a long way to go*, she told herself as she settled into her old bed that night, *but I will get there*.

"I'm going to try to come to see you more often," Clarissa told Lydia the next day as she prepared to leave. "I hate that you aren't going places and doing interesting things."

"I've had my life, and it's time you were having yours, but I will be happy any time you walk through that door."

She thought about those words as the big Douglas 80 roared through the sky en route to Toronto. Lydia had told her several times that her home was Clarissa's home. But how could she treat it as her home when she didn't work there and didn't want to appear to take advantage of the woman to whom she owed her career?

At the hotel, she stepped out of the taxi into swirls of big snowflakes that created a picturesque world all around her. "Nobody's coming to our show tomorrow night," she told the band members when they assembled New Year's Eve morning for a rehearsal.

"This isn't Kansas City," Raymond said. "Canadians don't run inside at the first sign of snow. They see almost as much of it as the Russians do."

"How's Cindy?" she asked Konny.

"Fine. She's upstairs in her room."

"What?"

"Yeah. How else could we spend New Year's Eve together?"

She stared at him. "Honey, you're a fast worker."

His shrug was meant to be off-putting. "Not necessarily, but when I'm hungry and I get some food, I eat."

Oscar's laugh could be heard in the next suite. "Right on, man. When the brother moves, he really makes time."

After the rehearsal, Clarissa rushed to Cindy's room on the twelfth floor. "I see you're a smart one," she told Cindy after their greeting.

"What do you mean?"

"I mean you're smart enough not to shack up with him here in front of his buddies."

"Honey, I'm not Konny's woman." Giggles poured out of her. "At least not yet, but that man is so sweet that I'm in danger of breaking every one of my rules—and soon. He's wonderful, Clarissa."

"Hmm. That's what he said about you. I'm glad you're here, not that I expect to see much of you. He got you a nice room up here on the floor with the bigshots."

"There was nothing else available. We're having an argument about who's paying for it."

"You mean, you . . ." Clarissa nearly swallowed her tongue. "What's that? Somebody's singing my song. My brand new song that isn't even published. *Turn that up.*" Cindy ran to the TV cabinet and turned up the volume on the radio.

"Hey, wait a minute," Clarissa said, groping for a chair. "Good Lord, that's me singing."

Cindy's eyes seemed to grow to twice their size. "That's you? Konny said you're the best jazz singer today." She eased herself to the bed and sat on its edge. "Gee, with that voice, you can sing anywhere. Girl, you're fantastic."

Clarissa sat there, shaking her head from side to side and rubbing her hands together as if she were washing them. "I hope I sound as good in person as I do on the radio." She jumped up, ran to the phone, and dialed Raymond's room number. "We're on the radio right now. How do I know what station it's on? Right now, I'm doing well to know what my name is. Do some surfing. Tell Konny and Oscar. No, I'm not losing my mind. 'Bye."

At their performance in the hotel's grand ballroom that night, they played to a crowd that filled the vast room and the corridors adjacent to it. Clarissa got her first taste of the downside of celebrity life when policemen had to escort her from her dressing room to a private elevator. She had wanted to mingle with the people, to thank them for their generosity to her, but when several fans grabbed at her and a crowd surged toward her with such strength that her band members couldn't protect her, the police moved to her rescue.

"I'm not sure I like that kind of success," she told Cindy and Konny during breakfast in her room the next morning. "Give me my Kansas City gigs. They're good enough for me."

"That's over," Konny said. "You're big-time now." She knew he was right, though she didn't want to accept that her peaceful, ordinary life would change so drastically that she would lose her freedom. Yet, she was soon to learn firsthand the truth of his remark.

They returned to Kansas City to reopen at Pilot III on the first Friday of the New Year. "They've been playing that song of yours on the radio ever since New Year's Eve," the club's owner told Clarissa. "People have been calling here from everywhere—" he gestured with his hands to include the world—"wanting to know if you were coming back here. What the hell went on up there in Canada?"

If he was perplexed, so was she. "Must have been the CD. Whatever it was, I'm thankful for it."

At their opening, a huge crowd welcomed her, and many waited outside in the cold, blustery weather, hoping to get into the club for her second show. Well, she wasn't going to look a gift horse in the mouth, and she definitely didn't plan to question God as to the reason for his blessing.

At the end of her second and last set, she slipped from the stage to her dressing room, didn't see fans anywhere, grabbed the fur-lined cape Lydia gave her, and headed for the exit. But as she stepped onto the street, fans waiting to purchase tickets for her next performance saw her and plowed toward her. She told herself not to panic as, to her amazement, a pair of strong arms lifted her and broke through the small group.

"Put me down. Where are you taking me? Stop."

"Don't worry. I wouldn't harm a hair on your head. That crowd would trample you."

His voice, deep, strong and calm, put her at ease, though he didn't set her on her feet until they reached the door of a small restaurant nearly two blocks from Pilot III.

"Thank you, whoever you are," she said. "You can please put me down now. Going out there was foolish, but I haven't gotten used to this."

He eased her to her feet and opened the restaurant's door. "They meant well. They only wanted to touch you, but the way they were shoving, they would have knocked you down. Let's sit over here. It's rather secluded, and you won't attract attention. What would you like?"

"Coffee, please. Who are . . . ?" She gasped. "Oh, m'gosh! *It's you!* I looked all over for you last night and tonight, but I didn't see you. I was so disappointed. Who *are* you?"

Close up, he fired her as a kiln fires porcelain. A big man with smooth brown skin, chiseled features, and large, expressive eyes that reminded her of someone. But it was his voice that unsettled her. It commanded her acceptance of him.

"I thought I was going to meet you at Christmas, but that didn't work out," he said, and a smile flitted over his face. "I'm Brock Stanton, Lydia Stanton's son."

"What? You're . . . how'd you—?"

"I live in St. Louis. My mother told me to keep an eye on you, so I went to hear you. I went back, because I loved to hear you sing, and then, I went because I had to, because you intrigued me. I stayed away for a couple of weeks, hoping to get you out of my system, but let me tell you it was easier to give up smoking. So I went back. Then, you disappeared, and I was disturbed about it until my mother told me where you were and what you were doing."

This couldn't be happening to her. This man who, from outward appearances, could have any woman he wanted, was telling her in so many words that he wanted her. She told herself to talk sense, to ignore all those silly and girlish things running through her head.

"If I hadn't gotten into trouble tonight, would you have continued to sit through my performances and leave without coming to see me?"

"No. After the night you sang `Solitude' and sang it directly to me, I knew I had to find a way to meet you that wouldn't make me seem like a stalker or an overwrought fan. I got the opportunity tonight."

She felt so comfortable with him, and she knew she would have been equally contented in his presence if he hadn't been Lydia Stanton's son. "I'm glad," she said, without reticence or the need for games or coyness. "I wanted to talk with you, to know what you're really like, who you are deep down inside."

"And I want to show you." He didn't smile, made no effort to charm or seduce her, and she liked that.

"Brock." She rolled his name around on her tongue. "I like your name." She said it as if she were nursing a memory, reminiscing about something pleasant. "I've never known anyone with that name. So to me, it's uniquely yours. It belongs to you. I mean . . . oh, I don't know what I mean."

Her cellular phone rang, and she grimaced as she removed it from her pocketbook. She glanced shyly at him. "Would you believe that Clarissa Mae from Low Point, North Carolina, owns a cell phone? The members of my band gave it to me for Christmas. Now they can pester me anytime they feel like it. Hello."

"Miss Holmes, this is Officer Cameron. Sorry to disturb you, but we've been trying to locate you. Where are you? Your band members are worried."

"I'm sorry, sir." She looked at Brock. "A policeman wants to know where we are. Seems my band members are looking for me."

"The Raven. Tell 'em you'll be at the hotel in a couple of hours."

"Officer, tell the fellows I left because I have a date. They could have telephoned me."

"Yes, ma'am, but they didn't think of it till I asked if you had a cell phone. Sure you're all right now?"

"Absolutely. Thanks." She hung up and turned off the phone. "Now they can't bug me." She leaned forward, aware that she wanted more from him than polite conversation, more than the satisfaction of her curiosity about him. "I've thought about you a lot," she said. "Brock, talk to me."

He reached for her left hand and began to play with her fingers. "These many weeks I've had a hundred things I wanted to tell you, but now that you're here with me, I can't think of a single one of them. I'm thirty-nine, single, and enchanted with you. For a living, I manage my own properties."

"Oh. Just like your parents."

"Not quite." He locked his fingers through hers. "They gave me a new car for a graduation present when I finished college. I sold the car, bought a bike, and used the rest for a down payment on a house. I rented out the house, got a job, and began saving to buy another house. That's how I got started. Dad inherited his first house from his grandparents, and I liked to remind him of that."

Pain clouded his brown eyes and his fingers tightened around hers. "My mother's whole existence changed for the better when you came into her life, and she loves you deeply."

"And I love her, more than she'll ever imagine. She introduced me to a new world. I'm here because of her."

They talked on into the night, past the time he'd said she would return to the hotel; talked until the restaurant owner came to their booth with three glasses and a bottle of cognac. He poured three drinks and lifted his glass. "I wish you a long and happy life together. But if I don't close up and go home, my wife will be in a rage and my own happy life will cease."

Brock clicked the man's glass with his own and then let the fiery liquid slide down his throat. "Thanks for your good wishes, brother. We're out of here." He stood, took Clarissa's arm, and dropped a bill on the table to pay for the coffee. "Thanks for your hospitality." To Clarissa, he said, "It's too late to go to the hotel. Call one of your band members and tell him I'm taking you home."

She called, but got a busy signal and hung up. Arm in arm, they strolled the short distance to the apartment building in which she lived. "When may I see you?" he asked. "You work nights and I work days. Can you join me for lunch? I'm going back to St. Louis day after tomorrow."

She stood beside him at the elevator, wondering how she could manage to get him to kiss her. She needed a deeper level of intimacy with him, but she wasn't ready to invite him to her apartment.

"Aren't you listening to me?" he asked.

"Yes. I mean, no. I was wondering . . . uh . . . what did you say?"

"Lunch tomorrow. I can be here at twelve-thirty or whenever you prefer."

"Make it one." The elevator door opened, and she reached up and quickly kissed his cheek. "Good night."

She stepped into the elevator, and both of his arms went around her, holding her tight and stunning her with the swiftness of his action. He ran his tongue across her lips and, giddy with joy, she parted them and took him in. He possessed her, shocking her with the force of his passion. When he left her at the door of her apartment a few minutes later, she had no doubt that, if he staked a claim, she was his.

Chapter 12

Inside the apartment with her back against the door and her eyes searching the darkness, she steadied herself and began groping for the ringing telephone. "Hello," she said in a voice strange for its unsteadiness.

"Where the hell were you, Clarissa?" Raymond wanted to know, as if he had the right. "With all that fracas in front of the hotel, we thought you'd been kidnapped. The police were all over the place."

"Oh, Raymond, I'm sorry. After all that applause and adulation, I was suffocating. I wanted to get away from it, to get some air and find my way back to reality. I went out the back way intending to walk home, but I didn't know about the crowd out there, and those people came after me like a wild herd. I'd have been trampled if Mr. X hadn't rescued me."

"If Mr. . . . who did you say? You mean that guy? Well, I'll be damned."

"I was with him, Raymond."

"Yeah? From the way you sound, I can see he made a hit with you."

"He did, indeed. Thanks for your concern."

She hung up and sat on the high stool near the kitchen door, reflecting upon the past months and Brock Stanton. It was as if she had always known him and always loved him.

"In his arms, kissing him, was so natural," she told Konny at rehearsal the next morning while Raymond and Oscar were revising an arrangement. "The first time I saw him, I had a premonition that he'd be important in my life."

She noted the vacant expression on Konny's face, his thoughts evidently elsewhere. He shrugged. "And you think you love him although you've only been with him once?"

Clarissa nodded. "I know I do. Almost from the first, his presence when I sang comforted me, and his absence always saddened me. When I'd see him again, my heart would pound, and I'd get a feeling of contentment—I guess you could call it that—a feeling I wasn't used to."

Konny answered his cell phone, put his hand over the receiver and said, "Excuse me, Clarissa, but the manager of Pilot III wants to see you in his office around one if you can make it."

"Sorry, but I have a one o'clock appointment. I can see him at noon today, but I have to be back in my apartment by ten minutes to one."

Half an hour later, Clarissa sat in the club manager's office, gazing at the original oil paintings, polished walnut furnishings, and deeply cushioned leather chairs and sofa. The man had great taste. And a lot of money, she thought, with which to indulge it.

"Thanks for coming, Miss Holmes," he said. And at that minute, two policemen entered the office. Her eyes widened and a feeling of apprehension stole over her.

One of them approached her. "At that melee last night, we arrested a man carrying two guns and a grenade. A waitress said he was about six feet from you and moving toward you." He showed her a photograph. "Do you recognize him?"

Annoyed at having been lulled there by a misrepresentation, she narrowed her eyes. "I would have gone to the police station, Officer, if you had asked me. This wasn't necessary."

The officer seemed nonplussed. "But ma'am, we didn't think you'd want to be seen entering a police station . . . a person with your status."

Taken aback by yet another reminder that her life had changed, she said, "Thank you, but I still think of myself as an ordinary citizen who obeys the law. I don't recognize that man."

"If you think that fracas threatened your safety, will you be willing to give us a deposition?"

"Of course, but could we do that day after tomorrow? I have an appointment at one o'clock today, and I hope I have one tomorrow at about this time."

"Sure," he said. "Whenever it's convenient for you. We'll be in touch."

She rushed back to her apartment, changed into a red woolen dress that had its own jacket, found some black accessories, and tried to slow down her heartbeat while she applied a small amount of makeup.

The doorman rang her buzzer at exactly one o'clock and, without giving thought to inviting Brock to come to her apartment, she put on her gloves and coat, walked out of her apartment, and locked the door. He waited for her at the elevator and, when she stepped out, he opened his arms and she walked into them.

He chose a small restaurant that served good food and sat beside her rather than facing her. "How about going to Washington with me weekend after next?" he asked her as they ate lunch.

Her spoon clattered against the dish that held her lemon parfait. "You want me to go with you to see Mrs. Stanton? You're kidding. I'm her aide, her servant. I can't do that."

He took a deep breath and blew it out slowly. "I told her I intended to bring you, and she let me know that her prayers were being answered. Besides, she told me last summer that she loved you as if you were her daughter. She's always regarded you as a friend, never as a servant, and you know it." His eyes narrowed. "Don't you want to go with me?"

She knew that her frown didn't send him the right message, but a bewildered person didn't smile, and she preferred not to mislead him. "If I do, what's she going to think?"

As if he had no misgivings, a smile brightened his face. "She said, 'Hallelujah.'"

Clarissa leaned away and stared at him. "About what? What did you tell her?"

"She asked how we were getting along, and I said you kissed me, and I kissed you back."

"You *what*? I didn't kiss you first—I just gave you a peck on the cheek."

The expression on his face bore no mirth as he gazed steadily at her. "Call it whatever you like. To me, it was a kiss, and I would have climbed a fifty-foot tower in order to cement it."

"If I insist, I'll lose. Right?"

His wink unsettled her. "Stick with me, and you'll never lose."

She thought of the struggle she'd had for so long, and told him of her plan to find her sisters. "You'll find them," he assured her. "They're probably looking for you, too, and the release of your CD ought to help them locate you."

She had never told anyone about her humble beginnings. Not even Lydia Stanton knew she had no idea as to the identity of her father. But she told Brock and felt his protective loyalty when he squeezed her fingers.

"You are a remarkable woman," he said. "Few people have traveled as far as you have with so little support." Holding both of her hands firmly in his, he said, in barely a whisper, "Do you want to go home with me?"

Chastened, her eyelids slipped down over her eyes. "Yes. I want to go."

He stroked her hands. "Get used to thinking of you and me as a couple, because that's what I want us to be from now on. I'll be back here Saturday, and I want us to be together that evening. Is that okay with you?"

She could hardly wait, her eagerness boldly obvious to him, and she imagined that her eyes sparkled with the joy boiling inside of her. "Yes," she said. "Oh, yes."

The following morning, sooner than promised, she gave the officer the deposition he had requested and hoped to hear nothing more of the incident. *I don't have ill feelings for anyone in that crowd, not even the man apprehended with the guns and grenade. If the incident hadn't occurred, I still might not know Brock.*

"We appreciate your cooperation, ma'am," the officer told her, "and I hope we won't have to trouble you further."

The doorman announced Brock at one o'clock that afternoon, and she didn't hesitate. "Ask him to come up, please."

She wanted to know what he'd do with her if they had complete privacy, how he would behave if he had her to himself. When the doorbell rang, she opened the door at once. He walked in and, without uttering a word, locked her body to his own and possessed her. When he released her, she grabbed his arms to steady herself.

"Let's go," she said, uttering the first words that passed between them.

He didn't smile. "Good idea."

But immediately, the doorbell rang again. She didn't miss the sharp upward movement of both of Brock's eyebrows just before his eyes narrowed. He stepped aside in a wordless suggestion that she open the door.

"Wh . . . what on earth are you doing here?"

Josh grinned, a slow, lazy and triumphant half-smile. She had almost forgotten how ugly he looked when his eyes gleamed with evil intent.

"Well, Clarissa Mae, you knew I'd find you. When you planning to come back home?" As if he'd just seen the man, he pointed to Brock. "Who's he?"

Her breath came in spurts. "You have no right to come here. Home? I *am* home, and who he is is none of your business. I am no longer your wife."

Josh walked farther into the apartment, glanced around, found a chair, and sat down. Clarissa forced herself to look at Brock, who leaned against the front doorjamb with his arms folded, his legs wide apart and his eyes in narrow slits. Breathing through his mouth.

My Lord! I'll lose him before I ever know him, she said to herself as she stared at Brock, his anger palpable.

Suddenly, she whirled around, raced to her bedroom, opened her top dresser drawer and flung its contents in every direction until she found the paper. Then, she sped back to the living room past Josh and straight to Brock.

"Here. Look at this," she said to Brock. "It's legal and it's final."

He opened it and read aloud the divorce decree. "Ask him to leave."

She turned to her ex-husband. "I want you to leave this minute, Josh, and I never want to lay eyes on you again."

"I ain't got no reason to leave here. You making all this money. The radio's playing you all the time. We married for better or for worse, and what God has joined, let no man put asunder.'"

She stared at him. "Shit. The Bible also says, 'Thou shall not commit adultery.' Get out, Josh," she said, but he didn't move.

Perspiration dampened her blouse when she looked at Brock, a man dangling on a precipice of violence. She lifted the intercom that connected her apartment to the doorman. "What do you mean by letting this man come up here when you knew I had a male guest?"

"Well . . . uh . . . he said he was your husband."

"Which means you're an idiot. Did you ask for identification? Did you check with me? He is not my husband. Send the police up here before somebody gets hurt."

"I'm sorry, ma'am."

"You could have gotten me killed. Get me a policeman, and hurry." Fearing a confrontation, she rushed back to the living room. "I'm telling you for the last time, Josh. *Leave*! You wanted Vanessa—you got her. Get out."

"Who's going to make me?"

Shivers raced through her as Brock moved away from the wall. The doorbell rang, and she raced to it and opened the door to two house detectives. After relating the problem, she showed them her divorce papers.

"You're under arrest for trespassing, buddy," one of the detectives said to Josh.

"You can't—"

The officer ignored Josh and handcuffed him while the other detective called the city police.

"This brother's missing a few screws," one said to Clarissa. "You'd better get a restraining order against him. Then, if he comes within a hundred yards of you, phones, or writes you, he'll go to jail."

Josh's top lip curled into a snarl. "You'd better make sure you never come back to Low Point," he said to her as he sauntered out between the two detectives with his hands cuffed in front of him.

They were alone, and in the awkwardness of the quiet that engulfed them, she prayed silently while she waited for Brock to speak. The blood ran icy-cold in her veins while he gazed at her, speechless and not moving a muscle. He must have detected her shivers, for he moved to her and gripped her shoulders, although with gentle hands.

"If that man interests you in any way, I want to know it this minute."

"He's nothing to me. Couldn't you see that?"

He held her so tightly that she could feel the beat of his heart. "When I get back here Saturday evening, we'll get together?"

She didn't act coyly or equivocate, because she knew that, given the chance, she would be with him. "Yes. Oh, yes."

It was not the warm, getting-to-know-each-other luncheon that they'd enjoyed the previous day. Their conversation—if it could be called that—was stilted, formal, and impersonal. "I'll be glad when the weather warms up," she said with her gaze locked on the lobster bisque that she prepared to sip.

"Me, too. It's been an unusually hard winter so far."

"I like this restaurant," she said. "I haven't been here before."

"I eat here once in a while. The food is good, and I like the atmosphere."

Meaningless small talk. *Neither of us is eating this food*, she said to herself. Clarissa didn't waste food or anything else; years of deprivation had instilled in her appreciation for the efficacy of conserving what she had.

"Would you be embarrassed if I asked for a doggie bag? I'm too full to eat, and I can't waste food. I'll eat it later."

He sat back in the booth and studied her. "If that's what you want, I'll ask the waiter. To be honest, I'm not hungry, either." He leaned toward her. "Are you worried about what your ex might do?" She shook her head. "I see. Are you thinking about Saturday evening?" He had a way of getting into her head and toying with her mind. Of course she was thinking about Saturday. She let a half-smile suffice for an answer.

As if he divined her thoughts, he said, "I figured that if anticipating our evening together had me tied into knots, you might be experiencing something similar."

God bless him. An honest man was hard to find. She let herself relax and smile. "Looks like we're together in this."

"Do you want to be with me?" Again, he didn't smile or try in any other way to influence her answer.

If she had any sense, she'd tell him she didn't know the answer to that because she didn't really know him, but deep down inside of her where she lived, he'd staked a place for himself, and she knew he would always be there. So what she said was, "Yes."

He walked with her back to her apartment building. "I'm going to leave you here at the elevator because I have to catch a train that leaves in one hour and twenty-seven minutes. If I so much as step into this elevator with you, I won't leave you until I've sated us both." He left without kissing her and with the heat of her libido singeing her loins.

Chapter 13

Once inside her apartment, she telephoned Lydia Stanton, hoping that a conversation with her friend would serve to ground her, that Lydia would be a stabilizing force. "Brock asked me to go home with him weekend after next," she said as soon as they had greeted each other.

"Well, aren't you coming?"

She heard the expectancy and, yes, the hope in the woman's voice.

"Uh . . . I uh . . . feel awkward about this."

"Nonsense. Why, for heaven's sake? Brock's besotted with you. When he was here at Christmas, he hardly uttered a sentence that didn't have your name in it. And mind you, he's almost forty, and he has never brought a woman to this house. *Never!*"

"We'll see."

"Now, you listen to me, Clarissa. I'm talking as your friend, not as Brock's mother. You've had a hard life, but you've made some mistakes, and marrying Josh Medford was one of them. You don't marry a man just to get relief from an intolerable situation, because you're only guaranteeing misery for yourself. You also don't walk away from a man you care for and who cares for you just because you've already made one mistake. You're a lot older now, and you ought to be that much wiser. Look at Brock for what he is; don't decide that he's a man, and therefore you have to run from him."

I can't let her think I'm foolish. I don't doubt that Brock is a decent man, miles ahead of Josh, and I believe he cares for me. He's not the problem; she is, and I have to tell her the truth.

"Don't misunderstand, Mrs. Stanton. I trust Brock, and I care for him, but I work for you, and you're his mother. It doesn't seem right."

"Hogwash." She imagined Lydia scowling and rapping the arm of her wheelchair. "You don't work for me, and even if you did, I've never treated you as less than a guest in my house, a friend. I've treated you as if you were my child. You ought to know that nothing would make me happier than to have you for my daughter."

Tears pooled in Clarissa's eyes and, as she groped for words, they spilled down her cheeks until she tasted brine at the corner of her mouth. "I . . . only my foster mother, Eunice Jenkins, gave me the feeling of a mother's love, the feeling I have right now. I guess you know that there isn't anything you would ask of me that I wouldn't do."

"I know you care deeply for me, Clarissa, but don't let our ties interfere with your relationship with Brock. Do you hear me?"

"Yes, ma'am. He's . . . he's important to me, Mrs. Stanton. What I'm feeling scares the beejeebers out of me."

"It shouldn't. No man is better than you are. You can admire a man without looking up to him. Never do that. You got it?"

"Yes, ma'am."

"Good. I'll see you weekend after next."

Clarissa dressed slowly for her performance that night. She didn't feel like singing. Her life was moving too fast, plowing along like a locomotive out of control. She was about to commit to a man she hardly knew, and the upshot of it was that she loved him and knew that what was happening between them was good and right But it went against everything that her hard and pain-filled life had taught her.

With her balled fists locked to her hips, she looked upward. *Josh Medford and four cruel or indifferent foster mothers are in the past. I've had so many blessings that I don't care about Josh and those women. Look where they are and look where I am now.*

She lectured to herself for a few minutes longer, but didn't succeed fully to lift her mood. Fifteen minutes before she was to leave for work, she took off the simple green evening gown and replaced it with a gold-lamé backless sheath. "If I don't sing well, maybe some sex appeal will take their minds off it." Realizing that she couldn't wear a bra with the dress, she tossed her head in defiance of custom. Not many women her age could boast of size 36-C breasts that stood as straight as those of a teenaged virgin.

"Coming. Coming," she sang out when the telephone rang.

"Is Mr. X with you?" Raymond asked without preliminaries.

"No. He's in St. Louis by now. Why?"

"Then I'll run over and get you. We don't want you to travel alone by taxi, and especially not at night. Never can tell what kind of ruse these weirdos will try to pull. It isn't safe."

She stared at the phone after Raymond hung up. She had achieved a good measure of success and fame, but in the process, she'd lost her freedom.

"You low-keyed tonight, girl," he told her when he met her in the lobby of the building in which she lived. What's the matter?"

"Nothing much. My mind's not on singing."

"What's that guy's name? You sure you can trust him?"

"Brock Stanton. His mother is . . . someone very dear to me. Until the night of that fiasco, I didn't know that, and I was taking a chance. He wasn't, though."

Raymond pulled away from the curb at his usual high rate of speed, unsettling her as he always did. But he didn't notice her case of jitters; he never noticed it. "A woman is always at more of a disadvantage," he said in response to her observation about herself and Brock Stanton. "That's the way nature set it up. Say, I thought our next gig was in St. Louis."

"That's three or four weeks from now, I think . . . or maybe four."

"You'd better perk up before you go on, Clarissa. They love you, but you're only as good as your last song. If they thought they weren't getting their money's worth, they'd jeer the angel Gabriel. You know what I'm saying?"

She did indeed. "I know. Chase wants us to tour Europe."

Raymond drove into the club's underground garage and parked. "Yeah? For a white boy, he sure knows the black circuit here in the States. I hope he's onto what's happening in Europe."

She glanced at the man who was becoming more than an employee and was gradually playing the role of a father or big brother. "I don't pay Chase to be ignorant, Raymond. He's our agent. Where in Europe do you want to go other than England, France, and Belgium?"

He got out of the car and walked around it to help her out. "I don't see how you got into this thing. You look like you're poured into it," he said of her evening gown. "Take me to *Scan-de-nay-vi-uh*. I want the same treatment that they laid on Pops."

She laughed. "Your teeth aren't as white as Louis Armstrong's."

"No, but I'm taller and better-looking. I don't blow a trumpet, but my guitar makes the angels sing."

She knew he was trying to cheer her up, and she wanted him to succeed. Nevertheless, when the band assembled, she told Oscar, "I want to change the program and open with 'Lover Man.' It fits my mood."

When the lights dimmed, she took a deep breath and gripped the microphone. As she sang the haunting song of unrequited love, she ripped the words out of her gut and flung her raw fears and anxiety at the patrons who sat like fossilized creatures, stunned at the power of her delivery. She hardly heard the applause, stomping, and cheering as she ran to her dressing room, fighting tears.

Minutes passed before she realized that the sound she heard was the ringing of the telephone, for she rarely received calls in her dressing room.

"I just want you to know that, according to my lawyer, nobody in Kansas—neither sheriff nor judge—has any jurisdiction over anybody here in Low Point, North Carolina," Josh said when she answered.

She would love to know who gave him the number of the phone in her dressing room. The sound of his voice was sufficient to jolt her from her low mood. "But if you put your foot in Kansas City," she told him, "you can be arrested, because you broke the law here when you dialed this number. Oh yes, and since you have decided to harass me, I am not going to give permission for my name to be removed from the deed on that house."

"You can't do that," he screamed.

She felt better with the passing minutes. "I helped pay for it, didn't I?" She hung up, repaired her makeup, put a smile on her face, and went back to the stage. Back to her cheering fans.

"What were you crying about?" Konny asked Clarissa as she drank coffee with her band members in their favorite bistro after the show.

"I've fallen in love, and I'm scared."

"Yeah. You told me that a few days back. What's different?"

"He'll be back here this weekend, and I—"

"If you feel it's not right, you can still walk away."

Her eyebrows shot up. "Not for a million dollars."

Konny's whistle split the air. "Go for it, then, babe. I wish you luck."

"What are you two mumbling about?" Oscar asked. "If I didn't know you were hooked on Cindy, man, I'd be suspicious."

She watched Konny drain his coffee cup and lean back in the booth with an air of self-assurance and masculine authority that he didn't possess when she met him. Did the love of a woman do that for a man? "When it comes to observing, buddy, I wouldn't pay you three cents for a week's work. I had a crush on Clarissa for over six months, and neither you nor Raymond noticed."

"No kidding? What happened?" Oscar asked him.

"Nothing. Then I met Cindy."

Oscar lifted his shoulders, shrugging it off. "I guess I didn't notice, 'cause I never thought you'd be stupid enough to fall for your boss. Not that it makes a difference; a woman may not be your boss before you marry her, but you can bet your eye tooth she's boss an hour after you say 'I do.'"

"Come on, Oscar," Raymond said. "Your wife isn't bossy."

Oscar reached into his pocket for his wallet and took out a ten-dollar bill. "No, but when it comes right down to the nitty-gritty, man, she's got the trump card."

Raymond stood, preparing to leave, and draped an arm across Clarissa's shoulder. "You heard what he said. Be sure you don't forget it."

Chapter 14

After a restless night, Clarissa got up before sunrise, made coffee, toasted a bagel, and sat down at the small table beneath her kitchen window to read the previous day's mail. She opened a letter from Lydia, curious as to its contents because Lydia had not written her before. The envelope contained not a letter but a clipping from *The Raleigh News and Observer*, one of the many papers to which Lydia had begun subscribing when she became wheelchair-bound. She scanned the clipping and saw that Helbrose Studios would close for lack of business.

Clarissa remembered the owner's kindness to her and telephoned him. "Mr. Helbrose, this is Clarissa Holmes. I just read that you're planning to close. You helped me when I needed help badly. Is there something I can do?"

After a brief silence during which she wondered if he knew who she was, or cared, he said, "Well, I'll be damned. I'm sixty years old, been in this business for nearly forty years, and this is the first time any singer I helped remembered it. You made it big just like I said you would. I know you got a record deal, but maybe you'd do a couple of shows for me. You'd fill up a big hall. I thought you were great when you made that demo here last year, and you're a hell of a lot better now. I'll take anything you can give me."

"Can you hold on for three weeks?"

"If help is coming, babe, I sure can."

"Count on it." She remembered that when she let him know that she was financially strapped, he cut his fee in half and added an extra tape of her demo. Of course she would help him.

At nine o'clock, she telephoned Raymond. "I may be a few minutes late for rehearsal this morning. I have to go to the library."

"Okay, but if you'd just back into the twenty-first century and get a laptop computer, you could save yourself a lot of time. Ten years from now, you'll be the only person who needs a library."

Her affection for Raymond did not cover forgiveness for his cockiness. "With that kind of wisdom, you're lucky you can play that guitar."

"When's your birthday?"

"It's already passed. October seventeenth. See you around eleven-thirty."

At the library, she got a copy of Gale's Directory and copied the information she needed on newspapers in a dozen cities and towns throughout the United States. Checking phone books in whatever location she happened to be in the hope of locating her sisters had netted her nothing but frustration.

"You're in a good mood this morning," Konny said to her when she arrived at Oscar's room for rehearsal. And she was, for she was about to take an important step toward locating her sisters. The following afternoon, she mailed an ad to papers in eight major cities scattered over the country. *"If you are black, a female triplet, thirty-three years old and born on October seventeenth, who was separated from her two sisters at birth, please contact me at this address."* She gave the address of a post office box that she rented for that purpose, enclosed money orders for the appropriate amounts to pay for the ads, and prayed that she would get a reply.

She dropped the envelopes in a corner mailbox and, immediately, the bottom seemed to fall out of her belly. She leaned against the mailbox and tried to calm herself. Thinking that she might be ill, she hailed a taxi, only to hear the taxi driver tell her that she was only a block from the address she gave him. She dragged herself home and, for the first time in her life, recognized a need to have a man's arms around her. A need that went beyond sexual desire and gratification. A need to be a part of one special man. And so, in a move that was another first, she telephoned Brock.

"Stanton speaking."

"I'm sorry to disturb you at work, but—"

"What is it?" He interrupted her, his tone sharp and urgent. "Are you all right?"

"Yes. I mean, no, I'm not. I . . . I need you."

She heard him suck in his breath. "What happened?"

She told him what she'd done. "If nothing comes of it, I know I'm not ever going to find them. I . . . I can't bear the thought of it."

"Stop right there. Suppose they don't read those papers. If we don't get results, we'll put ads in papers in other cities and towns, on radio and television. We're just beginning this search, and we won't stop until we find them."

"You're saying we? Don't mislead me, Brock."

"I said we, and I keep my word. We're in this together. Do you love me?"

She didn't hesitate. "Yes. I love you."

"And I love you. I'll see you Saturday afternoon. If I didn't have an appointment tomorrow morning, I'd be with you this night." For a long time after they ended the conversation, she savored those words.

Never had the days from Wednesday to Saturday crept along at such a pace. When Saturday finally arrived, she rushed home after the band's daily rehearsal, set the table, put the food in the electric warmer, and raced to the shower. He had said he would see her in the afternoon, and she knew him well enough now to be certain that he'd get there early. Dressed in a pink jersey overblouse and a pair of black wide-bottom pants, she opened the door when he rang the bell precisely at one o'clock. A smile spread over her face, and then she laughed, opened her arms, and went into his embrace.

"I thought we'd eat at Gates Grill, stroll through the park, and take in this great weather. I can't believe it's March and hardly a bit of wind." His gaze traveled over her. "But you're not dressed to go out."

She had plans for them, and she didn't want his good intentions to torpedo them. "I fixed us some lunch, but if you'd rather eat out . . ." She let the thought hang.

"No, indeed. I rarely get home cooking unless I go to Washington to visit my mother, and that isn't often. Thanks for going to the trouble."

She hung his coat in the closet near the front door and walked toward the living room. "I hope you like soul food."

"You can ask? I'm a black man raised by a southern black woman. If you baked cornbread, I'm your slave." He followed her into the kitchen and seated himself in a chair beside her little table.

"I hope I don't have to remind you of what you just said."

He leaned back and rubbed his chin as if in contemplation. "Many a slave has ended as master. I'd love being your slave. I like an earthy woman, and you're the epitome of one. I like everything about you."

She had leaned down to light the broiler, straightened up, and caught him with his gaze locked on her buttocks. He didn't flinch, but shrugged, as if to say, *Yeah. I like that, too.*

She put the crab cakes in the broiler to crisp them, and then looked him in the eye. "Am I going to get any surprises with you?" she asked him, suddenly nervous in contemplation of what they both knew would come at the end of the meal.

"Probably," he said, opting for the same candidness she'd displayed, "since no two people are alike. But I'll make the surprises as pleasant as I can."

"Ye-ess," she said, letting the word spill out slowly as if she were ruminating about its implications. "I don't doubt you at all. I trust you completely, and that bothers me. It doesn't make sense."

"I've said the same things about my feeling for you, but I know they're genuine, and I'm going with them."

She took the crab cakes out of the oven, put the food on the dining room table, and took his hand. "I've never heard of anybody serving soul food in courses, so if you'll say the grace, we'll eat." He said the grace, cut a slice of cornbread, and bit into it.

"You're a wonderful cook. This bread is to die for."

"Thanks. Just remember what you said."

His eyes darkened, and she knew that cornbread was no longer on his mind. "With pleasure," he said. "You have a seat somewhere while I clear the table and straighten up the kitchen."

She stopped herself from saying she'd do it, when memories of her resentment at Josh for refusing to wash a dish or a pot or even to clear the table floated through her mind. She got a bottle of pinot grigio and two stemmed glasses, put them on the glass-topped coffee table in the living room, sat down, closed her eyes, and waited for him.

Half an hour passed before she looked up to find him standing near and looking down at her with an expression that not even the smile on his face enabled her to fathom. She patted the place on the sofa beside her, but he shook his head.

"You said you needed me, and I've been able to think of little else since. Can you live in St. Louis?"

"Given the right circumstances, I could live most anywhere. However, I've tried it without running water, indoor plumbing, and central heating and, in my experience, that puts too heavy a burden on love."

He sat down, opened the bottle of wine, and filled their glasses. "I don't doubt it." He clicked her glass with his own. "Here's to our long, happy life together. Do you want us to live together for a while to see if we're temperamentally suited, or are you willing to marry me cold turkey?"

She looked at him from the corner of her eye, amused in spite of the apparent seriousness of his question. "Cold turkey? You haven't asked me to marry you, hot bird or cold bird."

His laughter wrapped around her like a warm blanket. He put their glasses on the coffee table and put his arms around her. "I've wanted to do this since the first minute I looked at you." With her head resting against the back of the sofa, he gripped her shoulder with his left hand, found her left nipple with his right one and eased his tongue into her mouth. Heat rushed through her, settling in her vagina and filling her with a wantonness that stunned her. With her left hand, she pressed the hand that rubbed her nipple, demanding more. When his tongue began to slip in and out of her mouth simulating the act of love, letting her know what he planned to do to her, the sound of her groans filled the room..

"Kiss me. Kiss me," she said. Her fingers clawed at his shirt until he slipped the blouse over her shoulders, unhooked her bra, and pulled her nipple into his warm mouth. When her breath became fast and heavy, he stood, locked her body to his, and let her feel his massive erection. Then, he took her hand.

"Where do you sleep?" He needn't have asked; she had already reached for his hand to lead him to her bed, for the pounding and clenching in her vagina demanded he put an end to it.

He got them out of their clothes quickly, turned back the bedding, and placed her on the lavender sheet. "If it doesn't work at first," he said, "don't worry. Before I leave here, I'll see that you're sated."

She didn't know that a man did those things to a woman, kissing and licking her all over, adoring her as if she were a princess. When he hooked her knees over his shoulders and thrust his tongue into her, screams poured out of her and tears flowed from the corners of her eyes. A strange weakness stole over her and she submitted to him totally as she had never done. She wanted to give him all that he was giving her, but he denied her. Every nerve in her body screamed for completion, and when she grabbed his shoulders he moved to cover her body. But he continued to refuse her until, frustrated beyond self-control, she wrapped her legs around his hips and took him.

When he finally collapsed in her arms, spent, she knew she would love him for as long as she lived. She didn't remember how many times she climaxed. She only knew that she had found with him what she missed in fifteen years of marriage.

"How do you feel?" he asked her. When she told him she was happy, since she didn't know how else to explain her feelings, he said, "I am, too, and I want us to get married. Will you marry me?"

"Aren't you supposed to declare your undying, never-ending love for me?"

She could listen to his laugh forever. "I'd do that and get on my knees, too, if I had the energy. Woman, you wore me out."

"You should thank God you had the strength," she said.

He braced himself on his elbows and gazed down at her, his face bright with a smile that could only bespeak joy. "Will you or won't you marry me?"

"I have to sing, Brock. It's as much a part of me as the beating of my heart."

"I know, and I will never do anything to hinder you. I take good care of what's mine."

She wondered at the implications of that statement, but decided not to question it, that to do so would amount to pettiness. "How are we getting together to go to Washington next weekend?" she asked him.

"I'll be here Saturday afternoon, and we can fly out Sunday morning. You still haven't answered my question."

"Don't you have a single reservation, Brock?"

He rolled over on his back and locked his hands behind his head. "Not a single one. You're what I want and what I need. I haven't had this feeling before, I like it, and I'm going to do my best not to let it escape."

With her head on his shoulder, she whispered, "I'll be proud to be your wife."

Chapter 15

The following Sunday morning at eleven-forty, the big Delta jet landed at Ronald Reagan Washington International Airport, and he stepped off the plane holding Clarissa's hand. Twenty-three minutes later, he stuck a key in the lock of Lydia Stanton's house, opened the door, and walked in with Clarissa at his side. At least he didn't have to worry about how his mother would feel about the woman he wanted to marry, but although it would have mattered if she didn't like Clarissa, it wouldn't have made a difference and his mother knew it.

They found Lydia sitting on the back deck in the warm sunshine. It didn't escape him that she raised her arms to Clarissa before greeting him. Dispensing with preliminaries, he said the words that made him feel like a colossus. "She has promised to marry me."

"Thank God. I prayed for it, because I know how much alike you two are. I know you're going to be happy together."

I hope you're right, Clarissa thought. *My life has changed so much in the past ten months, that I wouldn't be surprised to see myself singing in the White House.*

"I don't know when I heard such good news, Miss Clarissa," Sam said while driving her to the YWCA to see Cindy. "Miss Lydia's happier than I've seen her since Mr. Stanton died. I hope we'll see you more often now."

She thanked him and told him she would take a taxi back. Cindy greeted her with arms widespread. "Girl, I'm so glad to see you. We can't have a long visit, 'cause Konny will be here around three, and well, you know."

She didn't know why she was surprised. "Konny's coming this weekend?"

"He comes every weekend. Didn't you know that? No, I guess you didn't. I'll always be grateful to you for introducing us—he's everything to me."

"You're not thinking of shacking up with him, are you?"

"No. I'm guiding him toward marriage." When Clarissa laughed, she said, "Don't laugh. He seems willing to go, and I'm hoping we make some progress on that this weekend."

"I wish you luck. You get a powerful feeling when a man you love asks you to marry him."

Cindy's gaze locked on her, and then began to peruse her the way a jeweler examines a diamond. "Who is he?"

"Excuse me," Clarissa said, went into the ladies' room and, using her cell phone, telephoned Mrs. Stanton. "Will you and Konny have dinner with us tonight? She asked Cindy when she came out. We eat at seven." While Cindy's mouth hung open, Clarissa wrote the address and phone number. After a short visit, she left, because she knew that Cindy would like to prepare herself to greet Konny. That evening, Konny's approval of Brock Stanton was so absolute that she set aside any remaining reservation about her chance of happiness with him.

They sat in the Stanton living room, sipping cordials and after-dinner espresso. "He's the Rock of Gibraltar, and he's nuts about you," Konny told her in an aside. "That guy would go all the way for a friend, not to mention a wife. You hit the jackpot, babe."

"Thank you, Konny. Knowing that you feel this way about Brock means a lot to me."

"I want you to get married here," Lydia told her Monday afternoon as she and Brock prepared to leave. "If not in my house, at least here in Washington. I want my friends to see how proud I am to have you as my daughter."

"You ought to see her perform, Mama," Brock said.

"Yes. I'm singing in Raleigh next weekend. Maybe Sam can bring you."

"Sam *will* bring me. I wouldn't miss it," Lydia said.

Clarissa answered her cellular phone. "Hello.

"This is Chase. You won't believe what I got for you. May the thirty-first you and the band'll be in Carnegie Hall, and I'm getting you some TV dates to make sure you have a full house."

She grabbed the doorjamb. "*I'm going to sing in Carnegie Hall. Lord, what next?*" she fairly shouted.

She felt the nerve-rattling effect of Brock's arm so snug around her that his fingers touched the underside of her right breast. "Wonderful! And there'll be more to come, far more that you've dreamed of," he said.

She saw Konny take out his cell phone and knew that he was about to phone Raymond. "Our ship has come in, buddy," she heard him say. "See you tonight. No, Cindy isn't coming with me. She has to work, but Clarissa has some news for you."

She walked over to Konny, took the phone, and said, "We're playing a benefit in Raleigh next weekend." Then, with the phone an arm's length away, she stared at it. "Yeah. That's the news. Part of it, anyway." She handed the phone back to Konny, winked at him, and said, "Raymond has to know everything. Let him sweat."

As soon as she checked into the hotel the following Sunday morning, Clarissa asked for the Raleigh telephone book, settled into her room, and began calling the numbers listed for individuals named Holmes. But at one o'clock in the afternoon, tired, hungry, and disappointed, she didn't have one clue as to the whereabouts of her sisters.

I'm not giving up. I'll find them if they're alive, she promised herself.

That evening as the band tuned up, testing the sound equipment, Clarissa suddenly got a sickening feeling. "Raymond," she said, walking over to him in the dimly lit setting, "I've got an awful premonition. It's like somebody dropped a weight on me and won't let me get out from under it."

"That's not a good sign."

"You're telling *me?* The way I feel, it can't be. I'm going to ask Mr. Helbrose to put some extra guards or policemen here tonight."

"Sure," Helbrose said when she spoke to him. "Anything for you, babe. I'm sold out tonight and tomorrow night."

"I'm departing from my regular jazz program with this first number," she told her audience. "I'm going to sing 'For Once In My Life' as a tribute to a dear friend." She glanced down at Lydia, who sat in the front row with Sam on one side of her and Cindy on the other, and smiled. Lydia dabbed at her eyes with her handkerchief, and Clarissa began singing the love song to her. But the words soon took on a special meaning, a reflection of her love for Brock. Her voice rounded into a low, mellow torch and the words sprang from her heart. At the end, the audience rose to thank her with a loud and spirited applause. She didn't look at Lydia, for she knew that if she did, the woman would see her soul.

Near the end of the second half of her performance, she saw a man in the last row, far back from the stage, stand, and then he shouted, "Fire." Seconds passed before the audience took in the word, and then, to her horror, she witnessed what was no less than pandemonium. She also saw a guard who stood in the aisle near the offender's seat grab the man.

Raymond jerked the microphone from her. "There is no fire," he yelled. "Everybody sit down. There is no fire. That man is making trouble. There is no fire." Half of the audience turned to look toward the stage.

"There is no fire anywhere in this building," he said, his voice now calm and authoritative. "We will recess for a few minutes and resume the program."

"How can you be so sure?" Clarissa whispered to him.

"Because I recognize that man. When you were in Washington last Sunday, he came to the hotel looking for you, and told me he was your husband. The guy's either sick, or terribly reckless. He could have caused a lot of people to get killed." Slowly, the people returned to their seats.

"I'm sorry for this disruption," Helbrose told the audience. "The man who caused the commotion has been apprehended. Let's get it on with the best jazz singer in the country."

"It could have been a lot worse," Clarissa said to Raymond as she remembered her feeling of apprehension earlier in the evening. "If Josh did that, he's coming apart."

"You won't have to worry about him for years to come, because what he did constitutes a felony," Konny told them. "Good riddance."

Clarissa didn't like the idea of going to the police station the next morning to identify Josh. To her mind, if he was ill, he needed help, and the man she lived with for fifteen years wouldn't yell "fire" in a crowded hall if he wasn't sick. And if he wasn't sick, how could he hate her so much that he would risk jail to disrupt her concert? Still, she knew how Josh loved money, and the knowledge that living in poverty while she lived in comparative luxury was the price he had to pay for his sexual liaison with Vanessa Hobbs was probably making him crazy. Maybe she should thank him: if his testosterone hadn't made a fool of him, she might still be pumping water from an old iron pump in order to brush her teeth.

He's Josh Medford," she told the precinct captain. "I was married to him for fifteen years. I have a restraining order against him in Kansas City, Missouri, and he probably decided that it wasn't applicable here."

The policeman looked at Josh. "You really tore it this time, buddy."

"I'll get you for this," Josh said to Clarissa as he was led away.

"Maybe," the cop said, "but my guess is that when you get out of here, you'll be so old you won't have energy enough to hurt anybody."

"You make a misstep, just one, and you may ruin your life," Clarissa said to Konny after the show as they sat in Minnie's Grill, sipping coffee.

"Yeah, man, that's the history of the world," he said

"Well, you keep your good news from Raymond and Oscar, but I want everybody to know mine: Cindy and I are getting married, and soon."

"I'm so excited for you both. Cindy, this is great news."

"Yeah," Raymond said. "It's da bomb. You guys don't start pressuring me, now. Been there, done that, and don't plan to do that anymore. What's your news, Clarissa? Not that I can't guess. You planning to hang out with Stanton?"

She moved her head to the side and upward, drawing her shoulder close to her neck to suggest that she was looking down her nose at him, before a grin spread over her face. "Mr. Stanton asked me to marry him, and I said yes."

Oscar stared at Clarissa. "Well, hell! Yep. I'll be damned. The guy fooled me. Way to go, Clarissa."

She read the clipping that Raymond handed her. "You mean our CD has been nominated for a Grammy? Maybe there aren't many people recording jazz these days."

"You kidding?" Raymond asked. "With Reeves and Krall in there, we don't stand a chance, but this nomination will open doors for us, babe. You'll see."

Her career was in high gear and she had the love of a good man, but she knew that true happiness would elude her until she could find her sisters.

Chapter 16

Several days later, Clarissa stood at the registration desk of the Chase Hotel in St. Louis, gazing around at its opulence. She didn't like staying at a hotel other than the one in which her band stayed, but Brock had insisted that if she wouldn't stay with him at his apartment, she should stay at the best hotel. To make certain that she did, he paid for it in advance.

"I want to know that you're protected from adoring fans," he'd said, "and this hotel won't tolerate nonsense."

Her band members had balked at the price, so she housed them in a suite that consisted of three bedrooms, three baths, dining room, kitchen, and living room in a nearby hotel. "I wouldn't feel right in this posh place while you guys had regular fare," she told them.

She checked in and, on the way to her room, Brock waited with her at the elevator. "Will we have any time for ourselves while you're here?"

She digested the question, realizing it meant that he wouldn't interfere with her work or feel neglected because of it. "Every minute that I can find, beginning with tonight after the show."

"I know how important this engagement is to you, and I'll be satisfied with whatever you manage." She ordered breakfast for them in her room and, as they sat at the little table by the window, looking down at the lush green park, he said, "When can we get married?"

He didn't want it to happen any sooner than she did. "I thought the second weekend in June would be a good time."

The air seemed to seep out of his lungs and, although a grin rearranged the contours of his face, he said, "I don't know how I'll wait that long. I may go nuts in the meantime." His grin blazed into a smile. "I can hardly believe it. Let's eat."

She hated to use their time together for her own purposes. "Do you mind if I spend a little time checking the phone book on the chance one of my sisters may be living here?"

"Of course I wouldn't, but I've checked phone books for about every city in Missouri, and I haven't found one of them."

She put the telephone book back in the night table drawer and walked over to him. "You did that for me, as busy as I know you are?"

"I told you we would find your sisters, that I'm in this with you, and I keep my word."

In the two weeks that followed, she learned what it meant to have the support of a successful man who put her well-being on a par with or above his other interests. "We're booked into the Village Vanguard in New York for two nights," she told Brock, and my hair's been standing straight up ever since Chase told me."

"Great. You've got it made. Tell your agent to put you and the band in the Park Lane Hotel on Fifty-ninth Street facing Central Park. You'll be in a crime-free area near the heart of the shopping district, and fifteen dollars will get you a taxi to the club. I'll tell the concierge there to look out for you."

When she stepped out on the stage that Friday night, she looked out at the audience and gasped, for Brock sat at a table six feet from her. She could feel the glow inside of her, exorcising her every care, and she didn't doubt that his presence inspired her buoyant feelings. His thumbs-up sign further elevated her spirits. She wrapped her fingers around the mike, opened her mouth, and let the words of "Solitude" flow in sweet, velvet tones. Brock Stanton's smile was all the thanks, all the praise she needed, but there was more from the audience. Much more, as the patrons embraced her.

The next morning, she raced through the pages of *Variety* until she found the notice. "A new star in town. Clarissa Holmes takes us back to the days when singers *sang*, reminding us of Bailey, Holiday, and Fitzgerald, and the band backing her is proof that Kansas City still produces great jazzmen."

"I'll have to give the band a name," she told them at their morning rehearsal. How about Clarissa Holmes and the New Jazz Trio? That way, if I'm unable to sing, you guys can still make it."

"Works for me," they said in unison.

She didn't know how long she would sing or where she would be five years down the road, and she wanted to ease their way if they found themselves without her.

"Just imagine," she said to no one in particular. "My picture is in *Variety*. I'd give anything if Eunice Jenkins, my dear foster mother, could see it." The three men looked at each other, for they hadn't previously known anything of her background.

"That's right," she said. "I have no idea who I am, only what I've made of myself."

Raymond patted her on the back. "You've done great with whatever you had, Clarissa."

"Yeah," Oscar agreed. "You're special."

You're not going to believe this," Konny said, waving part of a newspaper when he joined Clarissa, Raymond, Oscar, and Brock at breakfast in their hotel the following Sunday morning.

Raymond held his coffee cup suspended between the saucer and his lips. "What?"

"The *Times* reported our opening Friday night. This cat swears there're no flies on us. Man, he compared us to Ramsey Lewis. I'll have a pot of coffee, two scrambled eggs, four strips of bacon, and lots of toast," he told the waiter without a pause. "According to this review, we can write our own ticket."

Clarissa looked at him. "That's one opinion. By the way, Chase insists we play Carnegie Hall. I told him he was out of his mind."

"Why not?" Brock asked them. "Even if the auditorium is half full, you'll be a success."

Oscar strummed his fingers across the table. "Tell her, man. I always wanted to play in that joint. Benny Goodman rocked it out of its staid snootiness back in 1938, and playing there has been the goal of jazzmen ever since. I want my turn."

She looked at their faces, bright with eagerness, and realized that they, too, longed for acclaim. "I'll tell Chase to go for it." She could almost measure their relief.

"I'm sorry to interrupt, Miss Holmes," the waiter said, but I have a telegram for you. Would you please sign here?" She signed and opened the message.

"Anything wrong?" Brock asked in a voice laced with anxiety.

She folded it and put it in her pocketbook. "Yes and no. The Raleigh police said my ex-husband is not mentally competent to stand trial, so I don't have to go to Raleigh. He's had a nervous breakdown."

Brock picked up the check and stood. "Poor fellow. I'd better pack. What about you, Clarissa?"

Raymond pulled air through his front teeth. "That poor fellow came damned close to getting us killed."

"I know," Brock said, "but I pity him for reasons you can't even guess."

"Hey, now," Oscar said. "See y'all at the airport."

Clarissa looked at Brock. "Pack your stuff, and bring your bags up to my room."

"They're already packed."

She kissed his cheek and whispered, "Hurry." When he entered her room, dropped his suitcase on the floor, and bolted the door, she dashed to him, and he wrapped her in his arms.

Two hours later, he said to her, "Roll over this way. I love to feel your breasts against my chest." She cupped her left one and held it, waiting, until the sensation of its feel inside his hot mouth shot through her. He paused and asked her the time.

"I don't know, and I don't care."

He went at her then as if in single-minded pursuit of that moment when she would erupt around him in ecstasy, and every cell in her body mated with him as she gave him all she had until he shouted her name, lost in her. Later, lying in his arms, she remembered that she was about to leave New York without having searched the telephone books in an effort to locate her sisters. She'd made the search on her previous trip there, but she could have overlooked a name.

"This will be the first time I've gone to a place without looking for my sisters."

His breath warmed her cheek. "I did it. I had plenty of free time, so I checked all five books. After we're married, we can place television ads. No point in doing it now without a publicist or other professional help. Okay?"

"I hadn't thought that far ahead, but yes. Thank you."

He released her, rolled out of bed, and yanked the cover off her. "We're in this together, and if we don't hurry, we'll miss that plane together. By the way, let me know who you'd like to have at the concert, and I'll see that they get there."

While she sat with Brock in the lounge waiting for the flight, her cell phone rang. "I got you some gigs on *The Tonight Show, The Today Show, The CBS Early Show,* and a couple of other big-time TV shows— *The Tom Joyner Show* and a notice in some big newspapers and magazines. How's that for a first-class agent?"

"You're the best, Chase. Just be sure my band goes wherever I go. I want to promote them."

"You bet. I'm pushing Clarissa Holmes and the New Jazz Trio."

She shared the news with Brock, who said, "With that kind of publicity, you'll have a full house."

I'm not getting on television in a t-shirt and jeans," Raymond said when they prepared for their first TV appearance. "I'm wearing what I always wear to work—a suit, shirt, and tie. I'm not nineteen, and I don't plan to pretend that I am."

"All right. The band will wear suits, and I'll wear an evening dress."

"This is a terrific band in its own right," Clarissa told the show's host after he introduced them. "Want to hear them?"

"Why not?" he said in response to the audience's applause.

As she hoped and prayed, the band's rendition of "Flying Home" brought prolonged applause and cheers. *Thank God. If they have to, they can make it on their own.*

"Don't forget to get your tickets now for Clarissa Holmes and the New Jazz Trio's May thirty-first performance at Carnegie Hall," the show's host said at the end of the applause, cheers, and shouts following Clarissa's rendition of "When Your Lover Has Gone."

"Well, what do you think?" Clarissa asked her band members as they rode back to the Park Lane in the network's limousine.

"We've got a whole week of these dates," Oscar replied. "How can we miss?"

"By getting cocky," Raymond said. "But, man, it sure felt good up there with those cameras worshipping us. You're a first-class human being, Clarissa. Not many singers would have done that."

Her left shoulder rose in a quick shrug, as if his words didn't matter, but she cherished every syllable. "You're my family."

May thirty-first arrived at last and, for the first time in a long while, sleep hadn't come all night. But she knew that once her fingers wrapped around that microphone, her nerves would settle and her jitters disappear.

I should have spent the night with Brock, she said to herself. *By the time he pulled out of me, I'd have been too drugged, too exhausted, and too besotted with him to stay awake.* She vocalized for half an hour, showered, dressed, and phoned Brock, who had offered to take care of the details.

"Mama, Sam, and Jack Helbrose are here, and Kenny said Cindy will arrive this afternoon," Brock told her. "Your friend, Jessie Mae, in Low Point can't make it, but she thanks you for thinking of her."

At precisely eight o'clock that evening, the lights dimmed in Carnegie Hall and the New Jazz Trio hit the first note of "Back Home In Indiana." *Lord, let there be some people out there.* She stood near the wings, praying, her eyes closed and her body tense. Encouraged by the loud, prolonged applause that followed, she laid back her shoulders and strode toward center stage. The rousing cheers forced her to look out at the packed house, and her gaze captured her friends seated in the front row directly below her. Brock smiled and made his thumbs-up sign simultaneously with Oscar's first note introducing "Fever."

She forgot concern that her red dress exposed over half of her bosom, forgot that she stood where some of the greatest singers rose to fame, forgot everything but the words and the music and her joy in making them live.

In her dressing room at intermission, Brock told her, "You've never sung like this."

"I know. I feel like I have to open up. It's as if everything in me wants to come out, to make room for something new and better. Oh, Brock, something good's gonna happen—otherwise I wouldn't feel so . . . so wonderful.

"Why shouldn't you feel good? You've made it to the top, and your friends are here to rejoice with you."

"Yes." She shuddered as what seemed like a chill shot through her. Something was in the air. She wouldn't call it a premonition, but she'd better beware.

"You have five minutes, Miss Holmes," an usher called to her.

"Give 'em your best," Brock said, kissed her cheek, and left.

She began the last half of her program with a rollicking version of "Any Old Time You Want Me" and ended with "Help Me Make It Through the Night," her fifth encore. An usher brought her a bouquet of red roses from Brock, and patrons threw flowers on the stage as they applauded and cheered, unwilling to let her go,

"I love every one of you," she said, "but I have no voice left. Please come back next time." Exhausted but happy, she rushed to her dressing room and dropped down on the sofa. Brock arrived as she knew he would, but seconds later, the usher attending her door knocked.

"Miss Holmes, a lady to see you."

She got up, went to the door, and opened it. *"Oh, my Lord!"* She grabbed her chest and fought for breath. "It can't be! It can't be!"

Brock rushed to her. "What is it?" His arm went around her, steadying her. After a minute of silence, he said, "It's all right, love." Still holding Clarissa in his arms, he stepped back. "Come on in—we've been looking for you."

With tears gushing down her cheeks, Clarissa opened her arms to the woman. "It can't be, but I know it is. I've looked and looked for so long. How did you find me?" she asked as they hugged each other.

"I saw you on *The Tonight Show*, and I knew you had to be one of us."

Clarissa could hardly contain herself. "Do you know where our sister is?"

The woman, who bore a strong resemblance to Clarissa and had her height and figure, shook her head. "I'd give anything if I did. I'm Leticia."

"And this is Brock Stanton. Wouldn't it be wonderful if—"

"Someone else to see you, Miss Holmes," the usher called.

Clarissa and Leticia bolted for the door and opened it to find their sister standing there. "I'm Jamilla, and I've looked everywhere for you. Thank goodness for TV." This time, no tears came, only joyous shouts of laughter as they hugged and inspected each other with a happiness that bordered on hysteria.

Clarissa dabbed at her eyes. "Lord, how I've prayed for this moment." They looked at each other, hugged each other, and didn't bother wiping the tears that glistened through their smiles.

They cried and hugged each other again and again. Suddenly, Leticia flung her arms wide and laughed. Laughed until, seemingly weakened by the experience, she dropped into the nearest chair, cradled her lowered head in her arms, and let the tears flow.

Jamilla's gaze wandered to Brock. "Only God knows how I prayed for this, dreamed of it, imagined it. It's happened, and it's almost more than I can bear."

Clarissa bowed her head. "I got so carried away, Lord, that I forgot to thank you. I knew you would answer my prayers. Thank you from the bottom of my heart for bringing us together."

At the touch of Brock's finger on her arm, Clarissa turned to him, and he handed her and each of her sisters a glass of champagne. Then, holding his own glass, he said, "Here's to the happiest day of our lives."

They drained their glasses and, with one eyebrow arched, Jamilla looked at Clarissa. "Who's he?"

"Oh. 'scuse me. This is Brock Stanton, my fiancé. We've found each other just in time for you to be bridesmaids at my wedding three weeks from now."

"I'll be there," each of them assured her.

"It's a miracle," Brock said to Clarissa.

"Yes. A modern-day miracle."

EPILOGUE

With an arm around each of her sisters, Clarissa gazed up at Brock through the tears that streamed down her face. "It can't be real. Tell me it isn't just another one of those nights when I'll wake up and find that I've been dreaming."

"Our prayers have been answered, sweetheart. Why don't I call for the limousine and the three of you go to your room at the Park Lane. After your fantastic success tonight, I hate not celebrating with you, but this night is for you and your sisters."

"But what about Mrs. Stanton, Sam, Cindy, and Mr. Helbrose?"

"They'll understand."

"Do you have time to go with me to my hotel room so we can talk?" she asked Leticia and Jamilla.. "I can't let you get away from me so soon."

"Right on," Leticia said. "This calls for more champagne."

"And champagne it will be," Brock assured them. "I'll phone you in the morning," he promised Clarissa.

"We could have walked these three blocks," Jamilla said when the limousine stopped at the Park Lane.

"Not with my public face," Clarissa said. "The last time I tried it after a concert was the night I finally met Brock when he rescued me from a stampeding crowd. No, thank you."

Once inside Clarissa's suite, it was as if reality dawned on them simultaneously, and they began to hug each other, their faces tear-streaked and mottled with powder and mascara.

As if weakened by the shock of the experience, Jamilla dropped to the nearest chair. "I've had so many nightmares about the two of you in some miserable place calling for me. It's as if this is just the beginning of my life. Tell me, what have the two of you been doing all these years? How did you grow up? Where have you lived?"

"I grew up in foster homes—five of them, in fact," Clarissa said, "and only one of my foster mothers was a real mother to me. She died last year. Three of the others were downright cruel. I left the foster-care system at eighteen and married the first man who asked me. I just got rid of that jerk. This time last year, I was living in the rural slums of Low Point, North Carolina, using an outdoor toilet and pumping water at an iron pump that sat on the back porch. I got sick of my husband's fornicating with a teenager, kicked him out, and hit the road. I never looked back. I worked for nothing on my first singing job in order to make a name for myself, and it paid off."

Leticia pulled out a cigarette, crossed her long legs at the knee, and leaned back in the soft leather lounge chair. Anyone could see that she was accustomed to comfort and elegance. She looked at Clarissa. "If you don't want me to smoke, say so." She lit the cigarette, took a drag, and blew out the smoke in big, floating rings." I'm not sure my story will do for your refined ears. You two sound pretty tame to me. You name it, I've done it. Of course, I haven't committed murder, stolen anything, or been in jail, though it's by my own smarts that I avoided the latter."

Jamilla's laugh reminded Clarissa and Leticia of their own. It was deep and throaty, right from the gut. "You did what you had to do, Sis," she said. "I have a law degree, but I don't judge. I write mysteries. Where'd you grow up?"

"In a succession of group homes in and around New Orleans, and you don't want to know what that was like. You could say I was mis-educated, and all I learned about social graces, I picked up myself. Street smarts? By the time I was fourteen, I had plenty of that. I've been a madam, an entertainment director on a cruise ship, and an entertainer—not for the public, mind you, just one client at a time."

Jamilla got up and sat on the arm of Leticia's chair. Understanding Jamilla's move as one of support for her errant sister, Clarissa walked over and sat on the other arm of the chair.

"We've all had it tough in some way," Jamilla said. "I grew up in comfort in the suburbs of Los Angeles with adoptive parents who treated me as if I had been born to them, and they educated me and gave me every advantage, but there was always a part of me missing, and I think that's one of the reasons why I'm a mystery writer. Not a day has passed when I didn't wonder where you two were and what you were doing, and I was always on the lookout for a female who looked like me. It's been debilitating in many ways. Still, I fared better than either of you."

Clarissa raced to answer a knock on the door, opened it, and gasped as a waiter wheeled in a table laden with champagne, hors d'oeuvres, petit fours, and three bouquets of yellow roses. The waiter refused a tip, saying that he'd been generously taken care of.

Leticia jumped up from the chair and surveyed the table. "Girl, that brother you've got is a class act. He knows how to operate. In my book, this speaks elegance."

The waiter opened the two bottles of Moet and Chandon champagne, poured a glass full for each of them, and left. "I don't know about the rest of y'all," Clarissa said, "but I have to thank the Lord before I drink this. "Lord, I thank you again and forever for answering my prayers." She raised her glass. "Here's to the hundred telephone books I've searched and the hundreds of telephone calls I've made to strangers whose last name was Holmes."

"This seems so unreal," Jamilla said. "I used to wonder why MaDear and PopPop hadn't chosen to take all of us or at least one other so I'd have you for company, but they didn't have that option. Anyway, that's behind us now. I want us to stay in close touch."

"Yes," Clarissa said, "and let's be there for each other. All these years not knowing who I am has been a drain. Now, at least I have this feeling that I'm somehow complete." She got a tablet and handed it to Leticia." Put your address and phone number there." They exchanged the information and busied themselves telling tall tales, drinking champagne, and eating the delicacies that Brock sent them.

I'm heading back to California tomorrow," Jamilla told them. "I have a book deadline, and that means I have to get to work. I'll send each of you a copy of a couple of my books."

"I've got a job lined up as a cruise director," Leticia said, "and I'll let you know when and where. I guarantee you a generous deduction anytime you want to cruise, and I promise to stay in touch."

"Not so fast," Clarissa said. "I'm getting married in a month, and you have to stand up with me. It's a formal wedding, because Brock's never been married, and I might as well not have been," she winked with a signifying look, "so I'm wearing a white bridal gown. Bridesmaids' dresses are on me. We're the same height and size, so I can do the first fitting. The colors are lilac and dusty rose. Who wants which?"

"Lilac," Jamilla said as her sister answered "Dusty rose" simultaneously. Clarissa laughed the laugh of one cleansed of all discomfort. She refilled their glasses, opened her mouth, and began to sing "Amazing Grace."

"I'd join you if I could carry a tune," Jamilla said.

"So would I, if I knew the words," Leticia said.

As Clarissa's dulcet tones caressed the words of the great hymn, the three of them sobered and looked at each other as if in awe.

Leticia's gaze shifted from one to the other of her sisters. "I still can't believe it, and the wonderful thing is that I like both of you and want to be with you. She gathered them to her. "I don't think I've ever been so happy."

"It's the greatest day of my life," Clarissa said.

"Mine, too. Let's get together often, but I suggest we always meet on May thirty-first," Jamilla said.

"Yes, but don't forget, we meet next in Washington on June twenty-eighth at my wedding. "

They agreed, and set about consuming the remainder of the fare before them, including the second bottle of champagne. Leticia sank into the deeply cushioned, silk-damask sofa, held up her glass as far as her long arm would reach, and kicked up her heels. "Way to go."

Precisely at six o'clock on the twenty-eighth of June, Counsel "Konny" Patterson, Jr. sent forth the first peals of the great organ at the All Souls

Unitarian Church on Sixteenth Street in Washington, D. C., and Leticia and Jamilla stepped into the aisle, side by side. Carrying bouquets of lavender and pink calla lilies, the sisters took their places at the altar facing Brock and his best man, a favored cousin. When Konny struck the first notes of "Here Comes the Bride," the congregation turned to see Clarissa, radiant in white and carrying white calla lilies, as she walked between Raymond and Oscar to meet her groom. Half an hour later, Brock's arms encircled his wife and his sisters-in-law, their tear-stained faces wreathed in smiles. Lydia Stanton sat on the third row, nodding her approval as tears of joy streaked her face.

DESTINY'S DAUGHTERS

DONNA HILL
PARRY "EBONYSATIN" BROWN
GWYNNE FOSTER

ABOUT THIS GUIDE

The suggested questions are intended to enhance
your group's reading of this book.

Discussion Questions

More Than This by Donna Hill

1. Leticia has some ambivalence about her choice of profession. Knowing that, why do you believe she stayed in it so long? What were her options?
2. After meeting her sisters, would she return to "the life?" Why or why not?
3. Was family really important to Leticia or simply something she needed to fill in some gaps?
4. Do you think that Leticia felt less worthy than her siblings? If so why; if not, why not?
5. Leticia is worldly in ways her sisters are not. Discuss what those ways are and how it will impact her relationship with her sisters in the future.

Life's Little Mysteries by Parry "EbonySatin" Brown

1. How would you have felt toward your adoptive parents if they had separated you from your siblings, who then grew up in foster care?
2. Was Jamilla right in her feelings of rejection though her adoptive parents loved her dearly? How do you think this affected her ability to maintain a romantic relationship?
3. Jamilla is obsessed with finding her sisters, though she has literally no information. Would you have continued this quest with such fervor or just let it die?
4. How realistic do you feel the ending was?
5. Now that Jamilla has found her sisters, do you think her physical pain and nightmares will stop?

The Journey by Gwynne Forster

1. When we meet Clarissa, she is a humble and uncomplicated person. In what respects does she remain this way throughout

the story? What are some instances in which she shows loyalty and support for others?

2. What, apart from loneliness, prompted Lydia Stanton to "adopt" Clarissa? As much as she needed Clarissa, why did she promote her career, in effect encouraging Clarissa to leave her?

3. How does Brock weave a place for himself in Clarissa's heart, and why does it seem so right when they are finally together? In what ways does he demonstrate his loyalty to and love to her?

4. Clarissa bears some marks of a rootless, rejected person. What are some of these traits?

5. Throughout her life, Clarissa tried to find her sisters. What was her principal method of searching? Why do you think she failed to find them? How did Clarissa's sisters find her?